GARDEN OF SECRETS

MISSELTHWAITE BOOK ONE

DRAKE LAMARQUE

GREY KELPIE STUDIO

A catalogue record for this book is available from the National Library of New Zealand.

Paperback 978-0-473-65093-3

Epub: 978-0-473-65094-0

Kindle: 978-0-473-65095-7

PREFACE

Content note:

This book contains sharing/multiple partners, death of parents, violence and bullying (not between the main characters).

It is also a slow burn, so... sorry about that.

*To the wonderful Gillian St Kevern, friend, YouTubing buddy,
enthusiastic cheerleader and fellow sad axolotl boy.
I couldn't have done this without you!*

CHAPTER 1

January, 1901
Derbyshire

There was absolutely nothing about Alistair Lennox
that made him interesting in any way. That was how
he felt and it was certainly how the world seemed to treat him. If
anyone were to describe him they would call him plain and
disagreeable.

But mostly no one described him for no one thought about
him at all. He spent most of his days shut up inside with his
mother in a manor house in the Derbyshire countryside, or in
their London townhouse. His father, Barnaby, was in and out,
sometimes away on 'business' and sometimes in the house.

Although his parents were always going to fancy parties of
her friends and social acquaintances, they never brought
Alistair with them, and they never invited their friends back to
the countryside to stay.

It had made sense when Alistair was young, when he was a

child with a governess, no one would imagine bringing him along to a party, but as he grew older he resented it.

On the eve of his twentieth birthday, he sat and watched his mother. His mother, Albertina, was fixing her hair in a stylish updo in the mirror. She had blond hair like his, but her's was warm and golden like sunlight, and Alistair's tended more to the grey side of blond.

Alistair knew she was a beauty for certain. From what he'd seen of her at the London parties the Lennoxes hosted, she was very much given to gales of laughter when she was with her friends, although she never seemed to be that way with him. She had Alistair's father quite smitten even though they had been married for almost twenty-four years, and he was just as excited to go to parties and plays and suchlike with her, and leave Alistair behind in the large, lonely house. On this night, Alistair decided to make his feelings known to his mother, while his father fixed his bow tie in the next room.

"Why can't I come to the party tonight?" Alistair said.

"You're too young," Albertina said. She had replied the same way every time Alistair had asked for something he very much wanted, using the same clipped tone. The same sense of finality to her words.

"I'm almost twenty. It's my birthday tomorrow, when will I be old enough?"

"Not yet," she said. She pushed a hairpin into place and turned to face him. "How do I look, darling?"

"Beautiful, mother," Alistair said, dully. He knew there was no other acceptable answer. If he said anything but that, she would scold him horribly.

"Good, tonight's an important occasion for your father and me." She hesitated and for a moment, Alistair fancied there was something like concern or fear in her eyes. But she shook it off in a moment, kissed his cheek, and breezed out of the room.

Within seconds, she and his father were gone and the house

echoed with the faint traces of her footsteps. Now it was just him in the house, alone with the servants, who would, of course, ignore him.

The house had books, and Alistair felt he had read all of them. The grounds were dull, mostly perfectly manicured lawn and lines of poplars, there was nothing to amuse him out there.

Alistair felt out of sorts, even more out of sorts than he usually did. In fact, he was usually suffering from a headache, which made him short-tempered at all hours of the day. He went to his bedroom and sat in the window, watching the carriage that carried his parents trundle up the driveway and away. They knew that they probably wouldn't be back the next day, which meant he had to face the prospect of a birthday where he had nothing to do and no one to share it with. No one to eat breakfast with, no one to give him presents.

My parents don't care about me any more than they care about those two horses pulling the carriage, he thought to himself. He frowned, feeling his headache worsen. The carriage turned onto the main road and was hidden from his view by the row of tall poplar trees that bordered the estate.

I hate them. Alistair was a little shocked by this revelation, but mostly because of how true it was. They were his parents, he was supposed to love them, but instead, he was consumed by an utter hatred of them. They didn't care for him at all, and they didn't care if he was sad or lonely. He hated them for it. He had read books, he knew that parents were supposed to dote on their children, they were supposed to help them to excel, send them to the best schools... instead, Alistair had had private tutors who came to the house and scolded him if he was too slow at his lessons. In fact, he should really have gone to college by this stage, but his parents didn't seem to care enough to send him to one. That or for some reason his mother wanted him shut up in the house, but that didn't make much sense at all. Surely they would want to introduce him to society soon?

Alistair picked up his journal and pen, and began to write. He had often taken to writing as a way to pass the time, and to express his innermost thoughts. He had no one to speak to, after all.

He began to write.

When I was a child I had an imaginary friend. A boy like me, and I would talk to him. I could tell him all the things I was thinking, all the things I wished I could do. I'm sure he was nothing more than a figment of my imagination, but he seemed so real to me at the time. I remember playing with my rabbit doll in the nursery with him, laughing together.

Later, when I knew for sure he wasn't real, I would conjure him up for fun sometimes. I would pretend as hard as I could that he was sitting beside me and give myself a headache from the effort of it.

What was his name again?

Now I wonder, is there someone like that out in the world for me? A perfect companion, a playmate, someone I could share my thoughts with? Alas, I fear I am doomed to live forever alone. That would certainly seem to be how my parents want me to be.

He looked up from his writing and glared out the window again. Letting the resentment he had for his parents well up inside him like a fire stoked by anger.

Something peculiar happened then. Alistair was sitting, feeling the power of his anger inside him, festering and boiling, and then the anger seemed to sharpen in his mind. He imagined the anger was stirring the clouds in the sky, making them dark and heavy with rain. He could just picture their faces as they looked out the window of their carriage and saw the sheeting rain and lightning piece the night, disrupting the ride as they made their merry way to London.

It was a strange fancy, which took his attention for a good few minutes, before he shook himself out of it. Disconcerted by the image he'd had of the carriage running off the road, he laughed, trying to believe it was nothing sinister.

"How odd," he said to himself. "Perhaps I am not at all above imaginary games, even at my age. Perhaps Mother is right and I am yet too young."

He sighed, closed his journal, and put himself to bed. For a moment, as he dropped off to sleep, he missed the small velvet rabbit stuffed toy he had owned as a small child. He wished he could hold it against his chest for comfort.

Outside a storm really had whipped up, and the howling of the wind and the rain pelting the roof made him feel cold and small as he fell into a restless sleep.

CHAPTER 2

*T*he next morning Alistair awoke when someone slammed his bedroom door open. This wasn't something that had ever happened to him before, as servants were always very quiet and respectful in the Lennox house.

"Terrible news, young master."

Alistair blinked awake to see the butler, Ryan, looking down at him. Ryan was a collected sort of man, and never seemed to be bothered by anything. This morning his face was drawn and white and his generous eyebrows furrowed.

Alistair sat up, half asleep and utterly confused. "What? Ryan, what on Earth do you mean waking me?"

"It's your parents," Ryan said. He thrust the letter he held at Alistair. "On their way to London last night their carriage went off the road and they both died."

⁂

*L*ater on, Alistair would remember very little of the days which passed after that startling announcement. The horses which had been drawing the carriage were brought home to stable safely, he remembered that. The connection between where the horses were bridled and the carriage held to them had severed somehow, but how no one seemed to know. His parents' bodies had been recovered, but he couldn't recall who had done it.

He could remember the joint funeral, the strangeness of sitting up the front of the church as the vicar talked about two people Alistair hardly knew. The church was full of mourners, and not one of them was familiar to him.

As he walked out of the church's graveyard, having tossed a rose each in the grave of his mother and father, Alistair felt himself lost at sea. What was his life going to be like without his mother telling him to stay home, to stay put?

What was it to be?

One moment Alistair was adrift, and the next he realised that his life could now be whatever he wanted it to be.

He didn't recall how he found the public house, but he could remember feeling grown up when he was welcomed in. The people in the place were not in mourning suits, and no doubt some of them looked at him askance, but he had money in his pocket and he could pay for ale.

He remembered that his first taste of ale wasn't good. It tasted strange, bitter and somehow wheaty. But then he loved it, and hours seemed to fly by in a blink. He remembered faces but not names, strangers who became friends, and he was telling them all about his writing and his dreams of finding a companion.

Then he remembered meeting someone out on the street. Perhaps meeting is the incorrect term, he considered as he thought back.

More accurately, he had collided with someone on the street. This encounter he could remember very clearly, it was highlighted with the clarity of anger.

He had been strolling out of the pub, and feeling exceptionally well, all things considered. He had been looking up, trying to see the stars, which were hard to spot in London, what with all the smog and smoke, and perhaps it was actually raining, when he walked straight into the chest of a man, and they both went sprawling onto the ground.

Alistair was stunned for a moment, very confused about how he had ended up with his hand in the cold slush of the gutter, his head sore from bumping it on the cobblestones.

The man he had collided with was swearing. "Watch where you're going, you imbecile!"

No one had ever, in his entire life, spoken to Alistair like that, and he sat up quickly, ignoring the spinning in his head to look at this person who dared insult him.

He was a good looking fellow, with a pale, sharp featured face and piercing bright eyes which seemed to catch the lamplight from the nearest storefront. His hair was black, and fell partially across his forehead, and he was dressed very well in a grey suit with a sort of half-cape over one shoulder.

For just a moment, Alistair forgot that he was angry and just gazed at how handsome the man was.

The man was not at all distracted, and got to his feet, brushing off his trousers in a fussy sort of way. "Well, nothing to say for yourself then? I expect that you're drunk aren't you? Well, if you're going to vomit please do it into the gutter and don't get my shoes any dirtier than you already have."

Alistair tilted his head. "Drunk? I'm not drunk in the slightest," he said. But having said that he wasn't entirely sure he was telling the truth. It was quite an effort to get to his feet, and to his surprise the grumpy, handsome man suddenly had his hand under Alistair's elbow and was helping him to rise. Alistair turned the wrong way and found himself in close proximity to him. All his thoughts whooshed out of his head as he gazed at the soft pink lips of this stranger.

"Pretty…" he breathed.

The man's lips twisted into a frown. "What did you say?"

"You're astoundingly pretty," Alistair said, a little louder since the man hadn't heard him.

The man's expression softened slightly and he shook his head. "You smell as if you've drunk all the beer in England," he said. His voice sounded sort of softer though. "Go home and sleep it off."

Alistair felt the anger in him rise again. "How dare you?" He said.

He placed his palms on the man's chest and shoved, creating space between them. "My parents are dead! They died on my birthday! I didn't even get to have cake! They're gone and I'm all alone!"

"Terribly sorry to hear it," the man said. "Goodnight."

He turned and walked briskly away, his heels rapping on the cobblestones.

He hadn't sounded sorry at all.

Alistair wanted to shout more at him, to tell him off for being so pretty and so rude, but his stomach was starting to roil in a deeply unpleasant way. He hailed a cab and gave the address of his parent's... no, that wasn't right.

His townhouse.

It was his now that they were dead.

CHAPTER 3

On Monday morning, the Lennox family lawyer called on Alistair at the London townhouse. He had been staying in town since the funeral, wandering the empty hallways and feeling terribly sorry for himself. His headache from the beer hadn't ever properly worn off, and he was filled with annoyance for everything in the world.

The family lawyer's name was Roberts and he wasn't someone Alistair had ever spent a lot of time with, although he was occasionally invited over to dinner. On those evenings Alistair was bored witless as Roberts prattled on about the finer points of some law or other.

But this was nothing like those visits. For one, Alistair had a terrible illness. Queasy in his stomach and a head that ached like nothing he'd had before. He was dreadfully thirsty but if he drank too much water he felt like he would be sick, so he was forced to take tiny sips.

He was in a foul mood, made worse by the memory of the man he'd met on the street the night before, with his strange cape and his knowing attitude.

He was still thinking about him when Roberts was let into the drawing room by the maid.

Alistair didn't bother to get up and Roberts hesitated before giving an awkward sort of bow and sitting down opposite Alistair.

"I'm terribly sorry for your loss, Master Lennox," Roberts said.

Alistair grunted by way of response, not at all concerned about seeming rude.

Roberts cleared his throat before continuing. "I have come to read your parents' will. I'm afraid there's rather a lot of paperwork for you to sign, and some rather bad news. Your parents have of course, willed you all their properties and wealth, it has all been put into a trust for safekeeping."

Alistair sat up, his heart thumping quickly because of the mention of bad news. "What's the bad news?"

"The bad news is that the trust is locked until either you marry, you turn twenty five or you complete a year's study at the Misselthwaite College."

"What?" Alistair couldn't believe it. His parents had never mentioned anything about college before, why on Earth would they only make it a requirement for him if they died? It made no sense at all.

"Indeed." Roberts showed Alistair the paper, and pointed out the pertinent phrases.

"What is Misselthwaite College?"

"It's a school for young men and women such as yourself," Roberts said. "I understand your father was, in the past, friends with the man who runs it. That's probably why they selected that particular school for you."

"I've never heard of it in my life," Alistair said. He sat back and squeezed his fingers together, confused and upset.

"You are of course permitted to remain in this house, or the country manor," Roberts said. "But there is only enough income to retain one housekeeper to keep the house in order. There wouldn't be anything for you to live off, however, the fees at

Misselthwaite College are already paid, and room and meals are inclusive. You may, of course, do whatever you choose, but I would highly recommend you attend the college for a year and then the trust would be unlocked."

Roberts paused and looked at Alistair, who had no idea how to respond. He had never in his life been given an important decision to make, and he had no idea how to even go about starting. He looked at the piece of paper and then at the lawyer and felt his aching head go utterly blank.

He shrugged finally. "Fine."

"Fine? So you'll go to university?"

"Yes, fine, whatever I need to do," Alistair said. He felt even more disagreeable than normal. "I can't live here with no money for food, can I?"

"No," Roberts said. "No, that's quite right."

The business of signing papers and sorting out arrangements took up most of the morning, and by the time it was done, Alistair's head was pounding and he had to retire to bed to rest. Roberts arranged a train ticket for him to leave the next day and with the maid's help he was packed and at the train station at the correct time on Tuesday morning.

Alistair had never taken a train on his own before. Indeed, he could hardly remember catching a train, although he supposed it must have been something he had done.

The station had been loud and confusing but at least Roberts had accompanied him through the crowd and to the correct platform. The train itself was loud and smelly, and far larger than Alistair had imagined. It seemed rather incredible he had never been this close to one before, since they were so large and noisy. But he had always travelled between the townhouse and country by carriage. They couldn't see any railways from the townhouse, either.

He had a little compartment in the carriage all to himself, and Roberts made sure the porter knew which bags and trunk belonged to Alistair and that he would need help with the bed when the time came to rest. Alistair couldn't imagine how a bed would fit into such a small space. On another day he might have been intrigued, but he simply felt irritated with the whole palaver.

Finally the train blew an almighty whistle and started to move. There was a lot of shouting on the platform, people saying goodbye to those on the train, and porters announcing their departure. Alistair slumped in his seat and gazed out the window. He watched the faces of those waving at the train and was surprised at the emotion he saw there. No one had ever waved him off with tears streaking their faces, or with such love radiating from their smiles.

Roberts was already lost in the crowd, presumably heading back to his office, and it made Alistair feel rather small to realise that the one person in all of London who knew he was leaving hadn't even lingered to wave goodbye.

The train pulled off and Alistair watched the faces of those left behind until they were quite gone.

He felt quite unusual as he sat back against the padded seat. He missed his mother only in an abstract sort of way. She had never been warm to him, and he hadn't known what he was missing of course. His father had been even more distant and his absence barely registered as a loss.

But knowing that other people on the train had people who cared if they were leaving or not had opened up a strange feeling in his chest. A sort of empty feeling, as if he had a hole carved out of him.

The feeling didn't leave him as the trip continued, it continued to ache in his chest and he puzzled over the meaning of it all. Perhaps he should journal about it, he considered. But he was more interested in watching the scenery out the window, which changed so quickly to things he had never seen before.

But after a time, he became bored which distracted him from puzzling out what the sensation was.

He watched the city of London thin out and become countryside, and he let his gaze then wander the interior of his carriage to examine every inch of it. There wasn't much to see. He investigated the small bathroom and the tiny basin, and eventually pulled back his door to look up and down the hallway. There were many such compartments, but the movement of the train made him feel slightly ill when he walked, so he sat back down by the window instead of investigating further.

Presently, he fell asleep and it wasn't until there was a knock on the sliding door that he woke again, some hours later to a woman who served him tea and a scone. Later, she came back to invite him to the dining car, and when he returned to his compartment, a porter had unfolded his settee into a bed and made it up with fresh white sheets.

Alistair didn't think he'd be able to settle to sleep, the train seemed too loud now, the dark world trundling past outside too unknown, and the whole thing rather uncomfortable and new, but he did sleep, and didn't wake until there was a knock on the door and the porter informed him his stop was coming up.

"But I didn't have breakfast yet," Alistair said, looking doubtfully around the room.

"That's too bad," the porter said. "You will need to be ready to exit the train in half an hour, sir."

So it was that Alistair was deposited on the platform of a country railway station, hungry, grumpy, and bemused, at a quarter past nine on Wednesday morning. There was no one in sight but the stationmaster, who eyed him suspiciously.

Alistair felt rather rumpled in the shirt, trousers and jacket he'd pulled out of his travelling bag, and he was starving for something to eat.

"Good morning," the stationmaster ventured. "I expect you're here for the university, although term's already started."

"That's right," Alistair said. "Misselthwaite College. How do I get there?"

"They'll send a carriage I'm sure," the stationmaster replied. "Most like, they'll be here shortly."

Alistair was forced to wait. There was an uncomfortable slatted bench to sit on. And with the train gone, and the stationmaster vanished into the office to do whatever it was station masters did, Alistair felt the yawning ache open up in his chest again. He had never felt so utterly and spectacularly alone in his life.

The station was quiet, nothing but the sound of the wind in the trees, rustling the leaves, and presently a bird began chirping. The morning was dull and overcast and Alistair felt as if he had left his entire world behind him. He found himself trying to remember the colour of the wallpaper in his room, and failing to recall it.

What lay ahead of him now was entirely unknown and he dreaded it.

He would have to meet new people, and he was sure none would like him, and that he would like none of them. He would have to attend classes, and although he had read a lot of books, he hadn't ever been to a proper school room. He had read about them but nothing more.

The time seemed to stretch and stretch until he was sure he had waited for hours, but the large clock hanging over the platform informed him it had been less than a half hour.

Finally, the carriage arrived, and two footmen loaded his luggage onto it. A tall woman with a stern expression and a grey bun pulled tightly at the back of her head came to greet Alistair. Her hair was grey, as if with age, but her face was quite young, her skin clear and dewy, and her eyes large and bright blue.

"Alistair Lennox?"

"Yes, that's me," Alistair said.

"I'm Honour Medlock, I'm the head of the house at Misselthwaite College. Please come this way."

She didn't curtsey, or smile or do any sort of thing to make Alistair like her, and he felt affronted, although of course, he hadn't done anything of the like to her either.

The carriage ride up to the manor was bumpy and Medlock didn't seem inclined to make idle chat. Alistair felt suddenly as if he had a hundred questions for her; What was the school like? How many students attended it? What was he expected to study? How soon could he eat something, as his stomach was gnawing at him.

But she stared resolutely out the window, frowning, and Alistair stayed silent.

CHAPTER 4

"There it is," Medlock said, abruptly. The carriage had turned a corner and Alistair looked out the window, a little startled. The trees lining the road thinned out and he saw the large and impressive looking house, standing at the top of a rise. It seemed to have a hundred windows all looking down on them, and a grey roof with several chimneys rising out of it. The house seemed to Alistair as if it were hiding something. Concealing secrets perhaps, or shutting up those who shouldn't be out in the world. It was a strange sensation, to look at a building like that, and feel such a thing. The ache in Alistair's chest seemed to increase, yawning wide so that he couldn't quite catch his breath. Medlock paid no attention.

"Misselthwaite Manor, now Misselthwaite College," Medlock went on. "I might as well warn you now that it's a queer sort of place. Although as you're enrolled in it I expect you yourself might be rather unusual."

"I beg your pardon," Alistair said. He tore his eyes from the view of the house and looked back at her, scandalised. Medlock met his gaze with a stern and unwavering blue gaze. Alistair's protest died on his tongue.

"Well, what do you think of it? I'm afraid the wind howls terribly off the moor, and may well disrupt your sleep."

Alistair felt confused and unsettled, and he shook his head. "It doesn't at all matter what I think," he said. "I have to attend this school whatever I think about it."

"Hmm," Medlock said. He had no idea if he had somehow impressed her with his response, or if it was just as she expected, her face gave no expression away. "It's a grand enough house, although terribly gloomy. But that's because of the Lord of the Manor of course. A gloomier man you could never hope to meet."

Alistair looked back out at the manor and sighed. It did look gloomy from the outside with heavy black shutters on the windows and a sort of looming aspect to it.

Inside was no better.

Medlock led Alistair into the house, and through the hallways. "I'll take you to your room first and then you can join the others for lunch."

"Am I likely to meet the lord of the Manor?" Alistair asked. Medlock led him up a grand sweeping staircase to the second floor of the building.

"Lord Carlisle? Not likely," she replied. "He's often away, so don't expect that he'll introduce himself to you any time soon. He acts as principal or chancellor when he's here, though, so if you get in trouble perhaps you'll see him then."

"I thought he was a friend of my father's," Alistair said, perplexed. "That he was expecting me."

Medlock shrugged. "Perhaps, although he doesn't entertain ever, and I am not sure that he really visits with people. Usually he's travelling, he likes to go places he's never been before."

Alistair's head hurt as he tried to make sense of it all. A friend he'd never heard of, running a school he'd never heard of. His parents insisted he attend for a year, and had no guidance for why or what he should study.

He set it aside for the moment and paid attention to where Medlock was leading him. The halls of Misselthwaite, of the university, were dark. It wasn't yet midday, but the windows didn't seem to let in much light at all.

Alistair's house had always been lit up with lamps and candles, fires burning in the hearth of each room. His mother had loathed the darkness, and couldn't stand for her house to be gloomy. Lord Carlisle obviously felt exactly the opposite, as there were more shadows than light within these walls.

Alistair and Medlock passed door after door, each one a heavy mahogany, stained even darker. The doors had elaborate brass doorknobs and keyholes, and a number plate affixed at eye height. All were closed, and Alistair assumed, locked. He could hear nothing behind any of them. In fact the only sound was the tapping of Medlock's shoes on the floor, half echoed by his own steps.

Finally, after turning several corners, Medlock led him to an open door. She fussed with the bunch of keys on her belt and extracted one which she handed to him. "This is your room, and this is your key."

Alistair took it from her and eyed the open door warily, as if afraid it was about to slam shut in his face or perhaps vanish altogether. The number on this door was 113.

"I expect a lot of people don't want this room because of the number thirteen," Alistair said. Medlock shook her head slightly.

"There are plenty of superstitions in this house, although some of them are based on absolutely nothing. Just settle yourself in. I'll send people up with your luggage. Lunch will be served in the large dining room downstairs. Go back to the staircase and downstairs, the doors will be open and the noise from the students will lead you to the right place."

Alistair was suddenly terribly aware that for the first time in his life he would be living with people of his own age. "How many students are there attending this university?"

Medlock was in the process of turning away, but she turned back to him. "Around forty board here. There are another two dozen who live nearby, either in boarding houses or townhouses. It's very small, very select. You'll soon find out the reason for that."

With those ominous words she turned on her heel and walked purposefully away, her back straight as a pin and her sensible shoes tapping on the floor. Alistair looked at the key in his hand, a small brass thing which would be easy to lose. He had never had to worry about such things as keys before, and he stowed it carefully in his waistcoat pocket, before venturing into the room which was to be his for the year.

It was unexpectedly large and beautiful, although it seemed as if it had been decorated a long time ago and never updated.

There was a large, high mattress, iron-framed bed against the far wall, and there was a wooden lacquered screen to change behind, a chair next to the washstand and a small wooden wardrobe with three drawers at the bottom of it.

On the other wall, under the window, there was a wooden desk with shelves along the back of it, and an uncomfortable-looking chair at the desk. The walls were papered with strange twisting trees and vines, the dark green colour was somewhat faded, but something about the design was unsettling to the eye.

Alistair heard movement in the corridor, people walking past. That must mean it was almost time for lunch, he assumed. He wished he had his trunk already, it would have been nice to change into something less rumpled, but he couldn't help that.

There was a knock on his door and a woman's voice said, "You must be the new student."

Two people stood outside Alistair's open door. He whipped his head to look at them.

There was a short woman who looked about his age, with

dark brown hair tied back with a green ribbon. She wore a copper-coloured skirt and a cream blouse with ruffles at the collar. Beside and slightly behind her stood a tall, rather muscular looking young man. He had large grey eyes and pale blond hair, and he returned Alistair's gaze with an air of annoyed boredom, as if Alistair's appearance had irritated him.

Alistair felt annoyed in response, for although the man was exceptionally good looking, he was looking at him as if he knew Alistair to be disagreeable.

Alistair realised she had spoken and no answer had been given. He straightened his back and tried to give himself an air of dignity.

"I am Alistair Lennox." His voice sounded stiff and strange, echoing in the large room. "I am a new student. How do you do."

"How do you do," she responded. "My name is Martha Kilpatrick, I'm in the room across the hallway, and this is Samal Bancroft-Dalton, he's in the room on your right. Number 115."

Alistair nodded at both of them. "It's a pleasure to make your acquaintance."

"We're just headed down for lunch now, if you want to come with us?" Martha said.

Alistair had no reason to decline, and in fact, felt a little comforted by the idea of going down to lunch with someone - that way he wouldn't get lost. So he nodded and went to follow them.

Samal eyed him, and Alistair was unnerved by his silence. He didn't feel quite brave enough to say something about it though.

Lunch was a strange affair. Martha insisted that Alistair sit with her and Samal, although Sam seemed to only communicate with nods and the occasional yes or no. He continued to stare at Alistair quite rudely, until Alistair was too flustered to be polite.

"Whatever are you staring at?" he said, setting down his fork and glaring at Samal.

Samal's forehead furrowed and he dropped his gaze. "Nothing."

Martha looked between them and huffed. "Honestly, Sam, you could be nice to the new meat."

Alistair bristled at that. "New meat, did you say?"

Martha waved a hand. "It's just what we call new students, it's not an insult."

"It's ridiculous," Alistair said. He looked down at the mutton and potatoes on his plate and shook his head. "Thank you for the invitation but I believe I shall sit somewhere else to eat."

"Oh, Alistair, don't be like that," Martha said. "I'm just trying to make friends."

"I didn't ask for friends, and I don't need your charity or your pity."

He desperately wanted to storm off and leave them in no doubt to his displeasure, but he was too hungry for that. He stood and lifted his plate, stalked across the busy dining hall, ignoring Martha's protests entirely.

The dining hall was dotted with tables set for eight people and Alistair chose on the corner of one which was largely empty. The other corner had a scruffy looking young man sitting at it. He glanced up at Alistair and gave a quick grin before ducking his head again and eating. He ate swiftly, as if he were afraid someone was about to snatch the food away from him. It reminded Alistair of a small animal, his movements swift and sudden.

This man's hair was warm brown, almost red and almost gold, although it seemed rather overgrown and moplike. His skin was a similarly warm colour, tawny and almost seeming to glow even in the dim light of the dining hall. With a start Alistair realised he was now the one staring rudely, so he set about eating his lunch. It was rather good, but Alistair at that point, would have enjoyed eating nearly anything set in front of him. He was so worn out from the travel and the new things.

The dining hall was chilly as well as gloomy, and Alistair felt it setting into his legs as he ate. There was ambient noise, the chatter of the other students, people making jokes and laughing out loud over the sounds of cutlery on plates. The ceiling was high and the noise seemed to echo back on itself, jarring Alistair's ears and aggravating him further. How could they all stand how noisy it was all the time?

He was only part way through his meal when his table companion pushed his chair back, making it screech on the flagged floors. Several people looked towards them then, and the man with the brown hair ducked his head, took his dirty plate across the room to a little window in the wall and fled the room.

The room had gone quiet at the sound, but slowly the noise rose again, and someone across the room laughed in a harsh sort of way. He had no reason to think it was at him, but he felt humiliated all the same.

He hunched his shoulders and ate the rest of his meal quickly, feeling now as if he was emulating the man who had sat at the table with him.

Once he was done, he took his dirty plate to the window and deposited it there. There was a kitchen and some people in white on the other side of the window. One looked up and met his eyes.

He turned away and almost collided with a pretty, blonde, young lady holding a folded piece of paper. "Excuse me, are you Mr Alistair Lennox?"

"I, yes, I am."

"This is for you, it's your timetable for classes." She thrust the paper into his hand. "Mr Carlisle said if you have any concerns about the schedule you should take it to Professor Barlow, and he will discuss it with you."

"Uh, who is Professor Barlow?" Alistair asked, pocketing the paper.

"He's the head of Magical studies," the woman said. "His office is just across the hall, next to the ballroom. He's usually there in the afternoon unless he has classes." She gave Alistair a fleeting smile, turned on her heel and walked away.

Alistair found he couldn't move. He must have misheard her, surely. She couldn't have said *magical studies*. Probably she had said *musical* and he hadn't quite heard her right.

He unfolded the piece of paper and looked at it. There were only four classes he was registered for it seemed.

An introduction to the History of Magic in England, Botany (practical), Spells and Hexes and *Magical Theory (first year)*

Below those headings was the schedule for study, which looked like rather full days on Mondays and Wednesdays with intro to History of Magic followed by Spells and Hexes, a two hour session in a greenhouse on Tuesdays and Thursdays and Fridays free.

He looked at the paper and then up at the students in the hall. Some were still eating. Some were bringing their dishes over to the window to deposit for washing. Across the room he saw Samal watching him, his gaze intense.

Alistair checked the paper again. It had to be a joke, he thought. A silly prank to play on the new student. He would have to go and talk to Professor Barlow, an actual teacher, and find out what classes he was *really* enrolled in.

He left the dining hall and made his way across the grand foyer to the ballroom. Beside the large doors to the ballroom, there was a smaller door with a brass plate screwed to it. It read 'Professor W. Barlow'.

CHAPTER 5

*A*listair knocked on the door of Professor Barlow's office feeling rather nervous. He had already met a number of new people and it was getting to be rather overwhelming. Alistair was used to going days at a time with no one to talk to but the staff and he'd already had conversations with the station master, Medlock, Martha, and the girl in the dining hall. He didn't count Samal in there, as he hadn't talked at all.

"Come in." The voice inside was young-sounding and slightly accented. He opened the door and saw Professor Barlow for the first time. Professor Barlow was a man of about thirty or thirty-five, and it was clear he had some sort of Asian heritage. He smiled softly at Alistair, another handsome man, but he looked distracted.

"You must be the young Lennox," he said. "Please take a seat." He gestured at a chair and Alistair lowered himself onto it.

"Yes, I'm Alistair. Listen, a girl just gave me this piece of paper but I think it must be a joke. I'd like to know my real class schedule, if you don't mind."

Barlow held his hand out for the piece of paper and Alistair placed it in his hand. It had gotten rather rumpled as he carried it.

Barlow unfolded it and gave it a cursory glance. "This all seems to be in order, were you expecting something else?"

Alistair froze in his seat. What kind of school was this where a teacher colluded with a student to trick someone new?

"You can't be serious," Alistair said. "It's a joke, I know it is."

Barlow leaned his elbows on his desk and his chin on his hands. He looked into Alistair's eyes and for a moment Alistair didn't know how to react at all.

"What kind of school do you think this is, Alistair?"

"I thought it was a university," Alistair said.

"It is. But it's not like Oxford or Cambridge," Barlow said. "You were expecting, perhaps, classes in English Literature? Philosophy?"

"Something of the sort," Alistair said. He felt quelled under Barlow's gaze. As if he were a slow child who needed to be explained things slowly. "To be honest, I'd never heard of this school at all before yesterday."

"I see, and I understand that your enrolment was a very special case, as well. How did you find out about this school yesterday?" Barlow quirked an eyebrow and watched Alistair carefully, although he didn't feel as if he were judging Alistair or annoyed by him. Alistair felt rather comforted and inclined to speak.

"My parents died," Alistair said. "And it was in their will. If I study here for a year then I can unlock the trust, get my inheritance."

Barlow nodded. "And neither of them ever mentioned magic to you?"

"Only in stories," Alistair said. Although it wasn't strictly true. His parents hadn't been the ones who told him stories, he had searched them out himself and read them in books. Alone in his room or sitting on the bench in the shade of his favourite oak tree.

Barlow nodded slowly. "This must all be a great shock to you then."

"I…" Alistair faltered a little. To say it was a shock seemed like an understatement. He still didn't believe in what Barlow was saying. There didn't seem to be any reason to pretend that he did. "I don't believe it."

"Well, you will in a day or so. Take today to settle in and get used to things. You can start in on your classes tomorrow and then you'll see the truth of it all." He sat back in his chair, spun to look at the shelves of books behind him and extracted a slim blue volume. "In the meantime, if you like to read, this one might make sense of things a bit."

Alistair accepted the book from him. It was a pale blue linen bound book with embossed gold lettering on the front. '*A Magical Primer*'.

Alistair swallowed hard. The book felt so very normal, mundane even, but it was real in his hand. It was as solid as the chair under him and the desk that Barlow sat at. "Professor Barlow, I hardly see-" Alistair began, endeavouring to try and explain how it couldn't at all be true.

However he was interrupted. The door slammed open and a student strode in. "Professor Barlow, forgive me for intruding, but I have to ask for an extension on this assignment."

Alistair looked up to see who this rude student was who had intruded on his meeting with Barlow, and all his protests died in his throat.

It was the man from outside the pub. He was a student here?

He was dressed less formally than he had been the other night, there was no cape, although he was still wearing a very fine suit.

Barlow looked up at the intruder with a mild expression. "William, I cannot give you an extension on every assignment. It's not fair to the other students."

"But sir," the man, William said, "I barely slept last night, I had an… an episode." He glanced at Alistair as if noticing that he was there for the first time. He gave Alistair a surprised expression. "What are you doing here?"

Alistair felt his cheeks warm. He had been about to ask William the exact same question. "I, I was.." he sputtered, unsure of himself all of a sudden. William's eyes seemed to sparkle as if there were stars caught in the pupils. It was most peculiar, he shook his head.

"Alistair is a new pupil," Barlow said. "William, the answer is no."

William groaned, although there was a fair amount of growl there as well. He raised both hands to his forehead and raked them through his dark hair, messing it up. "Sir, you have to understand the seriousness of my plight. I'm sure my father…"

Barlow held up a hand and shook his head. "William, don't bring your father into this. My answer is no. If the assignment isn't ready you will simply have to hand it in late and take a deduction in points."

"Perhaps I should go," Alistair said, uncertainly.

"Arrgh!" William turned on his heel and stormed out of the room in the dramatic fashion Alistair had wished he'd been able to achieve in the dining hall. The tension in the room didn't leave with him though. Alistair was now put out for a number of reasons. He was being expected to believe in magic, he'd been interrupted in a private meeting, and he'd run into the handsome but apparently entirely irrational and infuriating man he'd met on the night of his parents' funeral.

"I'm sorry about that," Barlow said. He didn't seem at all bothered by William's behaviour and Alistair began to wonder if anything at all was capable of upsetting the teacher. "William seems to think that the privilege he has to be the son of the principal means he should get special treatment."

Alistair frowned. William had mentioned something about an episode, perhaps he was also unwell in some form. If that was the case it wasn't just the fact of his father but his health that had kept him from doing the work, but he had no particular desire to defend him so he kept his mouth shut.

"Alistair, I'm sure you'll have a lot of questions, but I do think you need to spend some time getting used to the place. The Manor is an old house, more than six hundred years of memories in these walls, and plenty of ghosts along with it. The gardens are another creature altogether of course. So, don't make any rash decisions." Barlow stood up, and Alistair did as well, automatically. "Come and see me tomorrow after classes if you still have questions, but I think things will become clear to you."

Alistair left Barlow's office without thanking him. His mind was in too much turmoil for that. Across the entranceway there were a few students straggling out of the dining room. No doubt they had classes to attend, but Alistair had nothing to do until dinner time.

He made his way up the grand staircase. It looked different now that he knew it was over six hundred years old. Perhaps the poor light wasn't a choice on the part of the Principal's - William's father? - but simply a quirk of the building.

Alistair went upstairs and tried to find his room again. Thankfully the room's numbers were laid out in a sensible manner and he only took a few minutes to find it.

His trunk and travel bags had arrived, and for a few minutes Alistair amused himself by unpacking his things into the wardrobe. That done, he was at a loss.

Part of him wanted to go out, to explore the building, but this was overruled by the far larger part of him that was afraid and overwhelmed.

He sat on the bed, leaned back against the hard iron bed frame, and pulled his knees to his chest. It was a cold room, no fire had been lit in the small hearth, and the window seemed to be letting in a cold wind.

"I am sure I hate this place," Alistair said to himself. He sounded sour. He *felt* sour, and he indulged this feeling. "I hate it and I hate everyone in it."

He fished his journal out of the drawer he had stashed it in and got to writing.

Everyone here seems convinced that magic is real, or they are playing some kind of horrid joke on me. I don't know why they would bother to do that but here I am.

My room is dark and the building is dark and I am quite alone.

He paused his pen in for a moment, sniffed, and swiped impatiently at his eyes.

I should be surprised if I make any friends at all in this horrible place. It's like I have been transported into another world and I don't care for it at all.

CHAPTER 6

*a*listair had gone down for dinner when he heard a bell chime six. Unlike lunch it was a more formal sort of affair. A long table had been placed at one end of the room and Professor Barlow and some other older people Alistair took for teachers sat there to eat.

The food was laid out on another table in large bowls and platters, and the students formed a line to help themself.

Having made his way down, Alistair found he wasn't particularly hungry, but he took a few dinner rolls and a pat of butter and put them on his plate with a single chicken leg. Then he went to the same table he had eaten lunch at and sat in the same place.

The boy who had been at the other end of the table arrived soon after, although he moved a little closer to Alistair.

Alistair paid him no attention, although part of him was definitely fascinated by the boy with his quick movements, and quiet way. It wasn't worth worrying about, he told himself, and ate his bread and butter.

He went back up to his room and tried to read *the Magical Primer* but none of it made any sense, and soon his head ached so much that all he could do was lie down and go to sleep.

Some hours later he woke to a strange noise.

It was pitch black in the room, and there was no light from outside the window. Alistair's heart was racing, as if he had woken from a nightmare, but he hadn't been dreaming at all. He wasn't sure what had woken him.

Then it came again. A long howl. It was coming from... he couldn't tell where. He wasn't sure if it sounded human or animal, or something entirely unknown.

Barlow's voice came back to him, then. *"The Manor is an old house, more than six hundred years of memories in these walls, and plenty of ghosts along with it."*

It couldn't be a ghost could it? Ghosts weren't real. But then, Alistair didn't believe magic was real and apparently people in the building did.

The howl came again. It made Alistair's heart race and his skin prickle with fear. Whatever was making that noise sounded like it was in pain. In more than just pain. In agony.

Alistair pulled the covers tighter around him and closed his eyes, trying to will himself to sleep.

The howl sounded again and this time it sounded closer, as if it were approaching him. Was someone wandering the halls, howling? Surely not. Surely someone who did that kind of thing would be sent to a sanatorium or a hospital to get the help they needed.

The sounds faded away after a few minutes and Alistair dropped back to sleep, too exhausted to stay up and fret.

CHAPTER 7

*A*listair woke very early Wednesday morning. The sun was shining brightly in his window as he had neglected to pull the curtains and he felt curiously energetic. He got out of bed and looked out the window. His room was at the rear of the Manor and looked out over the back of the property.

He could see some bare garden beds, some paths in between them, to the left a palatial greenhouse, but closer to his window on the right, a stand of trees, and walls that seemed to stretch on and on. The gardens must be gigantic, he thought.

A peculiar sensation overtook him as he looked at the paths, bright in the morning sun, reflecting the dew. He had a powerful desire to go down there and walk the paths.

Checking the clock, it wasn't yet seven, the sun must have only just risen recently to shine in his window. He hadn't enjoyed the grounds at his parents' house at all, but they weren't anything like as organised and palatial as these ones. The Lord of Misselthwaite must truly love the gardens.

Alistair washed his face and dressed himself in his black suit, pulling on his boots. For the first time in days, he looked at himself in the mirror. Looking back at him was a plain, disagreeable boy. Pale skinned and sunken eyed, his dull, blonde hair lying lank and flat against his scalp. He pulled it back and tied it with a black ribbon.

He carefully locked the door to his room, pocketed the key and made his way downstairs. There was a corridor that led past the kitchens and out into the gardens at the back of the house and he took that route, hoping he wouldn't run into anyone so early.

The air outside was cold as ice. The last dregs of winter icing the tips of the blades of grass. The first part of the garden was walled with a knee-high brick wall, and full of a variety of fluffy and fragrant plants. This was the kitchen garden, although Alistair didn't know enough about plants to know that.

He was drawn up the path, so up the path he went, tucking his hands into his armpits to warm them, and wishing he'd thought to pack a scarf.

He made his way up the path, behind the first tall wall, which he liked. It hid him from the Manor house, in case anyone might be watching him from their windows.

He took turns at random, walking up the sandy white path between tall walls, past an apple orchard, until he came to a place where the path stopped and the gardens opened out to bare countryside. Well, not exactly bare. The land here was covered in shrubs and tangles of brambles. The plants looked strange and vaguely threatening to Alistair. He hunched his shoulders against the chill morning breeze and stared out at the land. It perplexed him, but it intrigued him as well.

"Hello there," a voice said.

Alistair startled so badly he almost fell over, although he had been standing quite still. His heart thundered in his ears and he turned to see the source of the voice. It was him. The tawny skinned young man who shared his table at mealtimes.

"You frightened me," Alistair blurted.

"I'm sorry." The man looked far more relaxed outside. The furtiveness had gone from his manner, and his shoulders looked loose and relaxed. He was wearing simple brown breeches and a soft looking linen shirt with the top buttons undone, showing off a muscled tan chest. "But I thought I ought to introduce myself. My name's Thomas Sowersby." He held out a hand which was smudged with dirt. "Pleased to make your acquaintance."

Alistair could tell from the boy's accent that he hadn't had the upbringing among society that the other students he had spoken to had. He glanced at the boy's dirty hand and cleared his throat.

Thomas looked down at his hand, then pulled out a handkerchief from his pocket and wiped it off before offering again. Alistair took it reluctantly.

"I'm Alistair Lennox."

Thomas shook his hand enthusiastically and Alistair felt the roughness of his grip. The hand which wasn't soft at all, but had obviously done a lot of manual labour.

"You're working class," Alistair said, before he suddenly thought that maybe that was a rude thing to have said. Thankfully Thomas didn't seem to mind.

"Aye, that I am. My mam's got a farm over east of the moor, and I'm the first in the family with the gift. She applied for one of the scholarships and here I am."

Alistair was disarmed by Thomas's forthright way of speaking, and not a little charmed by the dimple that showed when he smiled. He had a scattering of copper-coloured freckles across his nose and cheeks.

Suddenly he turned away and whistled, a sweet, high sound that Alistair was instantly envious of his ability to produce. Thomas raised one hand into the air and presently a small bird flew down and alighted on his finger.

"How did you do that?" Alistair breathed. He felt afraid all of a sudden. He'd never been so close to a wild bird before.

"Part of my gift," Thomas said. "Mam first noticed it when I was bringing home baby squirrels and lambs that had lost their mothers on the moor. Then I brought a crow back with me one day and she knew it wasn't just that I had a knack with animals, it was more than that."

Thomas moved his arm, bringing the bird closer to Alistair. "You can pet her if you're very gentle."

"So you have magic that makes animals trust you?" Alistair asked.

"S'right. What does your magic do?"

"I don't have any magic," Alistair said, although he wasn't entirely certain of this any longer.

"You must or you'd not be here," Thomas said lightly. Alistair very carefully, very gingerly, ran his finger down the back of the small bird. Under his finger she felt light and soft, her feathers as pleasant to the touch as the finest of linen.

He had no answer for Thomas and Thomas didn't seem to be waiting for an answer either. It was curiously refreshing to stand and talk with someone who seemed to have no expectations of him, no concerns over whether or not he was being polite. Thomas seemed at home in the open air, the wind tousling his curls in a way that Alistair envied. He never felt at home anywhere.

He dropped his hand to his side and the bird regarded him, her head cocked to the side as if asking him a question.

"I don't know what to do," Alistair said. He felt suddenly as if he could say anything at all to Thomas and he wouldn't think him strange. "My parents died, and they wanted me to come here, I suppose, so I did, and now people are saying magic is real and I thought it was only a thing in storybooks. And people here, I'm sure they have friends and study groups and so on. But I've never had a friend at all. I'm disagreeable and no one likes me-"

The bird trilled, interrupting Alistair.

"There, she likes you," Thomas said. "You've been through a lot, it's natural to feel unsettled, but it will pass."

Alistair breathed out and shook his head. "How do you know?"

The bird took flight and Thomas shielded his eyes from the morning sun to watch her fly towards the walled gardens. Thomas shrugged. "Everything passes, it's the nature of the world."

Alistair was so taken aback by this simple bit of wisdom that he was quite speechless. He turned to watch the bird fly off as well.

"She'll be nesting soon," he said. "She'll find a handsome lad, have some eggs, sit on them and they'll grow up and fly off. You think she'll sit around fussing about the changes?"

There was a pause and Alistair slowly shook his head. "No?"

"That's right, she just gets on with it. Most animals do. I like that about them, they just get on with things."

More wisdom that Alistair hadn't expected. "Right," he said. He had no idea what else to say. But the bird had disappeared, and Alistair was at a loss now. His stomach started to rumble, and Thomas gave a short laugh.

"Almost breakfast time."

"I suppose so."

"Come on, I'll walk with you," Thomas said, as easy and friendly as the bird had been. Alistair's chest warmed a little.

"All right."

They made their way side by side up the garden paths, past the various walls. Thomas filled the silence by describing each of the parts of the garden. Although presently they came to a wall entirely covered by a wall of ivy and Thomas fell silent.

Alistair looked up, he could see a branch over the wall, there was something on the other side of it. "What's in there?"

"No idea," Thomas said. "No one ever goes in there, it's forbidden."

"Forbidden?" Alistair had never heard of a forbidden bit of garden before. "Who forbade it?"

"His Lordship of course, Carlisle whose house this is. The principal or chancellor or whatever the word is."

William's father, Alistair thought. "I wonder why he did it."

Thomas shrugged and smiled, and it was clear he didn't give a fig about a forbidden garden, but something about it had caught in Alistair's head and he found it hard to let it go.

They helped themselves to eggs and potato cakes at the breakfast table and sat down to eat far more companionably than they had at dinner the night before.

CHAPTER 8

*I*t was a peculiar day of classes. First he had Introduction to the History of Magic which was absolutely confoundingly bizarre - apparently, Henry the Eighth had been a warlock who dealt in love spells?

After that, he had Spells and Hexes class where he was given an actual wand and told to wave it around like a fool. Alistair was perplexed.

One thing became increasingly clear though - these people could do magic. Real magic, sparks flying through the air, magic. He saw his classmate Martha transform a linen napkin into a fine-looking porcelain teapot.

Beside her, Samal fiddled with a wand which looked unnatural in his hand, too big perhaps, or too small. He seemed about as uncomfortable with it as Alistair felt.

The teacher, a Professor Laura Bernard, walked around the class instructing them. Alistair was very aware that he had missed some of the school term. Professor Bernard had written a list of spells on the chalkboard and instructed them to try them out.

Alistair, at a loss, stood quite still and watched the others.

"Mister Lennox isn't it?" Professor Bernard said. She had a

friendly, heart shaped face with bright brown eyes and her hair hung down her back in a simple plait.

"Yes," he said. "I don't think I can do this."

"Here," Professor Bernard took out her wand and tried to show him a basic spell. It was to clean the dust off the desk. Alistair, although he felt utterly foolish, tried his best to copy her. To no avail, the desk stayed dusty and the wand remained a lifeless stick in his hand.

Professor Bernard's wand made a soft musical note when it cast spells. Alistair's did nothing at all. Around the room, there were different effects from the spellcasting of the students. Some wands emitted light as they worked, some made sounds like the professor's, and from the sudden whiffs of honeysuckle or fresh bread, apparently, some made scents.

"Each person's magic is subtly different," Professor Bernard said. "As you have yet to tap into your own, perhaps it would be best if you just studied for the first few days, dear." She pulled out a textbook from a cupboard and thumped it down on the desk in front of Alistair. "Maybe it will help."

"Thank you, Professor." Alistair felt as dull and lifeless as his wand as he sat down and flipped open the dusty book. He couldn't concentrate on the words though. He was far too distracted watching magic occur around him.

He had been so sure, just the day before, that there was no such thing. But here it was, changing the very nature of things before his eyes. Thomas wasn't in this class, and Alistair found himself wondering if Thomas would agree to show him some of the basics of magic later on.

William was at the front of the class, casting each spell with apparent ease and something like boredom writ across his fine features. He was working alone although most of the students had paired up with each other.

Alistair found himself unable to stop staring at William. He was just as handsome in a simple white shirt, black waistcoat and tailored trousers, wielding his wand in the classroom with practised aplomb as he had been on the night they'd first met, walking down the street in his fine half-cape.

His cheekbones were so high and pronounced Alistair wondered if they would cut his finger if he was to touch them.

Not that he wanted to touch them, of course. William turned half away and Alistair's gaze dropped down his well-fitted waistcoat and to the way his woollen trousers hugged his rear end. It was a very fine shape, well rounded but not too large. He was a thin man, with a hint of muscles under his shirt and his rear was utterly distracting.

Alistair realised he was ogling his classmate and dropped his eyes, his cheeks warming.

He heard a noise to the side and looked up to see Samal was watching him. A hard expression on his face, he'd seen him staring at William, and now he probably thought Alistair was a lecherous creep of a man.

Alistair concentrated on the book very hard for the rest of the hour until William stopped glancing over at him and he felt he could breathe again.

❦

The day passed in a flurry of confusion. Alistair was overwhelmed, feeling rather a lot less capable than the other students, and by the time his Magical Theory class finished, Alistair could do nothing but retire to his room and journal about the day.

It appears magic is real after all. I have seen enough of it today to believe. But I am now more put out as it means mother and father were hiding this knowledge from me.

They insisted that I come here, to this college in the event of their early deaths, and they must have known the nature of the place. So why didn't they warn me about it?

Why did they spend all their time at parties and not... I don't know, casting spells about the house? I don't understand any of it.

And besides that something was howling in the night. Probably a ghost. Probably this entire building is stuffed with ghosts who will try and eat me in my sleep, or something of the like.

At least Thomas doesn't seem so bad. What was that thing he said this morning? Everything passes, and I should stop fretting and just get on with things.

Well, it's very easy to say something like that when you know how to work magic and I don't.

Alistair set down his pen, left his journal open for the ink to dry and went to bed where he promptly fell asleep.

CHAPTER 9

a knock on his door woke Alistair and for a moment he was utterly disoriented. He thought he was back at the country house he had spent so many years in and he couldn't understand why the window wasn't in the place he remembered it.

Then the day flooded back to him and a sharp pain sunk in behind his eyes. He had fallen asleep in his clothes and now, judging from the darkness outside his window, it was late evening.

"Mister Lennox?" someone called, and the door opened. It was Medlock. She gazed at him with a critical eye. "The Master of the house wishes an audience with you."

Alistair sat up at once and rubbed the sleep from his eyes. "I thought you said he wasn't likely to want to see me."

Medlock sighed. "I can't predict his lordship, and I should know better than to try."

Alistair ran a comb through his hair, adjusted the way his waistcoat sat on him and went to the door. "I'm ready."

"You have your key?" she asked, one eyebrow raised.

Alistair patted his pockets and found them empty. "No." He turned and found the key on the desk. He locked the door and pocketed it, following Medlock through the hallways to the stairs, and up. The top floor of the building, he had learned over the course of the day, was restricted to professors and the elusive principal.

The hallways were just as dark as on the lower floors, and Alistair took in the dark portraits and bleak landscape paintings that lined the walls. Some of them looked as ancient as the house itself and he wondered if they had always hung in just those places.

Outside the windows it was dark, night had fallen. Alistair must have slept through dinner.

Medlock led him to a tall door on the east wing of the house and knocked twice. "Mister Alistair Lennox to see you, sir."

"Come in." The voice sounded far away. Medlock opened the door and stepped aside. Alistair walked in, his steps tentative.

The room was even darker than the rest of the manor, with heavy purple drapes on the windows and dark wallpaper. There was a large portrait of a young woman, hanging over the desk, behind the high-backed chair that the man sat in. It was a curious positioning, Alistair thought, since he wouldn't be able to see her from his desk easily.

The man himself sat in the chair, hunched, one elbow on the arm of the chair and his chin resting on his hand. He was pale, as if he had never gone out in the sun in his life - rather like Alistair's own reflection - and he had long black hair tied back with a black ribbon. He wore a sombre black suit which was clearly very well made but had perhaps seen better days.

He eyed Alistair without moving. Alistair crossed the room slowly, his steps seeming to echo loudly in the silent room. Medlock closed the door and the thud jolted Alistair as if it was a thunderclap.

"Alistair Lennox," the man said. He sat up straight and his movements were beautiful, somehow, slow and graceful and precise. "Please take a seat. I am Lord Carlisle, owner of Misselthwaite and sometimes Principal of the school."

Alistair sat down on one of the visitor's chairs. "I'm pleased to meet you," Alistair said. He wasn't sure what else to say, so he folded his hands on his lap and waited.

"I'm sorry for your loss," Lord Carlisle said. "Your parents were…" he trailed off. Alistair looked up to see him gazing out towards the curtained window. "Very interesting people."

With that phrasing Alistair hardly knew what Lord Carlisle meant. It was good to be interesting wasn't it? But the pause, and the dryness to his voice made it sound like he was insulting them.

Alistair frowned. "Thank you?" he ventured.

"I expect you are having some trouble settling in." Lord Carlisle looked back at Alistair and his midnight blue eyes seemed to glint in the dim light. There was something unsettling about him. "Your mother said that you had no knack for magical arts at all. That's why you didn't come here when-"

Lord Carlisle stopped suddenly, apparently he had changed his mind about what to say. Alistair was utterly perplexed. "When what?"

The principal raised an eyebrow and Alistair realised he'd been somewhat blunt in his response. "I mean, I beg your pardon?"

"Your parents chose to send you here in the event of their deaths in case their absence would perhaps enhance your own weak connection to the magical realm. Sometimes it can happen, when the parents die the children or child get more of the essence, as some of us like to call it."

Alistair shook his head. "I beg your pardon, sir, but I never saw my parents do any kind of magic and they certainly never talked about it with me. Can you please… I don't know, explain a little bit?"

"You've been to classes, have you not?" Lord Carlisle said. "You must have picked up something about it by now."

"Well, yes I gather that magic is real and that I can try and wave my wand and nothing comes from it. But how can it exist? Why isn't it commonly known about?"

Lord Carlisle sighed and rubbed a hand over his forehead as if he had a great pain there. "This type of question would be best directed to Professor Barlow. But to put it briefly, my family has owned this house since it was built. As I had only one child, I became aware of how large this house is. My wife died." His eyes dropped to the table and he twitched one shoulder. Alistair wondered if he was tempted to look at the portrait behind him. Alistair's eyes flicked up and took in the lovely face. She had kind eyes and a soft mouth. The painter had captured something of her nature.

"My family also has a close relationship to magic. It..." he paused again. These pauses infuriated Alistair for they seemed to be revealing more than they hid. "Essence runs strong in my bloodline. There are other magical schools, but I wanted to open something that would welcome all sorts of students. Any gender, any upbringing."

That explained how Thomas had been accepted to the school then. It wasn't a school simply for the rich or noble classes.

"How would I know... if the magic had come through to me?" Alistair asked.

"You would feel it. You will feel it, simply being here with other magical beings will stir it out of you no matter how weak your talent may be. Your challenge will be to discover your talent, find where your magical essence leads you. Each of us have a speciality in our own way, and you will have yours too, in time."

There were a lot of things Alistair wanted to ask after that spiel but he started with perhaps the most startling one.

"Magical beings? What does that mean?"

"I think you should have another conversation with Professor Barlow. Interesting as this is, I have little time to speak with you, I'm leaving tonight."

"Leaving?" Alistair was more confused than ever.

"Indeed. I'll ensure that your allowance is issued and you can purchase new clothes when the others have a town day later in the month, should you wish to. It was good to meet you, Alistair. You may go."

Alistair stood up and hesitated. He felt like there was surely something Lord Carlisle had meant to say, about the circumstances of Alistair being there, or of his parents, but he had been summarily dismissed.

Lord Carlisle stood as well. "If you have any questions, direct them to Professor Barlow or to Medlock, one of them will help you."

Alistair turned and left the room. Medlock was waiting outside and Lord Carlisle's voice called to her. "Medlock please have my carriage brought round immediately."

"Yes, Lord Carlisle." She tipped her head at Alistair and they walked down the hallway together. Down one flight of stairs, she gestured for Alistair to go back to his room. "Well, then, that's about all you should expect from his Lordship."

Alistair wasn't sure if he should thank her. He certainly hadn't got much from the meeting except for additional questions.

His stomach rumbled and halfway up the hallway he stopped, turned back to the stairs and went down to the dining room. Dinner had been cleared away but on the table which usually held food, there was an urn of coffee, a pot of tea and some biscuits and scones laid out. He presumed this was for late night snacking and he was grateful for it.

He took two scones and was in the process of applying jam and cream when he heard a whisper and then a giggle. He glanced around to see Samal and Martha sitting in the far corner of the hall, some books and papers spread out between them as if they were doing schoolwork together.

Samal met his eyes and seemed to bore into him, the force of some emotion taking Alistair by surprise. He left his scones and stomped over to their table, feeling fed up after his encounter with Lord Carlisle.

Martha waved her fingers at him, smiling. "Good evening, Alistair, you all right?"

Alistair hardly even knew what he was going to say, but he was incensed and annoyed and he wanted to lash out at someone.

"Why are you looking at me and laughing?" He demanded. He planted his hands on his hips and scowled.

Samal tipped his head to one side. "We weren't."

"Do you want to join us?" Martha said, apparently not at all intimidated by Alistair's demeanour. "We were going over today's chapter from History of Magic."

"No, I don't want to join you," Alistair said. "I want to know why he keeps staring at me like I have personally offended him."

He jabbed a finger at Samal, who looked surprised, although his eyebrows remained furrowed.

"I am not staring at you."

"You were staring at me in Spells and Hexes! Is it because..." Alistair cast around for some possible reason and came up with only his own fears. "Is it because you can tell I shouldn't be here? That I have no magical gift whatsoever? Do you think I should be sent away?"

He blurted this all out and then to his horror felt tears welling in his eyes, already spilling over. His stomach clenched and his throat constricted with a lump and then, surprising himself more than anyone else, he started to sob.

"Oh my goodness, sit down." Martha was on his side of the table in an instant, guiding him by the elbow to a chair which he promptly collapsed into. Humiliated at the thought he was acting like an overgrown child and in front of these two people who he barely knew, but now that he had started he didn't seem to be able to stop. He put his arms on the table and his face on his arms and howled. He cried for his confusion, for being alone in a strange house where funny noises happened at night, for being the one without magic, and for the way that learning that magic was real had shaken him.

"There, there," Martha said. "I'll get your tea, and whatever you were fixing yourself.

Alistair sobbed, feeling restlessly alone and utterly miserable with it.

Then a soft, warm hand settled on his shoulder. It was so unexpected that it distracted him and he looked up. Samal was standing beside him, his hand on Alistair's shoulder.

"It's all right," Samal said softly. His voice had a calming effect on Alistair. He gazed up at the blond man and hiccupped. The warmth from his hand seemed to spread through Alistair, warming his chest and his legs, making him feel more secure somehow. More sure of his place in the world.

"You're going to be all right," Samal said. His eyes crinkled slightly, the tiniest of smiles, and Alistair rubbed his sleeve over his damp face.

"Thank you," he said. He pulled out a handkerchief and Samal dropped his hand away. The warmth remained in Alistair's chest and he was able to blow his nose and cease crying altogether.

"There now, I expect you feel a bit better," Martha said. "Nothing like a good cry, I think." She set the cup of tea and plate of scones Alistair had started preparing down in front of him and he wrapped his hands around the teacup gratefully.

"Thank you," he said, his voice a little strained. "I'm terribly sorry for... for all of that."

"It's fine," Martha said. "The stars know I had a good cry like that when I first started here. You'll get used to it."

Samal had moved back around the table and was packing up his schoolbooks and pencils. Alistair chewed on a scone, the warmth in his chest rapidly fading as he watched. He had obviously disrupted their studying with his emotional outburst.

He wondered if he ought to apologise to them but before he could sort out if that was a polite thing to do or if he'd just make it all worse, Samal spoke.

"I'm done in," he said to Martha. "I'll see you in the morning."

He shouldered his satchel of books and was gone. Martha blinked after him and then smiled sadly at Alistair.

"You shouldn't take it personally, Sam takes time to warm up to people."

Alistair swallowed the last bit of scone and shook his head. "It's fine. Thank you for your kindness tonight." He got up and left the dining hall, heading back to his room. He felt alarmingly like he might cry again and he wanted to be in private before that happened.

In his room he changed into his pyjamas, washed his face and got into bed. He extinguished the lamp and tried to settle down to sleep.

Instead of falling asleep, Alistair got his journal and brooded.

The day had been strange - long and full of surprises. He should have been exhausted, but his mind was whirling with thoughts and ideas. With concepts which needed to be unravelled, although he didn't have the tools to do so.

I feel as if I have unearthed the root system to a giant tree, and I can see the various strands tangled together, the dirt hanging in clods to parts of it, the roots branching off deeper and deeper... and I have no idea how to even make sense of it, let alone untangle it. Can such a thing even be done? One would never attempt to untangle the roots of a mighty tree.

Where even so little as a week earlier, Alistair's mind had been consumed with musings on himself, and what was wrong with him, now there was more to consider. The school had begun to open his mind up to turn him away from self-reflection into variations of the following questions.

Why was Thomas so kind to me when he had no reason to be? He is poor, poorer than most of the other students I've seen, judging by clothing at least. He didn't seem to have other friends, else why would he sit alone at mealtimes? Well, alone until I came to the school.

How was it possible that Thomas could communicate with animals? If I could talk with animals I might never seek human company again. I'm sure whatever animals have to say is much more interesting than humans.

The real question is how can I tap into the magic inside of me? Lord Carlisle had made it sound like a simple thing, tracking one's essence and finding a talent. Simple enough that he hadn't bothered to explain anything at all, instead acted as if I were a simpleton who needed the most basic of things explained to him.

And come to that... am I a simpleton?

Perhaps I am.

I had no idea magic existed a few days ago, and that was another thing; Why didn't my parents say anything, ever, about the existence of magic?

What did they know that they didn't see fit to tell me? If I went back to the London townhouse would I find diaries and journals about their secret magical lives that they'd hidden away? Had they really been going to society parties or secret magic rituals? How will I ever answer that question?

The people at this university are strange. Samal and Martha, they reached out to me, and apparently offered kindness.

Who are they to offer me anything at all? Are they perhaps, seeing me as something to be pitied? Something sad, and in need of charity.

That makes me feel even more awful. More lost, less likely to look kindly upon them. I don't need their charity.

Then there's the mystery of William Carlisle, who is as handsome as he is strange. I feel as if I ought to try and confront William - find out what he was doing on the street that night, find out what his apparent condition was, and what sort of magic he was especially good at. Why was he so happy to use his father as an excuse to get special treatment, and why in the world does he keep popping into my head?

Eventually Alistair set aside his journal, frustrated with the number of unsolvable mysteries, and went to sleep, but it was hardly restful.

CHAPTER 10

*A*listair woke in the early hours of the next morning to the sound of distant crying. Was it the same voice that he had heard the night before? He thought it was.

"How is anyone supposed to get a good night's sleep with that noise going on?" Alistair said to himself. Because it had taken him so long to get to sleep, and he had now been woken by something unsettling, he felt angry about it.

He got out of bed, pulled on a warm woollen dressing gown for the night was chill, and left his room. He left his key in the lock, so that he could easily get himself back in again. He took a candle in a holder to light his way and ventured out.

He looked up and down the hallway. All the students' doors were closed, of course, but out here the noise was slightly louder.

Could it be a ghost? He hadn't asked any of the professors if ghosts were real or not, although if magic was real there was no reason for them not to be. The thought sent chills down his spine.

Alistair pulled his dressing gown closer around himself and made his way up the hallway towards the grand staircase. It seemed as if the noises were coming and going. One moment loud and distinct, the next quite muffled.

Alistair crossed the landing and made his way up the hallway to the Eastern side of the manor, where he hadn't yet ventured. There were more doors with number plaques on them, just the same as around where his room was, although after a dozen or so, the doors were blank. Perhaps these rooms weren't for students' use? Or perhaps they had never had enough students to fill them all.

He turned a corner, the hallway had branched into two, and Alistair listened for a moment, before he heard the soft sound of moaning up one direction.

The floorboards creaked under his tentative footsteps, and Alistair startled at the sound of a shriek - something sudden and strange followed by silence. He felt sure that the noise had come from further up this strange, dark corridor, but his courage to explore was rapidly fading.

The corridor didn't seem as polished or clean as the one he lived on. Perhaps very few people ever came up this way?

With so many things unknown about this place, and about magic, who was to say what could be awaiting him up the hallway? There was a corner ahead, and he resolved to turn it and see what he could see in the next part of the hallway instead.

Around the corner the hallway seemed even less used than the one before. Alistair felt his nose tickled from the dust piling next to the skirting boards.

He took another step, trying to lay his foot slowly onto the ground to prevent further creaking. Ahead, he saw that the corridor branched again. He tried to make sense of it. How large the manor was seemed to boggle his mind, and he couldn't make the map make sense in his mind - surely he should have reached an outer wall by now? Or perhaps the building was simply bigger than he had realised?

He lifted the candle higher and looked around himself. In between the seemingly endless doors, there were framed art works and hanging tapestries. The people in the portraits looked severely down at him, and Alistair felt his courage waver even further. It was as if the ancestors of the current owners were watching him wander the corridors and were displeased.

Was it possible that the portraits were imbued with magic?

He shivered, and it had less to do with the chill in the air than his uncertainty.

He took another step and stopped. His candlelight had illuminated a tapestry that immediately caught his eye. The tapestry was of a garden scene, an incredible place with trees flowering pink and white, bright poppies, daffodils and so on burst from the green grass, and in the centre of it all, a boy who looked just like Alistair.

He was young looking, perhaps ten or twelve years old, with Alistair's golden-brown hair. His large brown eyes stared out of the tapestry and directly at Alistair. He was standing with one hand raised, palm out as if he was waving, or perhaps giving a benediction. His other hand was lowered, and seemed to be holding a bright star... the stitches of the tapestry radiated out from his hand in white cotton, as if too bright to look on.

Something quailed in Alistair as he looked into the eyes, picked out in thread the shade of which matched Alistair's eyes exactly.

He glanced up the hallway, towards where the sounds had come from, but he could hear nothing now. He looked back the way he came, glanced once more at his doppelganger in the tapestry and fled back to his room.

hursdays were one of the days when Alistair didn't have many classes scheduled, just spells and hexes, and then Botany in the greenhouse. At breakfast, Thomas was absent, and Alistair ate alone. All the thoughts which had been bothering him the night before were still whirling through his mind, bothering him.

He barely tasted his toast and butter and swigged down his tea without thinking so that it burned on the way down, but he hardly noticed. He went out into the gardens after eating - he had about an hour until his class, he reasoned. Perhaps he could find Thomas?

There was a gardener at work in the kitchen garden, but Alistair hurried on, paying him no mind. He took the same route he had before, the one which led to the orchards and down to the edge of the cultivated land. He looked out onto the moor and shielded his eyes from the sun's glare. There were things moving out there, animals moving through the underbrush and making it shake. The wind blowing made the moor move almost like water, and a chill went down Alistair's back. He had no idea what was out there, what the magic of this land could be and how it could affect him.

He took a step back, uncertain, remembering the strange noises in the night and then that strange tapestry with the boy who looked like him in it.

He turned, determined to go back up to the house, and had gone some way when he heard a friendly sort of whistle. He stopped, looked up and saw the bird that Thomas had introduced him to.

She perched on top of a garden wall. The same wall which was covered in ivy.

"Good morning," Alistair said. Then he felt foolish for talking to a bird.

The bird didn't seem to mind. In fact, she hopped back and forth and whistled again. Almost immediately, Alistair heard footsteps. Around the corner came Thomas, he walked with a fox at his heels, following as obedient as any dog.

"Good morning, Alistair" he said, his face lighting up with a smile.

"Hello, Thomas," Alistair said. He wasn't sure what else to say. He had been looking for Thomas after all, but he didn't want to sound like he was worried over him, or had searched him out... he faltered and blurted out the first thing which came to mind. "You weren't at breakfast."

"Oh," Thomas said, his eyebrows raised. "Right, I wasn't. I'm not used to anyone noticing if I'm there or not. Sorry if I worried you."

"I wasn't worried," Alistair snapped. But he had been, truly, and now he had no idea what to say. Again.

Thomas smiled softly and walked closer to him. "Would you like to meet Tod?"

He gestured down at the fox.

"Can I?" Alistair felt suddenly afraid. He had never seen a fox up close, and this one was so beautiful it intimidated him. Its fur shone deep red and its eyes were bright and intelligent.

"Sure, he's friendly as anything. I wasn't at breakfast because I wolfed it down, took some bacon and brought it out here for Tod. He was hurt a few weeks back and I've been making sure he's getting well again."

As he spoke, Thomas crouched down and pulled a rasher of bacon out of his pocket. He tore a bit off and offered it to Tod. The fox happily ate it from his fingers.

"I'm sorry he was hurt," Alistair said quietly.

"Ah he's all right, in fact he's perfectly able to hunt for himself again," Thomas said. He tore a bit of bacon and offered it to Alistair. "He just likes being waited on."

Alistair eyed the fox, crouched down like Thomas had, then rested one knee on the gravel path. Tod had trotted closer, and was looking at the bacon in his hand with profound interest.

Alistair offered the bacon, smiling as the fox took it from him, and then came back to lick his fingers.

"Ah, very good," Thomas said. "You made another friend."

Alistair looked up at Thomas and was suddenly overwhelmed with a desire to make Thomas his friend as well. He'd never made a friend before, but he wanted to very much. He cleared his throat, straightened up and took a deep breath.

"Thomas, will you be my friend?"

Thomas laughed a little. "You're very odd, Alistair. But aye, I'll be your friend. I'm very odd as well."

Alistair found himself smiling, on another day, perhaps an earlier day, he could have taken offence to being called odd, but he found it didn't bother him at all.

Alistair held his hand out and Thomas sputtered with another giggle before schooling his face into a serious expression. They shook hands. "Now it's official, is it?"

"Yes," Alistair said. He squeezed Thomas's warm, calloused hand and smiled so wide his cheeks weren't accustomed to it and they ached.

Thomas squeezed his hand back and then let go. "So, it's almost time for class, isn't it?" Thomas looked up at the sky and Alistair followed his gaze. Could Thomas tell the time simply from the position of the sun like a sailor could?

"I suppose it might be," Alistair said. "I haven't really gotten used to the schedule yet. I don't even know why I bother to go to the classes, as I'm no good at them," Alistair said. A bit of his old obstinate nature found its way into his tone.

"I expect it will just take some time." Thomas started walking up the path towards Misselthwaite and Alistair fell into step beside him. "Or more time out here in the gardens. Did you know there's a legend that one of these gardens is a place of power?"

Alistair's throat tightened and he shook his head. "What's a place of power?"

"Hmmm," Thomas stuck his hands in the pockets of his brown twill trousers and scrunched up his face as he thought. "I guess you could imagine it like a spring coming up out of the ground, only instead of water like you'd get in an ordinary spring, it's magical energy. The essence of the Earth itself, bubbling up in such a way that people like us, who can use magic, would feel it."

Alistair felt his stomach burst into butterflies and he clutched at Thomas's elbow. "Do you think it's true? If I could go to a place like that then maybe I'd be fixed and not useless like I am now."

"You aren't useless, Alistair," Thomas said. There was honesty in his voice, a bare sincerity that made it hard for Alistair to argue with him, although he wished to.

"I suspect that I am," Alistair said, his voice low. "I've never been good at anything at all, and now the professors expect me to wave a wand and make things happen. But it just feels like a stick in my hand."

Thomas pulled his hand out of his pocket and looped his arm companionably through Alistair's. It was a simple gesture and one that Alistair had seen other students do in the hallways. His heart sped up so quickly he had to catch his breath, every part of him that was in contact with Thomas felt warm and alive. Like the nerve endings had only just woken up.

For a brief moment, Alistair felt the urge to turn and kiss Thomas on the mouth, but he held it back. He was aware that he had been generously blessed with Thomas's friendship, and acting on an inappropriate impulse would put that into jeopardy.

They lapsed into silence and Alistair tried to get his heart to slow down again. Once they got to the hallways they split up, for Thomas had a different class to Alistair. But then they said goodbye, Thomas gave Alistair a quick, loose armed hug and promised to meet him later on, and Alistair walked to class with a smile on his face. An expression which felt foreign on his face, but welcome even so.

CHAPTER 11

*A*listair made his way into the Spells and Hexes room and took a seat by himself in the same spot he'd used previously.

Professor Bernard came in, the other students settled down and the chatter died off. Once it was quiet, Professor Bernard cleared her throat.

"Good morning class. Exercises this morning will be in pairs," she said. "Please find a partner and get to work on the spells written on the blackboard. There's an even number of you now that Mr Lennox has joined us."

There was a giggle from across the room and Alistair looked across to see two girls. They were leaning their heads together and whispering behind their hands. They were both looking at him, and when he met their eyes they laughed even harder, apparently not at all concerned that he had caught them speaking about him. One of them was the blonde who had given him his class schedule.

Alistair's cheeks burned.

But as he turned his gaze to the desktop in front of him, he couldn't find it in himself to blame them for laughing. Why shouldn't they? He was a terrible student of magic (he still struggled with the fact that magic was real, after all), and he couldn't make so much as sparks rise from the wand he had been loaned. No one in their right mind would pair with him.

Around the room, people were forming partnerships, laughing and starting to do the magical exercises, waving their wands or other magical tokens and speaking strange words. Samal and Martha were paired up, although Samal spared him a glance. His expression was again, inscrutable, but Alistair thought there might have been a touch of sympathy in it. It made him feel worse. Samal pitying him again.

The happiness, the excitement he'd felt in the garden with Thomas was a distant memory, and he felt dull and sour, the obvious last choice for any activity.

Someone moved between Alistair's desk and the window, casting a shadow over him. He looked up to see William, somewhat silhouetted in the morning light.

Alistair remembered how he had resolved to confront William, but he'd sort of become distracted from that.

"I suppose I shall have to partner with you," William said. His voice was cold and Alistair bristled, but a quick glance around the room showed him that they were the only two students not paired.

"I suppose so," Alistair grumbled. He got to his feet and pulled the borrowed wand out of his jacket pocket before removing his jacket and placing it over the back of the chair. It felt no different to a pencil in his hand. He sighed and looked up at the blackboard.

William pulled out his own wand with a flourish. It was carved of a beautiful pale grey wood, although Alistair wished to know what kind of tree would produce wood like that he simply had no idea. There were delicate swirls carved into the handle of it, and there were sigils etched up and down the length of it.

The loaned wand in Alistair's hand had been nicely made, but simply, and was of ordinary pine.

"Where did you get your wand?" Alistair asked, without thinking.

"I made it," William said. "Almost everyone in this room is using a magical conduit that they created with their own magic." He didn't say the rest of the thought, which was that Alistair alone was using something borrowed, but he didn't need to. Alistair's ears burned with the knowledge of it.

"Well, then, I suppose we had better get on with it," Alistair said. He looked up at the board and tried to imagine how those words were supposed to be said. "Maybe you should go first?"

"Very well." With perfect confidence, William flicked his wand and spoke the word. It wasn't any language Alistair had ever heard of, and although now he could understand how it sounded, it was going to be a challenge to get his mouth to reproduce the sounds. William aimed his wand at the textbook sitting on Alistair's desk and it rose gently into the air.

Alistair felt his grip on the wand tighten. There was no way he'd be able to make that same effect, he was sure of it.

William lowered his wand hand and the book settled gently back onto the desk.

"Your turn now, Mister Lennox." The way he said Alistair's name put his back up.

"I expect you're ready to make fun of me," Alistair said. Some part of him wanted to cut off the attack before it happened, although it felt rather vulnerable to do so. "Well, I'm just letting you know now that I don't care if you do. I don't care what you think of me at all."

William folded his arms. "I'm just trying to get through this class, honestly."

Alistair gritted his teeth and lifted his wand, trying to mimic the way William had moved his, and attempted to say the word. It was blasted hard on his tongue, and he could hear that he'd done it wrong. The book stayed utterly still, and Alistair felt foolish beyond words.

"That's not quite the right pronunciation," William said.

"I know." Alistair shook his head. "I don't have any magic, I don't know what anyone thought was going to happen."

"You do have magic or you'd not be here," William said. "When you do it again try for a glottal stop in the middle of the word." He demonstrated a strange clicking sound from the back of his throat and Alistair attempted it once and then shook his head again when he failed.

"Never mind, just go on to the next one."

"I am trying to help you," William said, raising one perfectly arched eyebrow. "Don't you want to prove yourself to all the people in this class?"

"No," Alistair lied. It was such an obvious lie that William's eyebrow shot up further.

"Don't you want to prove yourself to me?"

"Why on Earth would I care about what *you* think?" Alistair's defensiveness and the horror of being put on the spot, on being called out so accurately had ignited his ire. "Just because you're the heir to this ridiculous giant house, which is probably haunted by goodness knows what, going by the noises I hear at night!"

His voice had gotten quite loud, and most of the rest of the class had ceased their practise to watch him and William argue. Alistair was so humiliated that he found he didn't care. William however had gone quite pale. He looked around to see others watching, and Professor Barnard on the way over to them and cleared his throat.

"The next spell is simpler to say but requires complicated focusing of the will," he said, quickly. He pointed the wand up into the air and spoke a single syllable which was somewhat less bizarre sounding but still sounded more like he was being strangled than before. In fact he sounded a little like a caterwauling alley cat.

"Is everything quite alright here, gentlemen?" Professor

Barnard said. William had made a soft shower of rain fall from the ceiling. "That's a very good rain, Mr Carlisle," she said. "Now what was that yelling about?"

"Mr Lennox here thinks he's too good to do magic," William said. "Thinks it's beneath him, for some reason. Never mind that all the best families in England are magic, including his, and he's fond of going out at night and getting so drunk he can't walk."

Alistair was so incensed that his back straightened and he inhaled, ready to let William know exactly what he thought he was saying, but Professor Bernard stepped between them, both hands raised.

"Gentlemen, I won't have squabbling and petty grievances aired in my classroom. Please control yourselves and get on with the work as directed."

Alistair was fuming mad, his cheeks burning hot and his honour besmirched, but the Professor seemed to have had some kind of effect. He had forgotten exactly what he wanted to say, and William had taken a step back, looking abashed.

"I'm very sorry, Professor Bernard," he said.

Alistair swallowed and mumbled an apology as well.

"That's better," Professor Bernard said. "Now, Alistair, are you still having trouble with that wand? I would have thought you'd be used to it by now, would you like to try another one?"

"I'm not sure there's any point to that, as I have no idea what I'd be doing with it anyway. Nothing happens no matter what I do."

Professor Bernard smiled sympathetically. "I'm sure it will come to you with time, dear. In the meantime, feel free to read the textbook. William you can practise on your own for a bit"

Alistair flopped down at his desk even more frustrated than before. Everyone kept saying it would come to him in time, but how much time? How much longer could he stand being at this school where everyone but him could do incredible, unbelievable things?

"This whole magic business is ridiculous anyway." Alistair grumbled it, not quite loud enough for the Professor to hear, but loud enough for William. He could see William twitch, his face pulling into the frown of someone who had just been slapped with a glove. William turned away from Alistair and performed the rest of the exercises with what was surely perfect magical form and talent.

Alistair decided he hated William as much as he hated the school itself.

Once again he considered simply storming out, making his way back to London.

But he knew he had to stick it out for the year, or he wouldn't be able to unlock his fortune. He knew that, but at the same time, he wasn't sure he could bear it.

Alistair glared at the back of William as he waved his arms and said strange words, and perhaps his gaze slid down to the rear of William's perfectly fitted charcoal pinstripe trousers. But if it did, Alistair would never admit it.

As soon as class was dismissed, William was out the door, but Alistair hastily bundled his textbook into his satchel and gave chase.

William was taller than Alistair, and had longer legs, he was already quite far down the hallway. But Alistair was annoyed enough that he ran to catch up.

"William Carlisle!" he cried.

William stopped, turned, and arched that perfect eyebrow once more. His lip pulled up in a sneer. "What is it?"

"How dare you say that I like to go out and get drunk!" Alistair said. He had thought of various opening gambits as he stewed through the end of class, but that was the sentence which leapt out first.

"Isn't it true that you collided with me, stinking drunk, just a handful of nights ago?" William said, his voice marvellously dry. "Or was that some other lout?"

Alistair's fists curled and he scoffed with the outrage of it. "I think I am allowed to have some drinks on the night of my parents' joint funeral!" he fumed. "And what business is it of yours anyway? You're a pompous know it all, that's what you are."

William's expression faltered at Alistair's admission, but he screwed up his face at the insult. "Who even are you, Alistair? You sound like a spoiled, entitled brat and you've always got a sour expression on your face. Why are you here, if you hate magic so much?"

"Entitled?" Alistair's voice rose in pitch with his incredulity. "You're the one who asked for an extension on a paper because your father is the head of the university!"

William blushed a little at that. He took a breath and calmly started to roll up his sleeves, as if he thought he was about to get into a fistfight with Alistair. Alistair had never been in a fist fight but he thought if he ever would then now was the time for it. He swung his satchel to the ground and was about to roll up his own sleeves, but he saw strange markings on William's forearms. Black swirling vines seemed to be tattooed into his skin, interspersed with strange sticklike runes and weird circular sigils.

"What are those?" Alistair demanded. "Is that why you're so good at magic? You've had things inked permanently into your skin to ensure you are?"

"No, it's..." William faltered, looking around. There were a few other students watching now, and Samal was pushing past the two girls who had been laughing at Alistair in class. He looked like he'd intervene, going by the thunderous expression on his face and the direction of his stride.

William looked around, now looking almost panicked, a rabbit cornered by hunters. "Forget it. Just stay away from me."

William turned on his heel and strode briskly down the hallway. Other students parted ways before him, letting him through, and Alistair felt deflated although not quite disappointed. He hadn't got any answers from William, only confirmation that he was snobbish and rude. He hadn't exactly *wanted* to brawl with him, but he was somehow let down that they hadn't.

Samal was at his side in a moment. His hand brushed Alistair's shoulder. "Are you all right?"

To his horror Alistair felt tears welling in his eyes. He blinked them back and gritted his teeth. "Fine. I just..." he groaned, looking at the other students, who were slowly losing interest and wandering away. "I just really hate that man."

"Well, at least it seems to be mutual," Samal said. "Have you got another class? I'll walk you to it, if you like."

Alistair was taken aback but nodded. "Uh, yes, I have a botany class. I think it's outside?"

"In the greenhouse, I'll show you the way," Samal said.

Samal didn't say much, and Alistair spent most of the walk calming himself down. He didn't want to be thrown out of school for fighting, especially not for fighting with the Lord of the Manor's son. He had to get his inheritance.

CHAPTER 12

The greenhouse was impossible. It was too long, too warm and too full of strange plants. It was at least three times as long as it appeared to be on the outside, and although that should have bothered Alistair he found himself feeling strangely at home.

The atmosphere in the greenhouse was warm and damp, where the weather outside had clouded over and got rather chill. Inside it smelled pleasantly of rich soil and green growing things.

The teacher for botany was Professor Weatherstaff, a man who looked as if he had been outdoors every day of his long life, judging by the tan and leathery look of his skin. He had overgrown grey hair which looked as if it had never seen a comb, and piercing blue eyes under heavy brows.

His expression was forbidding, as if he hated all of them on sight, and instead of wearing a suit or a professor's robes, he wore a worn pair of overalls over a faded checked shirt. The overalls had grass stains on the knees.

There were workbenches instead of desks, and many students had already taken up positions around the benches, and Alistair looked around for a spot, smiling when he saw Thomas waving to him.

"Come share my bench," Thomas said, as Alistair approached.

"I didn't expect to see you here," Alistair said, feeling immensely relieved.

Across the room a boy and two girls were talking, and Alistair heard them mention his name. He looked over quickly and they all looked away. His heart sank. It was the same two girls who had been whispering about him in Spells class.

"I just about got in a fight with William Carlisle," he said, his eyes on the bench. "Thought I'd better tell you before you heard it from the others."

Thomas patted Alistair's arm in a conciliatory sort of way. "That's all right, he rubs lots of people the wrong way. He gets special treatment from the professors. I heard he even got an extension on an assignment from Professor Barlow, and he never gives out extensions.."

Alistair's head whipped up. "He didn't. I was there when he asked, but Barlow refused."

"Well, he might have changed his mind," Thomas said. "I heard he doesn't have to hand it in until Monday, now."

Alistair let this new piece of information kindle the fire of irritation he had burning for William Carlisle. It gave him a strange sort of energy.

"Alright, that's enough from you lot," Professor Weatherstaff said, his voice gruff. "This here's a practical class, but that doesn't mean you can just prattle on at each other the entire class."

His accent was broad, and certainly not from the noble classes, but Alistair found that despite this, he found himself liking something about the curmudgeonly professor. Perhaps they were something like kindred spirits?

Professor Weatherstaff thumped a stick against the smeared

blackboard where he had written in spidery writing the instructions for this class.

Repot Common sage seedlings
Pick the best specimen of yarrow blossom
Extract pollen and bottle
Press petals

"Get to it!" Professor Weatherstaff barked, and the students started to move towards the walls of the greenhouse.

"This way," Thomas said. "My seedlings are all on this shelf, here." He led Alistair to a shelf where sat a low tray of soil with half a dozen small green sprouts growing in it. The sprouts seemed very small to Alistair, just two or three leaves per plant. "Grab those little pots will you?" Thomas said, gesturing at a stack of terracotta pots. Alistair hastily picked them up and then looked at Thomas for further instruction.

"We need to fill those with soil from the barrel there," Thomas said. He held the tray of seedlings in his hands and nodded at the barrel where some students were already filling similar pots.

Alistair went to watch how other people were doing it, and when it was his turn, he scooped the pot into the soil and came up with it two thirds full.

Thomas appeared beside him. "I'll take the filled ones," he said. So they worked together quickly, Alistair filling six pots and Thomas ferrying them back to the bench. The transplanting of seedlings was tricky, because Alistair was afraid of tearing them, or otherwise killing them in the process.

He went about trying to dig one out of the tray with his fingers, when a voice startled him.

"Try using this." Professor Weatherstaff passed Alistair a tiny tool which looked like a spade but in miniature. "Slide it into the soil under the seedling and lever it out."

Alistair's forehead beaded with sweat but slowly, carefully, he did as the professor said, and the seedling came out of the ground easily. Alistair moved it to the pot where Thomas had already made a little hole in the new soil. He eased the plant in and gently patted the soil around it flat.

"Very good." Professor Weatherstaff said, and moved on.

Alistair felt something within himself that he'd never felt before, and couldn't name. A sense of purpose perhaps, or something satisfied inside him which had never been satisfied before.

Thomas and Alistair repotted the rest of the seedlings and moved on to the rest of the assignment for the class, which Alistair relied on Thomas for somewhat to know which plant was yarrow and how to extract the pollen from it. Although, it turned out that once Alistair had been told what to do his hands were quite clever at the actual work. This surprised him as much as it surprised Thomas, but it was a happy sort of surprise at least.

Something about the scent of the greenhouse, the fragile perfection of the plants and the way the soil felt under his fingernails just made sense to Alistair. He had no inkling as to why, but the satisfying feeling in his chest grew and expanded. He felt alive in a way he hadn't perhaps ever before.

Perhaps it was simply that this was the first of his classes at Misselthwaite that he had been able to follow and participate in? Alistair mused, as he carefully placed the tiny yellow petals between sheets of tissue paper with tweezers. Or perhaps this was something deeper.

Lord Carlisle had mentioned that he needed to find his magical essence, needed to tap into his talent... was it possible that green growing things would be the thing he had a talent for?

Professor Weatherstaff called the end of the class far too soon, and for the first time Alistair was disappointed to be leaving.

"I have to run to my next class," Thomas said. "But you were wonderful to partner with. Good work."

Before Alistair could respond, Thomas scampered away. He had wanted to thank him, perhaps, for being so patient when William hadn't been. He'd wanted to ask him to walk to lunch with him. He'd wanted to ... Alistair hardly even knew. He wanted to hug him and hold him close and never let him go?

Shaking his head, Alistair made his way back into Misselthwaite. What kind of class would take place over lunch?

There weren't too many students missing from the lunch hall, so whatever it was, it couldn't be too popular a class.

It occurred to Alistair, as he ate his slices of cold roast beef and boiled potatoes, that he could ask Thomas more about his particular magical talent. He had a way with animals, and could to some extent speak with them. Alistair knew that much, but he also longed to ask how Thomas had known that was his special talent. What did the essence of it feel like inside?

That would be a fine thing to know for sure. He went back to his room and updated his journal, trying to get as many details about the day recorded as possible. By the time he'd done that, his head hurt and he felt so overwhelmed by everything he pulled out one of the books he'd brought from home and read for the rest of the day.

CHAPTER 13

*A*listair's timetable said he had no classes on a Friday, which he presumed meant was supposed to give him time to study, do his homework and work on assignments. Since he had joined awkwardly in the middle of a week, he had no assignments and although he could probably use some time to study his textbooks, he had no desire to.

Once he had finished his lunch, he instead wandered the ground floor of the manor. There were students here and there, some lounging on benches and gossiping, some waiting to speak with Professor Barlow, or one of the other professors, but most seemed to have vanished.

Alistair didn't mind the quiet corridors, they were much less frightening in the daylight, although still not a lot of light filtered into the building. He made his way behind the ballroom to the far wing, and found the library. The door was standing half open, so he slipped in and took a moment to look around.

He found he had missed books. The mere smell of dust, leather and old pages comforted Alistair like an old friend.

The library was perhaps the cosiest room in the whole Manor. It was certainly the cosiest Alistair had encountered. There was a large stone fireplace with a merry fire burning in it, and several overstuffed armchairs dotted around it. The walls were covered with floor to ceiling bookshelves in a warm coloured wood which gleamed with recent waxing.

There were thick Persian rugs on the flagstones which warmed the room further. There was a small desk at the far end of the room from the fireplace. There was a person sitting at it, in front of a large open ledger, a quill and inkwell. They had long hair pulled back into a low ponytail and a severe pair of spectacles, although their face was fine featured. They wore a tailored brown suit jacket and a white shirt with a droopy bow tie which looked more like a neck ribbon than a normal tie.

They looked up at Alistair and gave a curious smile. He walked over.

"Excuse me," he said, keeping his voice lowered. "I'm a new student, just this week. I'd like to browse and borrow some books if that's all right."

The librarian smiled politely. "Of course. Here," they produced a piece of paper which looked like it had been copied with carbon paper. "This is the map. The general collection is down here by the library, that's where the novels and histories of Britain and so on are. Behind me and up on the mezzanine is all the magical collection. The things which are higher up on the shelves tend to be a little more temperamental so do be careful if you're using the ladders."

Alistair looked over the map, which had areas marked out by topic. The one which said *Magical Botany* caught his eye first. But he had all afternoon, and he wanted to explore some more.

"How many books am I permitted to borrow, Miss... er, Mister...?"

"Kincade St James, and I'm neither a Miss nor a Mister," the librarian said. "You may call me Kincade if you need to call me. And you may borrow as many books as you choose, I'll register them here against your name and room number."

"Thank you, Kincade," Alistair said. "I'm Alistair Lennox."

"It's a pleasure to meet you," Kincade said. "Please don't hesitate to ask if you're looking for something in particular. I'm here until five o'clock at which time the library will close until tomorrow morning."

"I understand, thank you," Alistair said again.

He examined the map and made his way first to the magical theory section, and then wandered through the various topics and histories, eying the titles and making himself a mental to-read list.

After perusing spell books and not finding anything which seemed to be geared towards the absolute beginner, he wandered to the magical botany section, browsing the titles with interest. He found one which particularly caught his eye titled *The Magickal Plants of Englande*.

He took it down and tucked it under his arm, determined to read it cover to cover.

After a while, browsing the shelves, he found another book that caught his eye: *Magical Gardens: how to plan a garden for maximum reward*. He put that under his arm as well.

He made his way up to the mezzanine, thinking just to peruse the collection and make mental notes for his next return.

The mezzanine was larger than it had appeared from the ground floor. A fine carpeted area with books lining the walls and a number of freestanding shelves loaded with uncountable volumes of magic. It was a little darker up here, and the shadows in the corners spread over the floor. It felt a little like the back of the mezzanine was warning him off somehow.

He swallowed his unease as best he could, and walked slowly around the standing shelves, which sported labels of the different kinds of magical books they contained. The label for *Healing* caught his eye, although some part of him suspected that would be far too advanced for him so he didn't pick any of those up. The same thought struck him looking at the books on shapeshifting and magical transformations.

Moving around the shelf to look at the other side he found *Curses,* and then an entire section on *Curse Breaking.*

"Fascinating," Alistair said, softly. From what he could tell there was no one else up there with him, but the shelves were tall and densely packed with books. So he spoke to himself as if he didn't wish to be overheard.

He set the two botany books down on a wooden footstool and trailed his fingers along the spines of the curse breaking books. He didn't much like the idea of learning to curse or hex people, but *breaking* that kind of thing was appealing to him.

He picked up a purple linen bound book called *Curses and the Breaking of Such* and flipped it open. The book had a particularly pleasing lavender odour, as if someone had pressed flowers between its pages.

The table of contents was long, Alistair ran his finger slowly down it when a voice startled him so badly he almost fumbled the book.

"What are you doing looking at something like this? Going to take your revenge on William Carlisle?"

Alistair gripped the book and turned to see Samal, tall and strangely pale in the light of the mezzanine. He breathed out heavily, once again perplexed by the appearance of this strange boy.

"What are you...?" Alistair's words abandoned him. Samal had removed his jacket and rolled his shirt sleeves up and for some reason Alistair was utterly distracted by the wiry muscles of his forearms and the fine pale hairs downing it.

"I beg your pardon?" Samal said.

"Uh, right," Alistair dragged his gaze up to Samal's face. "What are you doing up here? Did you follow me?"

Samal looked guiltier than Alistair would have liked, even as he shook his head. "Not at all, I'm simply looking for a book for an assignment," he said. He wasn't a natural liar. Alistair observed his eyes flicking to the side and Samal suddenly lunged, picking up one of the botany books Alistair had set down. "Here it is."

Alistair didn't hesitate, he snatched it back off Samal. "No, that's my book, I brought it up here. The botany section is downstairs and besides, you don't take botany."

Samal swallowed, his expression suddenly turning to something more raw, his eyes widening and his lips pulling down into a moue of concern. "Listen, I just need, I need you to be careful, all right?"

That wasn't the response Alistair had expected, not in a thousand years. "You need me to be careful?" he repeated it back, in case he had heard the boy wrong.

He picked up the other botany book and held both to his chest.

"I... yes, that's right." Samal lifted one of his muscular arms and ran his hand through his soft blond hair, mussing it up so a piece stood upright in the back. "I can't really explain, except that you need to be quite cautious, especially when it comes to William Carlisle."

Alistair huffed in annoyance. "I'm heartily sick of hearing William Carlisle's name," he said. "I'm hardly going to be seeking him out, or casting a hex when I can't do the simplest of magic as it is."

Samal chewed the inside of his cheek, eyes narrowing as he stared at Alistair.

"I... I know you've had a hard time adjusting," he said, stiffly. "And I don't want you to make the wrong enemy. Not after everything that happened."

"What do you mean after everything that happened?" Alistair was feeling more and more perplexed by the moment. "Do you mean my parents dying? My coming here?"

Samal shook his head. "I'm sorry, I know this must be absolutely infuriating but... you just... you need to be careful."

"Wait," Alistair said, a sudden idea striking him. "Is this about the noises I've heard in the night?"

Samal's eyes widened again and Alistair felt like he'd struck on something correctly. "It is, isn't it? What are those noises, what do they mean?"

"Just... ignore them if you can," Samal said. "And don't go out on your own at night. But, perhaps you're onto something with this botany. I..." he paused again, apparently struggling to find the right words.

"Spit it out, will you?" Alistair said, agitated now. "If you know something, just tell me. It's not like I have a wealth of friends I'm going to be telling secrets to, and if it concerns me for some reason then don't I have a right to know?"

Samal exhaled, dropping his hand. "You do. Of course you do, but it's not really my secret to tell, and it's for the best if you don't find out until you understand more about our society. I'm sorry. I've probably already said too much."

Samal turned on his heel and stalked off, turning around the end of the shelf.

"Please, wait!" Alistair cried. He gave chase, but Samal was nowhere to be seen. He couldn't possibly have descended the stairs already, but from the vantage point at the railings Alistair could see no trace of blond hair anywhere in the library.

He stomped downstairs, got Kincade to register the books he was borrowing and made his way back to his room. He lingered for a moment, before the door that belonged to Samal, and then the one belonging to Martha, but decided he'd had more than enough of people for the day, and went into his own room.

He locked the door behind him and sat down to look at the library books.

CHAPTER 14

*T*he *Magical Plants of Englande* was a jolly book to read through. It was written much the way a scientific dictionary would have been, with little figures depicting each of the plants. Alistair's foul mood soon evaporated as he read through the list of different sages, variations on hollyhock and other familiar sounding plants which also seemed to exist as magical varieties as well. He was inordinately pleased to discover that there was a breed of basil which could help one overcome shyness, if mixed into the correct potion.

Or that there was a nightshade species which could heal instead of poison.

He lost almost two hours reading the book, and he was still invested enough to know he would read it again that evening, however, his stomach rumbled, and reminded him that dinner was fast approaching.

*T*homas and Alistair shared dinner together, and although he had been irritated with people as a whole earlier in the afternoon, Alistair discovered he was glad of the company.

He was surprised, on some level, that he was glad to see his friend. Thomas was a sweet and warm dinner companion, who had a lot of amusing stories about the animals he had met on the moors.

"What is it like?" Alistair asked. "The animals must have so much of interest to say."

Thomas smiled and buttered another dinner roll for himself. "Well, it depends what you find interesting," he said. "Some times of the year, all they want to tell me about is where the best sources of hazelnuts are, or how to find the best burrow, or where to build the safest nest. Of course, they can all get into places I can't, so even if I did want to find hazelnuts they've usually already stolen them and hidden them away." He grinned.

Alistair thought back to the wall covered with ivy outside, a bird could fly easily over a wall like that. "I expect it must be nice to go to places where humans can't go."

"Oh, it is," Thomas said. He grinned wider, and there was something of Tod the fox in his smile.

"Your magic…" Alistair remembered the section on the library that was labelled shapeshifters. "Is your magic only communicating with animals?"

"Stars, no," Thomas said. "I can change myself into a dog and I'm learning how to be a bird as well, although that's very difficult. Maybe after that I'll try a wolf."

He said it so casually Alistair almost just accepted it as a perfectly normal thing to have said. But then his mind caught up to the words.

"You can turn your body into the body of a dog? Your human

body becomes a dog?"

"Sure," Thomas said. He chuckled at Alistair's consternation. "It's a pretty rare thing to be able to do, and I guess it's kind of looked down on, I mean, well. I don't know. The other students don't seem to like me much but I'm never sure if it's because of my talent or because I come from such a poor family."

Alistair's heart went out to this curious, well-meaning and matter of fact boy. He was gladder than ever that he'd agreed to be friends with him. He found him fascinating.

"Would you show me?" Alistair asked.

Thomas shrugged. "Sure, just not here at dinner. And, actually, not tonight. I was after heading home to visit mam after dinner, since it's the weekend and all."

Alistair felt a little disappointed, but he tried not to show it on his face. He had library books to amuse himself with after all.

They said goodnight after a generous helping each of bread and butter pudding, and Thomas wandered out into the night. Alistair climbed the stairs towards the dormitories.

The corridors were marginally busy. Mostly filled with students walking back from dinner, walking side by side and slamming the doors of their rooms as they turned in for the night.

Alistair couldn't go as fast as he desired, dodging around people talking about their homework. He was nearly to the top of the grand staircase when the crowd thinned out.

He looked up to see a girl sneering at him. She was coming from the dormitories. "Alistair Lennox, why are you here?" she asked.

Alistair paused, confused, and the silence stretched out between them. A passing student, apparently the last of the dinner rush, glanced at them as she hurried past, her eyes wide.

"I beg your pardon, I don't believe we've been introduced," Alistair said, finally. His stiff politeness seemed to amuse her and her friend.

"Oh, I am sorry," the one who had spoken to him said. Her voice lowered and made gruff, emulating his accent, before returning to normal for her introductions. "I'm Eleanor Violet Birch and this is my cousin Eulalia, and we don't think you belong at Misselthwaite."

A day ago Alistair probably would have agreed with them, but things had changed since then. He had the strange noises in the night to discover the source of. He had something to stay for now, he had a mystery.

Beyond that, he had a friend. He liked Thomas, and he wasn't sure he'd ever actually liked anyone before, let alone be liked by someone. Just the thought of that sent warmth through his belly.

He also had whatever Samal was.

He gritted his teeth, feeling his temper rise. "You are permitted to think whatever you like," he said. "It makes no difference to me. Now, if you'll excuse me."

He turned to go towards his apartment, pulling both hands out of his pockets to show he meant it. But Eleanor said a strange word and he felt hands on him, invisible hands turned him around forcefully, making him face her.

"I won't excuse you," she said. Her eyes were lit now with malice and her grin was nasty. To her side, Eulalia had pulled out a black wood wand, and was sketching circles in the air with it. Alistair's heart thudded and he struggled to move, but the invisible hands held him tight, forcing his arms behind his back. He looked around wildly but the other students had all vanished out of the halls, back to their rooms. It was just the three of them at the landing near the top of the stairs.

"These are simple spells," Eleanor said. She took a small step towards him. "A child from our society could have warded themselves against them..."

Eulalia whispered, the words forming mist which spiralled in the air, wafting towards Alistair's face. He very much didn't want to know what would happen when it touched him. He opened his mouth to shout for help, but no sound came out. An invisible hand closed around his throat.

"A child. You never learned the simplest of spells, you have no aptitude in class, I've seen it myself. And *everyone* is talking about it. Why are you here? To embarrass the school? To drag your family's name through the mud? Not that it wasn't soiled already, of course..."

Alistair was barely listening, his attention fixed on the mist that Eulalia had sent towards him, it was filling his vision now, cold droplets touching his skin. He couldn't see anything but the whiteness of the mist, and now it was pouring into his nose, through his open mouth, consuming him...

"Stop!"

The voice and the accompanying sounds were muffled to Alistair's ears, but it sounded like the flight of a flock of birds. Or perhaps one very large bird.

"This is none of your business," Eleanor snapped.

"Even still, cease your casting." That was Samal's voice, Alistair was sure of it, even if it was muffled.

The mist vanished, blown away by a pair of huge golden-brown wings. Alistair felt the invisible hands holding him clutched tight for a moment, choking him and squeezing his limbs hard enough to bruise, then they let go.

Samal stood in front of him, facing down Eleanor and Eulalia. The wings were his, sprouting out of his back, huge and beautiful.

"Samal..." Alistair whispered.

Samal raised a hand and Alistair blinked as the bright light of his magic flooded the hallway.

"We weren't going to hurt him," Eleanor said. She and Eulalia had backed up several steps. "But whatever, you can have him if you want him so much. Everett won't be happy to hear this, and you can bet you've made some powerful enemies tonight, Samal!"

They fled down the hallway, and Samal turned to Alistair.

"Are you all right?"

Samal's features were altered somehow. The bright light from his hand seemed to have lit his skin and clothing with a soft golden hue, making him even more beautiful than he usually was.

Alistair opened his mouth to say something, anything, but he coughed. It felt as if the mist were still in his throat, and the hand was still around his neck. He brought his hand to his chest and coughed again, struggling to get a clear breath.

"Let's get you outside," Samal said. Before Alistair could do anything at all, he was in Samal's arms, and then in a blink they were both outside.

"What..." Alistair croaked.

"Don't try and speak just yet," Samal said. "Can you stand?"

Alistair hardly knew what he could do. He was so afraid and confused and in awe.

And Samal's arms were strong, and his chest was warm, and Alistair felt... comforted. He felt safe being held like that. Safe and warm and something else. He wondered if that was what being cherished felt like?

Samal didn't put him down, just watched his face. "Try and take some deep breaths, the fresh air will help with the last of that spell. If it doesn't I can try some healing on you."

Alistair did as he said, sucking the air in through his mouth noisily, awkwardly, and flushing with embarrassment as his mind cleared.

Two girls had bullied him, had overcome him with two simple spells, and Samal had rescued him. He had scooped Alistair into his arms like he was a doll, and was *still* holding him. And Samal appeared to be an angel, and Alistair hadn't even been entirely sure that angels were real. He felt tears welling again, tears of humiliation and being utterly overwhelmed.

Samal noticed and quickly set him on his feet. "I'm sorry," he said. "Seeing my wings, my angelic form, it's sometimes too much for people, let me just..." He shook his head, sending his blond locks flying, and his wings folded into his back, the bright light faded as if it had never been there.

Samal stood before him again, quite ordinary in the same plain clothes he'd been wearing in the library, no longer gilded with divine light.

"Terribly sorry," he said.

"I don't understand," Alistair said. His voice was still hoarse but at least it was there now. "I don't understand anything at all!"

He curled in on himself, folding at the waist, his mind flooded with confusing new information and overwhelmed with emotions. He braced his hands on his knees and sucked in another breath of air.

"I suppose," Samal said, after a moment. "This is obviously a lot. I can explain a little, if you like?"

CHAPTER 15

"Yes, I would like you to explain, please," Alistair said. He straightened up, feeling the chill of the night air and wrapping his arms around himself. "Why have you got wings?"

"My mother was a human woman," Samal said. "But she fell in love with an angel. She said she was doing magic one night and they came down from the sky. The two of them fell in love instantly. Eventually, I came along."

Alistair swallowed. "So your father was an angel?"

"Angels don't really have genders the way we think of them," Samal said. "But... yes, I suppose you might as well explain it that way. And it's not like he stuck around long enough to be any kind of father."

Alistair's headache was back and he had no idea if it would ever go away now. He'd had to learn so many new things this week that he felt absolutely exhausted by it all. He decided it was easy to just accept it, and not worry too much, right at that moment.

"So, you're half angel and you can fly, and do magic," Alistair said. "And I suppose you've known about this all your life."

"Uh, yeah," Samal said. "It was terribly hard on Mother,

when my angelic parent left to return to heaven, she had to raise me without them, and my wings came in when I was nine or so. It was a trying time."

His wings. Alistair was glad he had decided to simply accept Samal's explanations because he might have been screaming or blubbering or something else undignified. Instead he felt a little bit like he was standing outside himself observing as he nodded along at what Samal was saying.

"Are you quite alright?" Samal asked. "You're not hurt are you? No lingering effects of those spells?"

"I feel strange," Alistair admitted. "And my head is thumping."

It didn't feel right to lie to an angel, even if he was only half an angel. And besides he had mentioned healing before, Alistair reasoned, perhaps he could help?'

Samal moved closer and the sensation that Alistair had been outside of his body and watching vanished. He was right there with Samal, who moved close enough that Alistair could smell the soft vanilla of him, which he recognised now, because Samal had been holding him just a moment before.

"Would you permit me to touch your forehead?" Samal asked, his low voice dropping soft.

Alistair swallowed a lump in his throat and nodded. "Uh, yes."

Samal's hand was deliciously warm, he laid his palm over Alistair's head and hummed softly.

"You're... you're not very relaxed are you?" Samal said.

Alistair didn't bother to reply. He felt like the answer to that question was entirely evident.

Samal hummed a little longer and the sharp pain in Alistair's head dulled and then faded entirely. The crick in his neck that he hadn't even been aware of eased. The tension in his jaw weakened and then vanished as if it had never been there.

Alistair felt lighter than he had since… he thought back. He couldn't remember ever feeling quite this at ease in his skin.

Samal dropped his hand and gave him a slow, gentle smile which seemed to communicate an affection that Alistair had never before seen. None had ever looked at him with such an expression. He felt his heart speed up, racing in his chest, and his breath caught.

He felt cared for. That was the feeling Samal had given him when he carried him earlier, and now he felt it again tenfold.

"Thank you," Alistair said. He hardly knew if he was thanking him for the healing, for the rescue or simply for the smile. Perhaps it was all of those things.

"It's my pleasure," Samal said. His eyes crinkled pleasantly at the corners as he smiled. This smile was utterly beautiful, warming his face into something friendly and becoming. Alistair suddenly found that he didn't mind too much about breathing. What he wanted was to keep gazing at Samal's face, and maybe move closer to him.

So that's what he did, taking a small step closer until he could feel Samal's breath on his face. Samal was a good two inches taller than him, and that was no good at all. Alistair wanted him closer. He reached up, a hand tentatively moving towards Samal's shoulder.

For a second, neither of them breathed. Samal leaned infinitesimally closer and Alistair's eyes wanted to flutter closed, but he also wanted to keep watching. He leaned closer in.

There was a peculiar noise from out in the gardens, a screech that made Alistair startle so badly he jumped, knocking his forehead against the side of Samal's jawbone.

"What was that?" Alistair said, breathless.

"I think it was just a fox," Samal said. "They make dashed strange noises sometimes. Almost sounds like a child shrieking."

Alistair shivered, his eyes scanning the darkness and seeing nothing at all. What had seemed a moment before to be a pleasant evening, providing them with privacy, now felt ominous and threatening to him. He stepped back from Samal and wrapped his arms around himself.

Samal's cheeks had gone pink, and his expression had shut down to the wary blankness Alistair was used to seeing on him.

"We'd probably better get back inside before they lock the front door," Samal said.

"Yes," Alistair said. He wanted to say something else, something *more* but he wasn't sure exactly how to phrase it. Samal was waiting for him, half turned towards the door, and Alistair realised he meant to escort him in.

Alistair walked towards the house and Samal fell in step beside him. Neither of them broke the silence as they walked into the house, up the stairs and to the respective doors of their rooms. The entire walk, Alistair's mind raced - replaying the moment before the fox's cry over and over, trying to decipher what it meant.

They had nearly kissed, hadn't they?

Was it just because Samal had rescued him and he was flooded with adrenaline? Because Samal had healed him and he felt so light and good?

Did he have feelings for Samal?

He was very handsome, especially when he smiled. He turned to say goodnight, but Samal had already retreated into his room and shut the door.

Alistair let himself into his own room, locked the door behind him and fell onto the bed. He couldn't even bring himself to set this down on paper, it felt too... private somehow, even for his journal.

School was turning out to be a lot more than he'd bargained for, in almost every way possible.

CHAPTER 16

On Saturday morning, Alistair had breakfast alone. It seemed Thomas's visit to his mother had kept him away from the Manor all night. Alistair felt sullen, eating alone. He had looked for Samal as well, but Martha was eating without him, chatting to some girls Alistair didn't know.

Eleanor and Eulalia were at breakfast, and Alistair was sure to give them a wide berth.

He ate quickly, barely tasting the scrambled eggs and bacon, before clearing up his plate and facing a whole day alone with no classes. He would have all the time he liked to sit in his room and read the books he'd loaned out from the library.

He made his way up to his room, locked the door and settled into a delicious weekend of solitude with the library books. He flicked through *Magical Plants of Englande* again, pausing on his favourite colour plates before setting it aside for a new volume.

He picked up *Magical Gardens: how to plan a garden for maximum reward*. It struck Alistair as a lofty title, especially for a student at a university which seemed to defy any kind of expectations. He wouldn't have his own garden until the year was up, and even then he had no idea if a magical plant would grow in the garden of his own country manor. He would have to remove a lot of lawn to even begin with plant beds... and he supposed the staff would look at him strangely for that.

He made a quick note in the notebook he'd been writing exciting discoveries into the night before.

Can magical plants grow in a normal garden? Do they require special situations?

Magical Gardens was a smaller book than *The Magical Plants of Englande*, but the cover was extra thick, heavy and cold to the touch. Alistair suddenly became aware of a slight ache in his back, no doubt from sitting leaning forward over the desk as he read.

He got up to move to the bed, thinking to sit up against some pillows, when the book shifted in his grip. He had no idea how to account for such an occurrence, he was holding it firmly enough, but the binding had seemed to ripple, causing the cover to pull under his fingers. He peered down at the book and realised that it had to be magic's doing.

The cover had changed a little - not the picture, but the texture of it. He sat down on the bed and ran his finger along the short edge of the cover from the spine to the corner. There was a distinct *click* and the cover of the book popped open, revealing a key hidden in a pocket carved out of the thick cardboard.

Alistair's heart skipped a beat.

He had done magic, hadn't he?

If he hadn't done it, he had at least set it off. That point couldn't be disputed. And what's more, he had found a key inside.

For a brief second he hesitated, Samal's voice in his head warning him to be careful. But Samal wasn't there, and besides, who was he to tell Alistair what he should and shouldn't do?

Alistair plucked the key out from the book's cover, and held it up to the light of his lamp. It was an old key, and rather on the large side. A brass key of some weight, with a carved leafy vine making up the top part of the key.

It was quite beautiful, and holding it, Alistair felt excitement bubble through him. Here was a secret that was just his, no one else's. No one could hide this key from him, it was his now, and he was going to find out what it opened.

He pocketed the brass key along with the key to his room and went out into the hallway. He took the turn towards the spooky corridor where he'd seen the tapestry which appeared to depict himself.

However, he realised at the very first door that the key he had discovered in the book was far too large to fit in the locks of any of the rooms in the hallway.

He frowned, trying to work out what that could mean. An external door perhaps? Maybe to the front door of the manor, or a shed outside?

But what was the purpose of having a key to a gardener's shed that was hidden in a magical book in the library?

Someone, at some time, had spent a good deal of thought trying to hide it. They hadn't wanted it to be found at all... which meant that it must lock up something secret.

Or perhaps... forbidden?

Once again the wall covered in ivy returned to his mind's eye. He hadn't been able to see any doors, but then, he wouldn't have. The vines had been so thick and long, a veritable curtain of leaves. A door could certainly have been concealed there. So what was the wall hiding?

Alistair turned the key in his hand. He'd been standing in the dusty hallway, holding the key and thinking so hard his head hurt.

Maybe he should go out right away and see if he couldn't find a door.

Mind made up, he turned and made his way back to the main hallway. However he caught sight of a blond head of hair, and heard the laughter of Eulalia and Eleanor Birch. All his resolve vanished. With Samal nowhere around there was no part of him which wanted to encounter those two again.

He turned tail back to his room and locked the door behind him, resolving to only leave the room only for meals for the rest of the weekend, and only when he heard other students in the hallway. There was safety in numbers after all.

The following week passed in a blur of confusion. Alistair was no closer to understanding magic, although the discovery of the key had given him a bolster to his confidence. He had meals and Botany with Thomas, which was companionable, but Samal continued to avoid him, and William was hardly worth paying attention to. The strange noises and howls persisted in the small hours of the night, but Alistair pulled his pillow over his head and ignored them, fearing some trickery from the Birches, designed to lure him out, vulnerable and alone.

The next weekend Thomas went home again and once again Alistair had his weekend meals alone. However, he was done studying the books he'd borrowed from the library and was feeling a bit more adventurous.

Alistair felt more at home in the Manor than he had been the week before, and although apparently failing all his classes was rather tiring, a sense of adventure had taken hold of him, refusing to be ignored.

In the grand entranceway he hesitated. He could go back to the library, which was rather appealing, but he could also...

He felt in his trouser pocket and felt the familiar weight of the strange key. He had been carrying it with him all week as a kind of lucky charm.

His gaze fell on the open front door. He imagined he could see the place where Samal had taken him the other week. Where they had stood together and spoken about Samal's strange parentage. Alistair still had so many questions. Was being an angel a common thing that lots of magic users encountered?

Did everyone at school know that Samal was half angel and had the most beautiful wings in the universe?

Were there other students who were secretly angels? Thomas was a shapeshifter, and Samal was half angel... what other oddities and unexpected things were happening with the students at this university?

Suddenly being inside felt like far too much. He strode outside into the morning air.

The grass still had a faint trace of dew on it, and there was a soft mist rising from the great lawn. Alistair skirted the house, taking the path that led away from the carriageway and past the kitchen garden to the walled gardens in the rear of the house.

The walk did him good - cool air clearing his lungs out and pinking the tips of his fingers. He walked briskly, warming himself up with the exercise, and tried to find his way back to the ivy-covered wall.

It took him some time - approaching from another angle confused his sense of direction, and he found a great number of orchards which he wasn't sure he'd walked by before. He might have given up, in fact, he probably would have if he had not had the motivating factor of wanting to find the door and try the key.

His stubbornness won out.

He felt as if he were close when he came to a little crossroads between the gardens. He looked up each path but they all looked as familiar as the next. He bit his lip and considered. Then he heard the whistle of a familiar bird. It could, of course, be coincidence, but Alistair decided it was a good omen. He turned down the path the bird had sung from, and it trilled again.

Looking up, he saw the same bird that Thomas had introduced him too, that strange morning out by the moors.

She perched on the wall, looking down at him as if asking what he was waiting for. The wall was covered in ivy.

"Thank you," Alistair said brightly. All his confusion and

irritation had vanished, swept up into a welcome excitement. This was surely the moment when he would solve one mystery at least.

He pulled the vines back from the wall, surprised at how heavy they were, how thick with leaves. Behind the vines was a red brick wall.

It took him some time, moving up and down the wall, fighting the ivy aside, and running his fingers over the rough bricks, but presently he found a wooden door.

There was a handle, and below it a brass keyhole. He held the ivy aside with one shoulder and pulled the key out of his pocket. He hardly dared to breathe as he tried the key. But it wouldn't go in to start with.

He bent to look and saw that some dirt or lichen was wedged inside the keyhole. He snapped off a dry bit of ivy vine and poked it inside, clearing the way. This time the key slid in easier, and he turned it.

There was some resistance, and Alistair felt a peculiar thrill. A tingle in his fingers from where he touched the key, which shot up his arm and made his arm hairs prickle with goose flesh.

For a fraction of a second, Alistair felt something outside of himself. A presence perhaps, or something judging him?

Then the key turned and he turned the door handle. He had no thoughts in his head about the warnings Samal had given him, or how Thomas had described this place as forbidden, or why that might be.

He pushed open the door with his heart in his mouth, every part of him feeling alive in an entirely new way. He *wanted* this, he wanted to see inside the walls and see what was there. He wanted it so badly.

The key had been stiff, but the doorhinges were screaming with their sudden use. Alistair in the back of his mind, knew he shouldn't make too much noise. Some part of him even wondered if he shouldn't stop, and listened to see if someone had heard and was coming this way.

But he was too excited.

He pushed through, shouldering the draping ivy to get it out of the way and found himself in the walled garden. *The Secret Garden*, he thought.

Looking around, he saw how beautiful it was. He thought it the most enchanting place he had ever seen at first. But as he walked further in, fear touched his heart - for the trees were bare of leaves, the ground was covered in a carpet of dead leaves, the shrubs were scratchy looking bramble and the place seemed to be shades of grey rather than growing green things.

The door, which he carefully closed and locked behind him, opened onto a path lined with white pebbles and crushed seashells - although many of them were covered with moss, or lost under brown leaf skeletons. The pebbles looked grubby, the odd one stood out gleaming like a pearl but Alistair had the sudden urge to clean them, buffing each pebble one by one until the path glowed with white as it had evidently been planned to do.

The garden was large, he had imagined it was a walled square, but the path led a winding way into the distance. The wall he had come through seemed mundane enough, but surely magic had been employed in the building of this place. As he walked up the path, delighting in the crunching sound under the soles of his shoes, the path wound around a corner, the wall jutting out to hide the door he'd come through once he'd turned around it. The path diverged into three, one leading through an arch overgrown with thorny vines. The second led into a thicket of trees, their bare branches had grown uncomfortably close over the path, and Alistair would have to stoop to go through there. The third path was the one he felt most drawn to, it led to some steps leading down, past a large, gnarled tree.

"Might as well start with this one," Alistair said to himself, and made his way down the third path. The steps were cut into the clay of the ground, and set with two long cobbles across each step - but the cobbles were soft and slippery with moss so Alistair took them slowly. He was wary of falling and injuring himself in this place where no one knew where he was, and no one could access.

That thought though was comforting rather than alarming. He got to the bottom of the steps and allowed himself a moment to exult in his discovery. He had solved one of the mysteries on his own, and he had discovered this wondrous garden, too big to be real, and no one knew about it but him. It was his and his alone, and all the students in the school had no idea that it was here, right under their noses.

Now it was his.

This part of the garden, at the bottom of the steps, was an overgrown lawn. The grass had reached knee height and had become a sort of meadow, scattered with wildflowers.

This part at least, was alive. It was a proliferation of life, just not the right kind to be in a proper English garden. Alistair liked that about it. He liked that it was a wild meadow contained secretly within the walls. He waded through it, inhaling the fresh scents of grass and pollen, and even enjoying the way it tickled his nose.

In the centre of the meadow there was something standing erect, and he made his way towards it. The meadow seemed subdued closer to the thing, and he realised why as he approached. Worn cobbled paving surrounding the structure.

It was a fountain. It had clearly once been very beautiful with a large, round shallow pool walled with carefully placed and fitted stone. There were carved stone frogs placed at equal intervals around the low wall. Their mouths were round and open, showing that if the fountain had been working, water would spout out of them and into the pool.

In the centre of the pool rose a marble pedestal, wound

about with carved ivy, and green with moss. Atop the pedestal, and weathered with countless rainstorms and winds, stood the figure of a woman. Her face was tilted, slightly downturned. Alistair followed her gaze to see a carved fawn pressed against her skirts, looking back up at her.

She had long flowing hair and wore a Grecian style robe. On one hip she rested a basket with flowers inside, all very cleverly carved out of marble, white shot with copper veins here and there. Her other hand reached lazily down to the fawn, as if she were about to scratch its head.

She was lovely to look at, although she needed a good clean.

Alistair moved closer in, until his toes pressed against the stone wall so he could gaze on her face. She looked familiar in some way. He tried to make her features map to his mother's, but it wasn't that. Mother had never left her hair loose over her back in this manner and the statue's features were sharper, her brow heavier, her cheekbones sharp and beautiful in a very different way to his mother.

He rested a hand on the closest stone frog. His excitement and exultation from earlier had rapidly developed into an affectionate fondness for this place, and the knowledge that he had only discovered a small part of it so far filled him with serenity. He only hoped that the rest of the garden could somehow be brought back to life.

Slowly, he became aware of a sensation in his fingers where he was touching the frog. It felt sharp, like pins and needles, or as if he had touched his fingers to a flame and quickly pulled them away. Not pain exactly, but something uncomfortable, something unusual.

He swallowed, his mouth dry. Becoming aware of it seemed to have increased the effect's rapidity, and he let go of the frog to feel the pins and needles shoot up his arm and swell in his chest.

He gasped, quite unable to breathe as it felt as if the bones of his ribcage were rearranging themselves. Curiously it still wasn't painful, although it was incredibly unpleasant. He had the sudden sensation of something within himself tearing free, and his head tipped back of its own accord.

His ribcage settled back into place, and he took a mighty breath in, then exhaled, letting his head fall forward again. There was something lodged in his throat and he bent forward, resting one hand on the frog again as he coughed.

It was in his mouth - cold and hard, and utterly alien to him. He spat it out into the empty pool of the fountain. A small black shiny stone lay there, glistening with his saliva.

"What in the world..." Alistair gazed at the thing. Had he swallowed it at some point? How had it come out now? And what could it possibly be?

Should he take it with him? Show it to Professor Barlow perhaps? Or should he leave it where it lay and never touch it again?

There was so much he didn't understand about the magical world.

He rubbed his hand over his chest, relieved that it still felt exactly how it had always felt.

Straightening up he took stock of himself. Whatever had happened it was definitely over now. He felt utterly normal again.

Except... no, there *was* something different.

His shoulders felt lighter, his head clearer in some way. He felt an increase of energy inside himself. Far more than he had possessed that morning, or the day before. He felt ... capable.

Swallowing, hardly daring to voice the idea, even inside his own head, Alistair turned to look for a sprout, some tiny little plant like he had been tending in Botany class. There, between two of the cobbles on the ground, a pair of small green leaves pushing up towards the light.

Alistair crouched on one knee and stroked a finger over the tiny leaf. He felt the energy inside him warm his skin, and under his hand the plant grew. He watched as the main stem grew thicker and taller, and two more leaves sprouted above the first one.

It happened so fast, and it had felt so simple to do, that Alistair lost his balance and fell sideways, crashing into the overgrown grasses of the meadow.

He laughed then, surprising himself with the sound, and startling a bird out of a nearby tree. He had found the garden, and within it, he had somehow solved the problem of his own magical talent.

What a grand day it was turning out to be.

He spent the next hour exploring all the parts of the garden, trying each path and finding the various sections of the garden. At some point someone had spent a great deal of time arranging flower beds, and designing this place. He wondered who it could have been, and why the place was locked up and forbidden now.

Perhaps it was because of the fountain? Whatever had happened to him, it had only happened when he had touched the fountain.

Here and there he noticed a tiny green spike pushing through the leaf litter. When he saw these he indulged himself to bend down and clear a bit of ground around it. Giving it room to grow, and then gently touching the spike, delighting every time it responded by growing taller, pushing further out of the ground.

Presently he started to feel unaccountably weary. Dinner time must be approaching, although he hadn't taken a pocket watch to keep an eye on the time.

It didn't feel right to leave the black stone behind in the fountain, so he went back to retrieve it. He didn't want to touch it with his bare fingers, so he pulled out his pocket handkerchief and used that to pluck it out of the fountain, wrap it up and stow it safely in his pocket.

He needed to visit the library again as soon as possible.

There had to be some books in there which would explain what had happened.

Thomas was absent at dinner, so Alistair ate alone and quickly. Samal arrived late, just as Alistair was leaving, and he avoided Alistair's eyes. Alistair wasn't sure what to feel about that, except he wasn't terribly surprised.

He had barely managed to keep his eyes open over dinner, and as the library was definitely closed for the night, he went immediately up to his room.

He didn't have the energy to do a proper journal entry so instead he made a list of all the beautiful and wondrous things he'd seen that day, or that popped into his head.

A Secret Garden

The fountain of the lady, with frogs and a fawn

Peculiar feeling, and a black stone coughed up

New connection to the world?

A tiny green spike pushing its way out of the ground

The winding path in the Garden

Thomas

Samal

He gave up, went to bed and fell into a deep and dreamless sleep.

CHAPTER 17

On Saturday night, Alistair's sleep was broken by a strange sound.

For a moment, he considered pulling his pillow over his head and just ignoring it. Let the mysteries of Misselthwaite Manor sort themselves out in the small hours of the morning.

He wanted to. He even tried it briefly.

But the sound came again, and he knew he was too enmired in the mystery of it to ignore it now. He had to know what it was, and hopefully put a stop to it so he could sleep all the way through the night for once.

He pulled on his dressing gown and slippers, picked up a candle and made his way through the corridors once again. He retraced his steps to the far wing of the Manor, ignoring the tapestry which depicted him or someone who looked like him, and moving further down the hallway.

This time he wasn't going to be deterred. The knowledge that he'd somehow unlocked his magic in the Secret Garden had bolstered his courage and he made his way into the darkest part of the corridor with stubborn determination, although his hands were still trembling.

The cries had varied from an unearthly shriek to wails of despair. Someone or something was howling into the night.

He had no idea how the other students could ignore the sounds... perhaps they were simply accustomed to them, having lived with them for years? The thought was a depressing one. Someone was clearly in distress.

Samal had known what he was talking about, but he had told Alistair to ignore them. That was another confounding mystery. Samal was a healer, wasn't he? Surely he should be trying to help someone in distress.

The sounds got louder, until Alistair found himself at a door. He was certain the sounds were coming from behind there.

He reached out to touch the door handle but when he did, the door lit up with runes and sigils, they glowed bright blue in the dark corridor and a flash of pain shot up Alistair's arm.

He let go of the door handle and knocked on the door instead. His knuckles flared with magical pain with each rap.

"Hello in there!" he called out.

The sounds had ceased, and the door dulled back to looking quite ordinary when he stopped knocking.

There was the sound of movement inside but no response came.

"I can hear you in there!" Alistair said. "What are you crying about?"

He paused to listen. But now there was no sound at all. Not movement, not noise... whoever was in there obviously was trying to ignore him.

Or was hoping he'd go away.

Alistair found this even more annoying than constantly being woken up. Here was another mystery to solve, but the answer wasn't cooperating with him. He had no idea how to read the runes and he was sure he'd need to do something of the sort before he could break the lock on the door and go in.

But the riddle of what was behind the door prickled at his curiosity.

"Who are you?" he tried. And then "what's your game, making all this noise in the middle of the night? Do you need some help?"

No response.

"If you're doing this for fun, then I want you to know it's waking me up."

Alistair frowned. He knew where the door was now, he could go and look in the library for books on magical locks and how to open them the next day... or he could just wait out here in the corridor until whoever it was came out.

He looked up and down the hallway and yawned, despite himself. No, his bed was calling him.

He gazed at the door, wondering if he ought to tell the occupant that he was leaving, but that might inspire them to start howling again. He shook his head, tsked his tongue against his teeth and made his way back to his room.

CHAPTER 18

*S*unday was traditionally a day for staying in bed late for Alistair. His parents had not been particularly pious sorts, and they hadn't ever gone to church in his memory. But on this particular morning he wanted to get up and visit the library. He had no idea if the library even opened on a Sunday, but he didn't want to risk missing out if it was. He scrambled out of bed, washed his face and decided he couldn't be bothered with brushing his hair and simply tied it back with the same ribbon he'd worn the day before. He pulled on black trousers which needed pressing, a cream-coloured linen shirt and a black waistcoat, left his jacket on the hanger and hurriedly grabbed his room key.

He went to the library first, although the smells wafting from the dining hall were very tempting. His stomach rumbled, but he turned down the corridor which led to the library.

The doors were closed. He tugged on the handle anyway, just in case, but they were locked. He felt the same sort of shivering sparkle of energy up his arm that he had felt at the door in the middle of the night, although not nearly so painful.

"That must mean it's magically locked, or uh, warded,"

Alistair said, remembering the word from his reading of the basic textbook.

He stepped back from the door and spotted a brass plate etched with the library's hours. It said that on Sundays the library was only open from midday to four.

Alistair sighed to himself. It was disappointing, but at least he had time for breakfast now, and could come back later.

He made his way back up the hall with less haste, and went into the dining room.

Thomas was sitting at their table. Alistair was flooded with relief, seeing him. He hadn't quite realised how much he missed his friend when he went on these weekend trips home. He helped himself to a bowl of porridge, sprinkled it liberally with brown sugar and dried apricots and went to join Thomas.

"Good morning," Thomas said. His cheeks were ruddy, as if he'd been out running.

"Good morning," Alistair said. "Where have you been?"

"Ah, mam asked me to stay and help out around the house a bit," Thomas said. "So I stayed all Saturday and last night too. But this morning I took off before she could ask me to mind the little ones."

"The little ones?" It occurred to Alistair then that he knew very little of Thomas's life, save that his mother had a farm and lived somewhere in the moors. Or over the moors.

"Mmhm." Thomas had finished a bowl of porridge and was working on a plate of smoked kippers and toast now.

"Would you tell me a bit about your family?" Alistair asked, feeling a bit shy, and rather ashamed he hadn't asked before.

"I'm the eldest, and then there's Simon, he's two years younger than me. Jonathan's just turned eleven, and the twins are just five, and they're Esther and Madrigal."

Alistair tried to imagine having that many younger siblings, and found he absolutely couldn't.

"I'm an only child," Alistair said. "It must be so busy and loud at home."

"It is, and the house isn't big, so if it's rainy it's awful, everyone crammed in on top of each other. At least the twins aren't babies any longer, it was really noisy then." He spoke with good natured affection, even though the situation he was describing sounded rather horrendous to Alistair's ears.

"Is your father still around?"

Thomas shrugged one shoulder. "Well, sometimes he is. He comes and goes."

Alistair could at least relate to that. His own parents had largely been absent from his life, after all. "What does he do?"

"Oh, all sorts of things," Thomas said. "When I was a kid I thought he was a forest god, but mam says he's just a wanderer, can't be stuck down for too long in one place."

Alistair blinked. "You thought he was a forest god? I'm sorry I don't understand."

Thomas grinned around a mouthful of kippers, swallowed it and grinned again, fox-like with his teeth showing. "Aye, he often has an animal's ears instead of human, usually a fox or a wolf, poking out of his hair. I got my shape-shifting from him y'see, and he uses it to do odd jobs. Helps out in hunting season, finds missing kids, goes town to town and see what needs doing."

Alistair felt his mind expand again. There were so many new things he had to learn about. "That's honestly amazing. My parents just went to parties and to London and left me alone."

Thomas's forehead furrowed and his mouth turned down. "I'm sorry to hear it."

"It's fine," Alistair said, ignoring the flare of pain in the centre of his chest. "But they never told me about magic and I'm a bit angry about that now, especially since -" he stopped himself. He had been about to share what had happened in the Secret Garden with Thomas.

But *should* he share it?

He had wanted to keep it a secret, but on the other hand, Thomas knew far more about magic than Alistair did and maybe he could help him to understand it better.

He looked Thomas over, drinking in his golden-brown skin, his freckles and his large, clear eyes. He liked Thomas, and he thought he could trust him. He decided to go for it.

"Thomas, can you keep a secret? It's a deadly secret, it must never be shared," Alistair said, lowering his voice. His heart was thumping, excited about the prospect of sharing what he'd found and strengthening the bond he had built with Thomas at the same time.

"Of course," Thomas said. He leaned in closer. "You can trust me. I won't tell anyone, except maybe mam. I've been telling her all about you, and she's very curious."

That was another surprise and Alistair was distracted from his purpose. He tried to imagine Thomas talking about him and couldn't really picture it. "You did? She was? What did you tell her?"

"Oh, all about you and how you turned up in the middle of the term and didn't seem to know anything about magic. She was really interested, she said she'd heard of your parents."

"She did?" Alistair leaned forward on his elbows. "What did she say?"

"Oh, that there'd been some kind of tragedy. We got interrupted before I could ask about it, because Jonathan had brought in a hare that had twisted its ankle and I got to work mending it up."

Alistair tilted his head. "How does a hare twist its ankle?"

"I don't really know," Thomas admitted. "But it was a tricky thing to heal, because it kept wanting to bound off as soon as it felt better, but it needed to rest."

They both contemplated their cups of tea, and the

circumstances in which a hare might twist its ankle for a moment.

"Anyway, what was this deadly secret you wanted to tell me about?" Thomas asked.

Alistair looked up at him and smiled. He dug the key to the garden out of his pocket and placed it on the table between them. "I stole a garden."

Thomas eyed the key and then looked up at Alistair. "You what?"

"I got a book out of the library on gardens, because I've been enjoying Botany the most out of all my classes," Alistair said. Then he described all the rest of it, the trying doors and then the ivy -overed wall, and finding the fountain and coughing up the black stone and how after that he was able to magic the plant seedlings. He kept his voice low, so that others wouldn't overhear, and Thomas was a rapt audience, his eyes wide.

"That's a curse," Thomas said, finally.

"What is?"

"The stone," Thomas said. "It's evidence that someone, at some point, put a curse on you. They must have bound your magic power."

Alistair felt a shiver down his back and he leaned back in his chair. "Is that even possible?"

Thomas shrugged his shoulder. "It must be, because they already did it."

Alistair couldn't argue with that line of reasoning. "I suppose they did."

"But I'm happy for you, that's a great thing to have discovered." Alistair smiled and pocketed the key again.

He wanted to let Thomas in. Give him more than just the knowledge of the secret. He wanted to get closer to him, and perhaps now, he had a good opportunity to do so.

"If you're interested, perhaps you'd like to come and see the garden?"

"I'd love that," Thomas said. "I bet I could tell you if those plants are really dead, or if they're just hibernating, too. We could identify all the things you've found, and work out what it will be like when Spring comes properly."

Thomas's words were like energising music to Alistair's ears and he felt his excitement well up all over again. "Wonderful, perfect, let's go today!"

"Going into town are you?" The now-familiar voice of Eleanor Violet broke into their conversation, and Alistair's excitement died, replaced with tension and fear.

What was she going to do now? Was she going to attack him in front of Thomas? In front of half the school.

"Not to town," Alistair said stiffly.

"Good, I'd hate to have you on the train with us, stinking up the carriage. I see you've made an appropriate friend." Eleanor sneered at Thomas, who blushed and looked down at his plate, chewing his lip.

"I don't know what you're insinuating," Alistair said. He felt his temper rising. It was one thing to pick on him, but quite another to pick on Thomas. "But I won't stand for you insulting Thomas."

Eleanor scoffed at him. "Well, if you wish to be friends with a dog, that's your decision of course. I hope you enjoy rolling about in the mud together."

Eulalia laughed musically. "Oh, that's perfect. Rolling around in the mud, sniffing out rabbits and wading through mud puddles," she said.

Thomas seemed to be shrinking, his shoulders hunching up under his ears as he curled forward. Alistair stood up so fast his chair made a loud scraping sound on the flags. If anyone hadn't been watching this exchange they certainly were now.

"Stop it this instant!" Alistair shouted.

"Or you'll what, bark at me?" Eleanor asked. She had her wand in hand, Alistair realised with a sinking heart. Alistair hadn't even tried the borrowed wand since he'd found his magic. He had no skill, no way to fight back if it came to that.

"What's all this fuss about?" Professor Barlow strode into the room and Eleanor hastily pocketed her wand. She composed her face instantly into a sweet and innocent expression.

"Nothing, Professor."

"Eleanor was just being hateful," Alistair said, without thinking. Eulalia and Eleanor looked at him, scandalised, and he wondered if there was some rule of etiquette he'd just broken. But the Professor had asked, and he'd answered honestly.

Professor Barlow looked like he was trying not to smile. "Please all of you, return to your breakfasts. It's Sunday, don't you all have homework you can concern yourselves with?"

"Yes, Professor," Eulalia and Eleanor said, in unison.

"Yes, Professor," Alistair said, a beat too late. The girls flounced away, sending Alistair scathing looks over his shoulder.

Professor Barlow examined Alistair for a moment, his expression pensive. "How are you settling in, Mister Lennox?"

Alistair wasn't sure now how to answer that, so he cleared his throat and made a polite answer. "It's an adjustment, Sir."

Barlow smiled and nodded. "I imagine it is. Hang in there. And don't forget you can come to me with any questions you have, all right?"

Alistair nodded. Professor Barlow looked at Thomas and then shrugged, seeming to give him up as a lost cause before he walked away.

Alistair sat down again, Thomas hadn't looked up from his plate yet.

"I'm sorry," Alistair said. He reached a hand out to Thomas, patting his where they were clasped on the table. "I didn't mean to embarrass you."

"You didn't," he said. "I'm grateful that you stood up for me. But I usually just get by without them noticing me." He unclasped his hands and slipped one into Alistair's, holding it gently. Alistair's cheeks warmed and he felt a warm energy from Thomas. Something like the energy from the doors... it must be Thomas's magic, he realised.

It was pleasant, warm and wild. Alistair almost fancied he could smell the fresh scent of green leaves and a cool breeze.

"No wonder you were willing to take me as a friend," Alistair said. "If you're used to everyone treating you like a dog."

"I mean, I can turn into a dog," Thomas said, wrinkling his nose. "That's where they get it from."

"Well, I think turning into a dog is a wonderful thing to do," Alistair sniffed. "They're probably just jealous of you."

Thomas smiled and squeezed his hand, and all of Alistair's fear and tension evaporated. Alistair wondered if he should ask Thomas to see his shapeshifting again, but perhaps it was rude to have asked, and that's why he hadn't offered to do it. He decided against it.

As they got up to put away their plates, Alistair caught sight of Samal and Martha at their customary table. Samal was watching him with an unreadable expression.

Alistair would perhaps have waved, except he was bundling his plate and breakfast things through the window into the kitchen and when he turned back, Samal was in deep conversation with Martha.

Alistair frowned, he didn't know at all how to handle what had happened with Samal, and he didn't want to betray his secret - if it even was a secret - to Thomas.

Thomas and Alistair went into the main entranceway . "Are you ready to go look at the garden now?" Alistair asked.

"Sure," Thomas said. "But I actually do have some homework that I need to get done, so I won't be able to spend all day there..."

"That's fine," Alistair said. "I want to get to the library this afternoon."

The promise of a morning in the garden with Thomas stretched before Alistair and he felt his cares drop away again, exulting in the prospect of a pleasant time.

Unfortunately, it was not to be.

Medlock hurried down the stairs and fixed her eyes on Alistair. "Mister Lennox, I'm glad to have caught you," she said.

"Good morning Medlock," Alistair said. "I was just about to head out into the grounds for... a walk."

"You'll have no time for that," Medlock said. "Lord Carlisle wants to speak with you."

"He does? I thought he was travelling?"

Medlock sighed, shook her head and wiped her hands on her apron. "Well, he's returned now. Come along, he doesn't like to be kept waiting and you 'll need to put on a jacket before you meet him."

"I'll find you later," Thomas said. He gave Alistair a rueful smile.

"Right, all right," Alistair said. "I'll hopefully not be long."

Medlock had already started to hurry off, and she turned back to beckon impatiently at Alistair. He hesitated, wanting to offer Thomas something, a hug perhaps... or even a kiss on the cheek, but it felt presumptive, and wrong, so he waved and turned to follow Medlock.

CHAPTER 19

*A*listair was once again confused and uncertain of himself. Breakfast had been going so beautifully with Thomas, and then Eleanor and Eulalia had ruined things. Professor Barlow had been kind, but then the news that Lord Carlisle wanted to see him had been so confusing and abrupt.

He fussed in his room, brushing his hair and retying the ribbon before pulling on his black jacket, which also needed a press.

Medlock stood in the open door, sighing every thirty seconds to indicate that he was taking too long and that he was keeping her past her patience.

He hurried out finally and followed her up to the office he'd visited with Lord Carlisle before.

Medlock rapped on the door and the voice came from within. "Enter."

Alistair walked through, feeling unaccountably nervous. Had Lord Carlisle heard of his altercation with William, his son? Was he about to be told off?

Had he heard about his behaviour at breakfast? Was he about to be expelled for brawling with anyone who spoke to him the wrong way?

Or…did Lord Carlisle somehow know that he'd found his way into the Secret Garden? Of all the possibilities that was the one which frightened him the most. He had only just discovered it, and there was so much he wanted to do there… if Lord Carlisle knew about it, perhaps he'd never be allowed back into it.

Lord Carlisle was standing this time. The drapes in the room were closed, giving the grand study a close and stifling air. It was sunny outside, and Alistair felt the call of it, and wondered why Lord Carlisle was so insistent on having his room as gloomy as a tomb.

"Mister Lennox," Lord Carlisle said. "Please, sit down. I've had tea delivered, please help yourself." He waved a hand listlessly at a low table between two overstuffed chairs. There was a tea service, complete with shortbread biscuits on a silver tray on the table. The chairs and table were positioned near the drapes, as if they expected to sit in a pleasant sunbeam. As it was, it felt like Alistair had been suddenly transported back to the middle of the night.

Alistair poured a cup of tea and added a little milk before sitting where Lord Carlisle had indicated.

"Thank you Lord Carlisle," Alistair said, feeling quite perplexed. This didn't feel like a scolding, but then again, he had never been to a university before and didn't know what to expect.

Lord Carlisle sat opposite him, poured himself a black tea and sat back, holding it carelessly in one hand.

"Mister Lennox, I understand that you have been moving about the manor in the nighttime."

Alistair had been in the process of sipping his tea and now he gulped it down guilty, burning his tongue. "Ah! Ah, yes, uh, I'm sorry sir, I didn't know I wasn't supposed to."

Lord Carlisle, gimlet eyed, examined Alistair's face. "Are you prone to sleepwalking?"

"No, Sir," Alistair said. "It's just I've been hearing these strange noises. Like, well, like someone crying. I didn't know what it was, but once you've heard something like that it's hard to ignore it and go back to sleep."

Lord Carlisle set his cup down and steepled his fingers, leaning his head back against the chair. "You've heard strange noises."

It wasn't a question, and Alistair didn't know how to respond. So he set his teacup down and picked up a biscuit and gave no response at all. Lord Carlisle seemed to think for a minute and then continued.

"You are the only student who has ever reported such noises," he said.

"They are there, I didn't make it up," Alistair protested, his mouth partially full of shortbread. Hastily he swallowed, flushing because he was pretty sure he wasn't supposed to argue with a lord but then, he didn't like not being believed either.

"I know they're there." Lord Carlisle sighed softly. "What do you know of the Carlisle family, Alistair?"

"Almost nothing, sir," Alistair said. "My parents never took me to society gatherings, and I only found out about the existence of magic when I arrived here a couple of weeks ago."

Lord Carlisle nodded slowly and eyed Alistair over his peaked fingertips. "There is a curse on my line, one that has unfortunately passed down to my son. Would that it were not so, but it is. The curse cares not for personal preferences."

Alistair couldn't imagine that any curse cared for anything at all, but he knew to hold his tongue in this case, at least. But some sort of response did seem polite.

"I'm terribly sorry to hear that," he said.

"Indeed. It took my wife from me," Lord Carlisle said, his voice dull. His eyes flicked briefly over Alistair's shoulder, towards the desk and a large portrait of the smiling lady. "And now it plagues my son. We have had doctors, magical specialists, witches, wizards, mages from various countries in Africa, and the Hindu practitioners of medicine from India... anyone who thought they might be able to help has seen him. And none have been successful."

Alistair remembered William begging Professor Barlow to be lenient due to his 'condition'. If he was cursed, that would certainly explain it. But what did being cursed actually mean? He assumed it wasn't whatever Eleanor and Eulalia had done the other day, or William wouldn't be walking around and speaking.

"What uh, what form does the curse take?" Alistair asked, slowly. Not at all sure if he was allowed to be asking this, but Lord Carlisle must have brought it up in conversation for a reason.

"It varies," Lord Carlisle said. "I would be loath to betray William's trust by speaking on private matters, however I am intrigued that you were able to hear him through the wards and protections placed on his door. It speaks to something peculiar about you."

He stared at Alistair again with those piercing eyes and Alistair felt desperately uncomfortable. He picked up his teacup again in order to have something in between the two of them.

"Tell me, Alistair Lennox, have you found your connection to magical essence?"

Alistair swallowed, and nodded. "Yes, I believe I have, sir."

"Indeed. Have you any idea what your talent might be? I haven't heard anything from the professors about it."

Alistair stared into the cup, but he knew there was only one answer he could give. "I, I'm not entirely sure, but I think it might be Botany. I felt at home in the greenhouse the other day, and yesterday..." he thought hard, not wanting to give anything away that he didn't have to. "Yesterday I was out in the gardens and I made some little seedlings grow."

Lord Carlisle's expression which had been intent and tense, sagged into disappointment. "I see."

Alistair felt the sudden need to apologise. Whatever Lord Carlisle had been hoping for, he hadn't delivered it, and the man seemed haunted, desperately in need of some good news. But he didn't wish to apologise for having a connection to plants, he was proud of that.

"I don't suppose," Alistair said slowly. "That the curse on your family takes the form of small black stones, inside the body?"

Lord Carlisle tilted his head to the side. "No, indeed it does not. It is embedded in our blood."

"Ah." Alistair grimaced. "That sounds deeply unpleasant."

Lord Carlisle waved his hand, dismissively. "I wish to understand how you can hear my son in the night... it is up to him what he does with the information. I spoke to him shortly before you arrived, and he said he would think on it for a while. Perhaps, even if your magical skill lies in plants as you say, there is something you can do to ease his suffering. Perhaps."

Alistair, although he now felt somewhat sorry for William, he couldn't forget how arrogant and condescending he had been. He didn't see why he should have to help him.

"Perhaps," he said, since it didn't promise anything at all.

"I should like to hear of any progress you make," Lord Carlisle said. Alistair's heart sank in his chest. He would have to do *something* now.

"Right, sir. I'll uh, well, I'll try."

He finished off his shortbread and Lord Carlisle lapsed into silence, gazing at him a while longer. "There are some books which perhaps would help you, I've spoken to Kincade to set them aside for when you next visit," he said.

"Oh, well, I had planned on visiting the library this afternoon anyway," Alistair said. He dusted off his hands and cleared his throat. "Uh, I suppose, I'll let Medlock know if I have anything to update you on?"

"That would be fine," Lord Carlisle said. "I expect to be called away tonight, and may be gone another night or two, I am not sure. But Medlock will know where I am."

"Right," Alistair stood up. He wasn't sure how to end the conversation. Lord Carlisle stood as well.

"Thank you for your help," Lord Carlisle said. "I don't know what you may be able to do, but perhaps there's something."

"I'll go to the library then." Alistair felt increasingly awkward by the second and the urge to flee, to run to the Secret Garden was growing stronger.

"Keep me updated."

Alistair managed to maintain a steady walk out of the study and resisted the urge to bolt.

CHAPTER 20

*M*edlock wasn't waiting outside this time, which meant that Alistair could close the door to the study, lean on it and catch his breath.

How had he got such a responsibility lumped on his head?

If William had been seen by so many talented people from all over the world, what was Alistair expected to do? It was utterly ridiculous. Still, the idea of new books to read was intriguing.

He made his way slowly down the hallway. There was too much to think about, even more than there had been the night before, and his head had started to hurt again.

The biggest question, which had been nagging at him, and now felt the one most pressing and most frustrating was why on Earth his parents hadn't told him about magic before?

Obviously they must have known something. He'd had magic himself, after all, but somehow that stone had cut him off from it. He'd been locked away from the world, perhaps on purpose? Now that he thought about it. Maybe he had been kept out of society for a reason.

Was it possible that his magic was harmful in some way?

Or was there some connection to the curse on the Carlisle

line which his parents wanted to sever. Did they hate Lord Carlisle?

If there was a chance Alistair could help then they surely must hate him, to have kept him away from magic, and from any schooling in magic.

He groaned out loud, annoyed and frustrated and full of impossible questions. His parents were dead, and could tell him nothing at all.

He turned onto the grand staircase and made his way down to the dormitory level. William was waiting outside his bedroom door.

Dressed in tailored bottle green trousers, a pale cream shirt and matching green waistcoat. The look came together with a striped green and crimson tie. He looked like a fashionable man's dream. Alistair envied him the confidence to be able to wear colours like that, and knew he would never be able to pull off such a look himself.

William leaned carelessly against the door frame to room 113, one hand in his pocket as if casual, but his posture was tense, taut. He met Alistair's eyes.

"Well?" he demanded.

Alistair was in no mood to be ill-treated. "Well, indeed. What a true gentleman you are to greet someone like that," Alistair said. He tried a sneer but wasn't sure he had quite achieved it.

William folded his arms and huffed. "Good morning, Alistair, how do you do. What did you conspire with my father about?"

Alistair rolled his eyes. "Excuse me, I should like to access my room if you don't mind."

William stepped aside but didn't leave. Alistair glanced at him as he fumbled his door open.

"So, what did he say?"

Alistair sighed, seeing he wasn't going to deter William, and frankly, if he was to have any progress at all with this curse, it would be easier to have William's cooperation, he supposed.

He went into his room and held open the door. William sauntered in.

"He said that you have a curse, that your entire family is cursed and there's perhaps something I can do to help, since I can hear you screaming at night."

William at least had the good grace to look shamefaced. "Ah, so that was you outside my room last night."

Alistair huffed and picked up the books he had to return to the library, a blank notebook with a soft cardboard cover and a pencil. "Of course it was."

"You didn't say your name," Will said.

"You didn't answer me at all," Alistair said. "In fact, you pretended you weren't there, if I'm not mistaken."

William looked away. "Anyway, I have no idea what Father is thinking of. You have no magic to speak of, and no idea about any of our society."

Privately, Alistair agreed with this sentiment, but he didn't like to hear William say it. He was so condescending and frustrating.

"I am going to the library now," he said. He'd hoped this would give William the hint to leave him alone, and indeed he did walk out of the room, but then he waited in the hallway. Alistair locked his door and started walking to the library. William fell into step beside him.

"How much did Father tell you?"

"Not much," Alistair said, sighing. "Just that the curse had been passed down to you, it's in your blood and that no one had been able to break it."

"Well, that's true enough," William said. "I've had so many different people giving me advice, now I just don't follow any of it."

"That doesn't exactly seem like a wise course of action,"

Alistair commented. Perhaps if he was particularly caustic William would leave him alone?

"Hah, that just shows how little you know of the situation," William said. "One doctor may suggest that I get a few hours of sunshine in the morning, and then a witch comes in and says I should stay out of the sunlight at all costs. One says the spores from the blossoming flowers may aggravate my pains in the night, and another says that only a tonic made from pollen may ease my suffering."

Alistair watched him out of the corner of his eye. He had never seen William quite so animated, it was as if he was taking joy in explaining the lengths of his suffering. It aggravated Alistair even further.

"I should think, if it were me," Alistair said slowly. "That I should pay attention to the things which made me feel better and do those."

"If there were such things perhaps I would, but nothing has helped. I am likely to die before I turn twenty-five."

That shocked Alistair to the core and he actually stopped walking. "What?"

William turned back, and his expression was odd - blank and accepting but his eyes were wide.

"Yes, that's what the curse will do. It killed Mother, and it will kill me. It's already trying to, but my own magic has kept me alive so far." His smile seemed nonchalant, uncaring, but there was something fearful around his eyes. Alistair's heart squeezed in his chest and he realised that however annoying William was, he still wanted to help him. No one deserved to live with a curse, and no one should be so careless about their own death.

"How do you know it will kill you?"

William shrugged. "They've all agreed, all the specialists. Many think it's a miracle that I've lived as long as I have, but I expect I shall die within a year."

Alistair's mouth had dropped open but now he snapped it

shut. "If someone had said that I will die, I wouldn't do it. I'd keep on living, just to spite them."

William's eyes widened in surprise and he laughed, a curiously warm and musical noise which Alistair liked immediately. He wanted to hear it again.

"Curses don't really work like that."

"I don't care," Alistair said. He started walking again, he had renewed his determination to get to the library and read about curses. "I don't know what curses do, what they're capable of, or how to break them, but I am going to learn everything I can."

William hurried to catch up with him. "You're very odd, you know," he said. "No one else who knows about my condition is so, well... casual when talking about it."

"Why do you call it a condition?" Alistair asked.

"I just always have, I think that's how Father always described it with the specialists and doctors and so on."

They got to the library and reluctantly, Alistair set down the two books on magical botany on Kincade's desk. "Thank you for these, they were lovely," he said.

"Oh, done with them, are you?" Kincade smiled and pulled out their ledger.

"I might borrow them again," Alistair said. "But I've read them both through, a couple of times."

"Well, you know where they are next time." Kincade smiled at Alistair and then nodded at William. "Welcome Mister Carlisle."

Alistair noticed the difference in Kincade's demeanour. They had become icier, which showed Alistair that they had been treating him relatively warmly. That was a nice thing to know. He liked Kincade, largely because of their proximity to books, but still. They certainly weren't as happy to see William as they were to see Alistair.

The curse itself was clearly well known, even if people didn't know the nature of it, or hear William's cries in the night.

Alistair wondered how any of them got anything done at all, with known cursed people in the building and no one doing anything about it.

Obviously it was fate that he'd ended up here.

"I believe Lord Carlisle had some books set aside for me," Alistair said.

"Ah yes. One moment." Kincade pushed their chair back and turned to retrieve a stack of books from a set of low shelves behind them. "These ones."

Their face was carefully schooled to show no expression as they passed the books over. Alistair took them and made sure to give Kincade as warm a smile as he was capable of.

"Thank you. Now," he turned to William. "If you're not going to leave me alone, you might as well help look through the curse section of the library. I saw it on the mezzanine the other day."

"There's nothing useful in there," William said, trailing behind Alistair as he strode towards the stairs to the upper level. Alistair dearly wanted to stomp his feet, but he respected the quiet of the library too much.

"Well, you never know," Alistair said, waspishly. He had assumed that William, if he had any sense at all, would have already scoured the curses section of the library. But he was also coming to realise that a lot of these magical people didn't notice things that were right under their noses. Perhaps common sense wasn't a common trait for magical people.

Maybe they needed an outsider to solve their puzzles for them.

"I do know, actually," William said. "I've looked through all of them, and there's nothing of any use. If the answer was in the library don't you think I'd not be cursed anymore?"

Alistair ignored him, set the books Lord Carlisle had suggested down on a low table and started reading the spines of the curse books on the shelves, picking out the ones which had promising looking titles and adding them to his pile.

"Oh, I don't recognise this one," William said.

"Hah!" Alistair exclaimed, before realising it sounded rather undignified. Well, never mind that. He was too irritated to excuse himself.

He caught a glimpse of something moving outside the nearest window, and turned his head to see a blackbird flying near the window, looking in, perhaps trying to find a perch. It was a lovely day outside, and it looked warm. He longed to visit the Secret Garden... but as long as William was following him around he couldn't go down there.

Unless... he stopped moving and touched the stone, hidden in the other trouser pocket to the garden's key. The fountain in the Secret Garden had solved his curse for him and he hadn't even known he was under one. Could it be as easy as taking William down there and getting him to touch the fountain?

Maybe he should have told Lord Carlisle about the garden... asked if he had ever tried the magic of the fountain.

He picked up the notebook and wrote 'fountain?' on the first page. Then he returned to examining the spines. He didn't want William in his Secret Garden, he was too annoying and arrogant. He'd probably spoil it, somehow.

He took down a generous armful of books and added them to the stack. William was leaning on the next shelf over, flicking through one of the books. He looked different when he wasn't sneering. His expression smoothed to something even more beautiful than normal, his full lips pouting a little as he concentrated.

Alistair's chest tightened and he had to force himself to breathe. No, he wasn't going to be distracted by how pretty William was, he was going to solve this problem and then be done with him.

"Well, I suppose I'll check these out, take them back to my room and start studying tonight," Alistair said.

"Tonight?" William blinked at him, as if waking from a

dream. His eyelashes were long and black, like the fringe of a curtain, highlighting the strange colour of his eyes.

"Yes, well, I want to... go for a walk, while it's still sunny," Alistair said. "And the library is only open for a handful of hours, so we can't sit here and read."

"Oh come on," William said. "You can't offer to help, and get all these books and then just do nothing all afternoon."

"I could," Alistair said. But he couldn't help feeling guilty about suggesting it. He took in William's stricken expression and nodded. "All right, how about you tell me what you know about curses and then when I'm walking I can kind of puzzle it out."

"Very well," William said. There were two stools on either side of the low coffee table and they sat down. The library was quite quiet on a Sunday afternoon and it didn't at all feel like they could be overheard by anyone. They could see the stairs leading up to the mezzanine from where they sat, which made it feel especially safe.

"Well, what would you like to know?" William said.

"What does the curse do?" Alistair asked. He had his notebook open on his lap, ready to make notes.

"It causes me great pain at night," William said. "It makes me ill, so ill sometimes that I fall into a deep sleep, or a coma, and sometimes those last a long time." Alistair made notes and then frowned at the words.

"Comas?"

William shrugged a little. "I start to feel very faint and then I pass out. Honestly, it would be better than the agony, except that I lose time to it. Well, except I'm never particularly sure if I'll wake up again."

"That's ghastly," Alistair said, meaning it. "And this has been going on for how long?"

William hesitated before answering. "My whole life."

Alistair sighed. He wished the magical world was simple, but there they were, two men who had been cursed from birth, apparently.

"I don't know if it's any comfort," Alistair said, surprising himself. His emotions towards William seemed utterly inconstant. One moment he wished he'd leave him alone and the next he'd feel so sorry for him he wanted to take him in his arms and tell him everything would be all right. Well, he'd started now, he might as well blunder on. "But it turned out there was a curse on me as well."

William leaned forward, his elbows on his knees. "I beg your pardon."

"I know, I had no idea. But it broke, or... something, and now I can do magic, a little bit. Although I've obviously got no training in it."

"Huh," William tilted his head. "How did it break? Did you break it?"

"I..." Alistair very much didn't want to betray the fountain in the Secret Garden. But perhaps it could help William? "I found a place. It was a special place, and there was energy there." He stopped himself from saying more, terribly conflicted.

"A place? Perhaps the intersection of ley lines or something similar," William mused. "Where did you find this place?"

"Er, on the grounds," Alistair said. He looked away from William's piercing gaze. His eyes were so bright all of a sudden that it was like looking into two stars.

"I don't go out on the grounds much," William sniffed. "Still, perhaps there are some answers there."

Alistair was torn, terribly, between the desire to help William and the desire to keep the Secret Garden just to himself.

He had thought that he would take Thomas there, but Thomas was his friend. William was... what was William? A rival? A nuisance? A project given to him by the principal?

No, he was more than those things. He was someone in need. Someone that there was a chance Alistair could help. But, he decided, there was nothing to be gained from barrelling into any one solution without consideration.

"I'll think about taking you there once I've learned more. What happened was I connected to the energy and I coughed up a black stone. Listen, how do you think the curse on me was done? To remove the magic from me?"

William sat back and almost overbalanced. He'd clearly forgotten he was on a stool and not a sturdy chair with a back on it. He flailed his arms and caught himself, looking so silly that Alistair couldn't help giggling.

"I didn't fall at least," he said, looking stung.

"You looked very silly," Alistair said, then tried to school his features. He was rewarded with a brief and sweet flash of mirth from William.

"Let's see. Magic is the energy of the world around us, so I guess to curse someone like that you'd just need to create a barrier to that energy," William said. "A ward inside a human... I wasn't aware such a thing could be done."

Alistair noted down 'ward inside of a human' and then looked at the words.

"Is it possible that's your problem too? That the curse is creating a barrier between you and...well, you have your magic. Perhaps a ward between you and your life... essence?"

William frowned deeply and shrugged. "Perhaps. I have definitely inherited it from Father, though, so I don't think it's something someone has directly done to my body."

There was something here that wasn't making sense. Alistair thought hard, thought back over what William had said, something didn't add up correctly.

"Wait a moment," Alistair said, he had it. "If you inherited it from your father, and he's still alive, how do you know that it will kill you?"

"Father," William looked away. "... Father's condition is different to mine."

Alistair folded his arms. "I can't help if you don't tell me everything."

"I don't think I can," William said. He stood up abruptly. "I'd have to talk to Father and... then I don't know. I'll... I suppose I'll come and find you."

"All right." Alistair tried and failed to keep the exasperated tone out of his voice. "Didn't you think to discuss this with him this morning?"

"Sorry." That word coming out of William's mouth was perhaps the most startling thing of the day.

Alistair blinked at him, no words on his tongue. William nodded once. "See you later." Then he was gone, hurrying down the stairs and out of the library as if Alistair had set fire to the tails of his coat.

Alistair looked over the brief notes he'd taken, picked up his pile of library books and went to check them out.

CHAPTER 21

*W*hen he got back to his rooms, there was a piece of paper pinned to his door. He had an armful of books which he had to juggle to wedge between his hip and the doorframe so he could retrieve his room key. It wasn't in the pocket he usually kept it in because the curse stone was, meaning he had to awkwardly twist and check his other pockets before finally turning it up.

Alistair unlocked his door, went in and placed the books carefully on his desk and then went back to retrieve the note. It was a piece of lined paper torn out of a notebook.

I'm in room 148, please come find me - Thomas

And he'd drawn a little cartoon sketch of a cheerful dog underneath the words.

Alistair smiled at the note and the sketch. There was nothing in his way now, he could go and find Thomas and then show him the Secret Garden.

He forgot all about William and his woes, too excited about the prospect of going out and seeing the Garden, as well as spending time with Thomas out of doors.

He pocketed his key, patted the pocket with the garden key in it and went to fetch Thomas.

Soon enough the two of them were leaving Misselthwaite through the back door and heading down the path to the gardens. It was mid-afternoon by this time, and the light wasn't likely to last much longer. Alistair, for the first time in his life, was aware of the changing of the seasons and yearning for spring and then summer. Then he'd be able to happily stay outside in the garden after dinner time.

Thomas had companionably slipped his arm through Alistair's again, and asked him about his conversation with Lord Carlisle. Alistair wondered if he should keep it a secret, what he'd been asked, but decided that as William's condition was relatively common knowledge there was no apparent reason not to.

He gave him a quick rundown of how the interviews had gone, first the one with Lord Carlisle and then the one with William himself.

"I suppose it is possible that the fountain might help him," Thomas said. "Perhaps it's some kind of Wellspring of power, or a convergence of ley lines."

"William mentioned ley lines, too," Alistair said. "But I didn't really understand. What does it mean?"

"Ley lines are like..." Thomas considered for a moment. "Rivers that trace all over the land, but they're not rivers of water, they're rivers of energy. Of magical essence. If you stood on one you'd feel it, connecting you to the energy of the earth and everything in it."

"Can you see them?" Alistair asked. He looked left and right as they walked down the path towards the ivy-covered wall.

"Some people can, I think," Thomas said. "But not usually. Usually it's just you feel nice around them. Then the places where two or three cross each other, the energy concentrates and it's even better."

"I think I understand," Alistair said.

"There are meant to be a few around here, that's why

Misselthwaite Manor was built here, they say, and why it's a school for magic now." Thomas tipped his head up towards the sky and smiled, seeming more relaxed out of doors than he ever was inside. Alistair felt the same way, and after watching Thomas for a moment, he lifted his face as well, letting the sunlight warm his skin.

"It'll be spring soon," Thomas said. "I can smell it."

"Good," Alistair said. "Only I hope I can get the Secret Garden ready for it."

"I'll help, if you like."

"I think I would like that very much."

They found their way to the ivy-covered wall, and Alistair showed Thomas the place with the hidden door and let him through.

Seeing Thomas's reaction to it was almost like discovering the garden all over again. He couldn't help but get excited, showing Thomas all the things he'd discovered from the path, to the little green spikes he'd made space for, to the arch and finally to the fountain. Thomas was a worthy audience, seeming to be just as excited as Alistair was about the place.

"That there's a climbing rose," he said, pointing to the vine tangled over the arch. "It will want pruning but it looks like it's going to flower just fine."

"Is it?" Alistair asked. He felt a surge of triumph through him. "Maybe I could help it to bloom even though it hasn't been pruned?"

"I'm sure you could."

Thomas knew the names of a lot of the plants. He knew which branches of the trees needed to be cut off and which were well. He said the green spikes were almost certainly from bulbs, although it was too early to tell what kind of flowers would bloom from them.

When they got to the meadow and walked through it to the fountain, though, he became quite quiet. Alistair was pleased. It felt like a sacred place to him, and Thomas being quiet was the proper awe-struck response.

"I wonder who she was," Thomas said, softly.

Alistair looked at the statue of the lady again and was struck by her resemblance to the portrait in Lord Carlise's study.

"Thomas, do you think this garden has been shut up for a terribly long time?" He kept his voice soft as well, matching Thomas.

"I'd heard that it had been dozens and dozens of years," he said. "From where some of it is overgrown, it could have been. But I don't know for sure. Mam would probably know better, or maybe Professor Weatherstaff, although it's not like either of them have been around that long."

Alistair laughed. "Professor Weatherstaff could have been, he does look rather old."

Thomas tittered and elbowed Alistair and then they both subsided into quiet again.

"You just touched it and then the stone came out?"

"Yes," Alistair moved closer to the fountain but didn't touch it. He pointed out which frog it had been. "Perhaps you ought to touch it as well, Thomas. Just to see if there's something you can feel."

He didn't say it out loud but he also wanted some reassurance that it hadn't been a fluke. That whatever the magic the fountain possessed it hadn't only existed for him alone. He'd been singled out by Lord Carlisle but he didn't want it to have happened here as well.

Thomas nodded and moved closer, moving towards one of the other frogs, and gently stroking its head.

"Oh yes, there's magic here," he said, his voice soft again. "I think... yes, I think it's a Wellspring."

"So," Alistair thought hard about what that would mean. "A spring of magical energy? Which bubbles up here?"

Thomas nodded and turned back to smile at him, his smile

even brighter than ever, his eyes sparkling. "It's very powerful, no wonder it lifted your curse from you. I can feel it giving me energy too, connecting me to the energy of... well, everything. But this garden in particular."

Alistair moved to stand beside Thomas and touch the fountain, his hand on the same frog as before. Perhaps it was superstition to want to touch the same place, but Alistair didn't mind it. Now that he understood a bit more about what he was feeling, the energy passing into him was a welcome feeling. No hint of pain at all, just tingling energy and exhilaration.

He looked around him, at the trees and the plants, the thick long grass and wildflowers of the meadow and for a moment he could see traces of green light, pulsing through the living things, connecting them to the ground, shedding particles of light up into the air.

It was awe-inspiring, and Alistair felt his eyes water as his chest expanded with the feeling of connection. He was truly a part of the world, he was a part of the garden.

He opened his mouth to speak but all that came out was a dreamy sigh.

Thomas took his other hand, and he turned to look at Thomas. He could feel his magic through their fingers entwined, and he could see the energy pulsing through Thomas as well. Not green but warm copper light, sparkling here and there with gold.

"You're so exquisite," Alistair said, his voice still more sigh than anything else.

Thomas smiled shyly, his cheeks going pink, and moved closer to Alistair. For a moment they gazed at each other, watching the pulsing light of magical energy flow through each other's eyes.

Thomas inhaled, and Alistair's heart leapt with anticipation, although of what he couldn't be entirely sure. He felt as dazzled by the lights as he was by Thomas himself, and his brain couldn't seem to make sense of it.

The potential in him welled up, and his heart raced, but then something passed through Thomas's expression and he pulled back. Dropped Alistair's hand and turned to look out over the meadow, stretching his arms up over his head.

"I'm full of energy. Let's get some gardening done, see if we can't wake up those roses a bit as well. Although it would be easier with some tools."

Alistair let go of the fountain and let the world around him dull itself back to its normal colours. It was still pretty, but there was a certain disappointment in it as well.

Or perhaps the disappointment was because of whatever had just happened with Thomas. He had hoped, he realised belatedly, that Thomas would kiss him.

Silly, perhaps, to think that. But then Thomas had smiled so sweetly, and moved in closer as if he wanted it as well. It brought Samal to mind. That moment when it had seemed like they might kiss each other, before he decided to avoid Alistair for an entire week.

Probably best to focus on the garden, it was far less confusing.

"I expect there'd be tools in the greenhouse," Alistair said.

They exchanged an uncertain look. "Professor Weatherstaff isn't likely to have unlocked the greenhouses today. He goes to church on Sundays," Thomas said.

"He's a wizard and he goes to church?" Alistair asked.

"I wouldn't call him a wizard," Thomas said slowly. "There are all sorts of words used to describe our kind, and wizard, well, it's a certain type of person. Someone very studious who spends their lives surrounded by books. Of course, he must have passed the Baccalaureate if he's a teacher, so…"

Thomas trailed off.

"I understood very little of what you just said," Alistair said.

"But I'm still surprised, I suppose I thought the church would look down on people like us."

Thomas shrugged. "I'm sure they would if he went in there and did magic. Mind you, a church around here, they're bound to know of the school. I don't really understand it all that much, but I do know that magical society has a lot less rules than the mundane folk do."

This was the first Alistair had heard of there being fewer rules. But he decided not to ask right that second. Thomas was already walking towards one of the overgrown flower beds, and the magical energy from the fountain was thrumming in his veins. The garden wanted attention, and he very much wanted to give it that attention.

They spent a companionable two hours in the garden, clearing more space around the green spikes Alistair had found and made great progress.

The sun started to drop and Thomas sat up, shielding his eyes from the last rays. "We ought to go in if we want to get cleaned up before dinner."

Alistair was loathe to stop. He had dirt under his fingernails and the knees of his trousers were surely ruined from kneeling in the grass and dirt and leaf litter, but he had never been happier. He felt the energy of the world all around him, his own magic responding to it with warmth and light. He felt *alive* and joyful, and with Thomas alongside him he felt the Secret Garden could be truly beautiful again.

But his stomach rumbled, noisily, and he had to agree it was time to go in.

Eleanor and Eulalia were lingering in the main entranceway as they walked in, along with a young man Alistair wasn't familiar with.

"Oh my goodness, look at the state of their clothes!" Eulalia laughed, her voice shrill and piercing.

"Have you been rolling around in the mud-puddles with your dog, Lennox?" Eleanor said.

"Just ignore them," Thomas whispered. He squared his shoulders and moved quickly past them. Alistair slipped his arm through Thomas's to show allegiance and strode past them, nose in the air.

Eleanor and Elulalia fell about laughing, but when Alistair chanced a glance back over his shoulder, the boy was watching him intently. Alistair didn't like the look of him at all.

"It's horrid that they called you my dog," Alistair said when they were up on the dormitory floor.

Thomas shrugged one shoulder. "It's not the worst thing I could be, I suppose." Then he flushed deep red and fled to his room. With a hurried "see you at dinner!" called over his shoulder.

Alistair watched him run off, a queer feeling in his chest which wasn't quite as outraged as it probably should have been. Thomas not minding being his... anything... well, that wasn't as disagreeable as it might be.

With a sigh, he went into his room to clean himself up and change for dinner.

CHAPTER 22

*D*inner on a Sunday turned out to be a magnificent roast side of beef, a pork roast, mountains of roasted potatoes, carrots and parsnips, steamed peas and carrots with melted butter, and a huge basket of dinner rolls beside. Alistair, hungry from the afternoon spent out of doors, and all the confusing conversations, heaped his plate high and drowned all the food in the delicious smelling rich gravy.

Thomas was already at their table, waiting for Alistair before he started eating. His own plate was well stocked and his napkin on his lap. He grinned at Alistair as he sat, clearly ready to pick up their conversation about the garden as soon as possible.

Alistair sat and was shaking out his napkin when a third chair was pulled out from their table and William sat down.

His plate was modestly filled, only two slices of roast beef, and a single potato with a pile of peas which were carefully arranged so as not to touch any of the gravy.

Thomas and Alistair blinked at him silently.

"Good evening," William said. "How did it go, your walk on the grounds?"

"I, uh..." Alistair swallowed. He had utterly forgotten about William and his predicament, his thoughts had been too swept up in the garden and in spending time with Thomas. "Well, the walk was lovely. But when it comes to your curse, I'm afraid it's going to take some time."

"I should think so," William said. His tone was bright although there was an edge to it that Alistair couldn't ignore. "I've only been trying to deal with this blasted curse for my entire life. I hardly thought you'd solve it in one afternoon."

Alistair wondered at those words, because he felt the weight of responsibility settle over him as William spoke. He had expected something. And Alistair hadn't delivered it.

Alistair floundered a little, wondering why he felt like he'd let William down, when that was utterly ridiculous and he'd only really found out anything about the situation that morning.

"The roast beef is very good tonight," Thomas said, pointedly changing the topic of conversation. Alistair shot him a grateful look.

William glanced at Thomas, rolled his eyes and picked up his cutlery, starting to eat with them. Alistair got to work on his own dinner as well, although it did feel peculiar not just being the two of them. Besides that, he had dearly wished to talk with Thomas about the Secret Garden, but he hadn't told William about it yet and he wasn't sure what to say instead.

After a few awkward mouthfuls, Alistair became aware of a distinct feeling that he was being watched.

Brows furrowing, he looked up. Across the room, at his usual table, Samal was staring at him. Martha didn't seem to be present, and Samal sat with a dish full of dinner, untouched. His gaze seemed electric, aimed right at Alistair. Alistair looked quickly away as their gazes met, and then looked back over. Samal was still staring at him, one eyebrow slowly raising as if casting judgement on Alistair's tablemates.

Alistair looked away again and chewed a bread roll. He had no idea what Samal meant by staring so. Alistair wondered if he ought to wave to him, or invite him over to join them, or just ignore him... Maybe he ought to ask William and Thomas, after all they knew Samal better than he did.

Alistair swallowed his mouthful and cleared his throat. "I say, uh, William," he said, slowly. "What do you know of Samal?"

He had asked it but was suddenly afraid. He didn't want William or Thomas to know that Samal had angelic blood, that felt like something private between him and Samal. And he was also aware that it was a foolish thing to feel that way. Why should he be the one who knew all the secrets of the people at the university?

William chewed thoughtfully and cast a quick glance towards where Samal sat. "Him? Oh, he's a strange chap. Didn't talk to anyone for the first few months he was here, and then Martha took him under her wing I suppose. Since then the two of them have been thick as thieves. His parentage is a bit of an unknown." William tapped his fork thoughtfully on the edge of his plate.

"What does his parentage matter?" Thomas asked, his hackles up.

William cast him a particularly disdainful look down his long, perfect nose. "Alistair, being as clueless as he is about the world of magical practitioners, may not be aware of how these things work," he said.

Alistair's own hackles raised. "What do you mean talking of parentage, I thought this university took everyone, regardless."

"It does," William said. "But if you had experienced schooling in the magical world before now, you'd know there are certain families which have been upholding the ways for generations."

Alistair shifted uncomfortably. He still had no idea what his parents' role had been in the magical world, but if William was spouting on about it he decided he may as well ask, even if it was awkward.

"What about the Lennoxes?"

William blinked at him, his eyes large and beautiful, pools to get lost in. Alistair looked away.

"A strange family," William said slowly. "One that has a lot of secrets, I should say."

"Lots of secrets seems to be totally normal for people around here," Alistair sniffed. "I don't see why that should make my family strange."

William laughed then, a sudden gale of sound that seemed to startle all three of them.

"He's not wrong," Thomas said, and started to laugh as well. Alistair, although still uncertain, felt he could see the funny side as well. He laughed along with the two of them.

William shook his head and quieted his noise to a giggle, and Alistair was astonished to see that tears had welled in his eyes. Alistair wondered when the last time he'd laughed like that had been.

"All right," William said, finally. "You're right, everyone in this blasted community draws secrets around them like they're dressing gowns. To be honest with you, I don't know much about the Lennoxes at all. My father might, though, if you are lucky enough to have another interview with him, you might ask."

The word 'lucky' was laden with irony, and Alistair felt a wave of satisfaction. He understood William now, he thought. He had been raised in a certain way and it was hard to let go of the things you'd been taught.

"I'm from the wrong kind of family altogether," Thomas said, smiling. "I try not to let it bother me, since it doesn't have any effect on my spellwork at all. I get better grades than some of the students who come from what some would call the best families."

"Mmm, well," William shrugged one shoulder. "Father's intent with the university was always to make it a welcoming place. I think he was so tired of people making a big deal of the

Baccalaureate and places like Minchin's, that he wanted something else. Especially given..." he looked between Alistair and Thomas. "Given my family's situation."

"Living under a curse, you mean?" Alistair said. It was perhaps a little blunt, but if William had decided to sit down and eat with them then he could put up with a bit of bluntness.

"Quite," William said. He eyed Thomas as if afraid he'd say something but Thomas just kept on eating.

"I suppose it makes sense," Alistair said. "If you want to break the curse, you need the widest possible pool of people to help or to research. There's more chance of hitting on the right solution if you don't limit the people you're inviting to the school."

Alistair cleaned off the last bit of food from his plate and wondered if he'd put that sentence together as eloquently as he could have. Ah well, it was out in the world now, and he was feeling quite weary now that he'd eaten his dinner.

"I suppose so," William said.

"Well, I'm glad I didn't have to go to a school like Minchin's," Thomas said. "I learned just fine from my mam."

"What is Minchin's?" Alistair asked.

"It's a private school for magic, in London," William said. "I was there three years before things got too bad with my condition and father pulled me out."

"They learn etiquette and things as well as magic," Thomas said.

"I don't understand," Alistair said, miserably. He hadn't really meant to say it out loud but Thomas and William were both looking at him.

Thomas's expression was a warm, sympathetic smile. He placed his hand over Alistair's. "What don't you understand?"

"Why didn't I know about any of this? Why was there a curse on me to keep me from feeling magic? Why is... why is any of this happening at all?"

He was determined not to cry and fall apart the way he had the other night, so he chewed on his lower lip and swallowed the lump in his throat down.

"I'm sure we'll work it out," Thomas said. He shifted his chair closer to Alistair's, moving around the corner of the table so he could lean his shoulder against his.

His presence against him was soothing, a solid wall of friendly boy who seemed to be genuine. Alistair was coming to realise that being genuine was a trait that might be hard to find in the halls of Misselthwaite.

He leaned his weight against Thomas's shoulder. His cheeks warmed as he looked up to see William watching them with a pensive expression.

"What is it?" Alistair asked.

"You two are very...." William moved his dinner plate to the side and leaned his elbows on the table, gazing at the both of them. Alistair had no idea what he was going to say, that they were cosy together? A bit too close for two new friends? "Endearing," William finished.

Well, that was a lot more of a surprise than Alistair had counted on.

"Endearing?" Thomas chuckled and slung an arm around Alistair's shoulders. "Why is that?"

"Because you're..." William leaned further in, looking between them both, his eyes shining like stars. "Thomas, you're sweet and kind and warm, and Alistair is. Well, I think he's those things too but he's not used to showing them. And Alistair is blunt and fearless and strange. I like it. I believe I shall be your friend."

Alistair swallowed. He wanted to object to this although he didn't exactly know why. Hadn't he asked Thomas to be his friend a few days ago? But that was the difference. Alistair had asked politely, William had sort of proclaimed he would be their friend. As if it were an absolute given that they would accept him in.

"Steady on," Alistair said, his voice wavering.

Thomas laughed. "You two are so weird," he said. "Fine, I'll be your friend, William. But I'm going to call you Will, if we're friends and all."

Alistair smiled at that. Perhaps it wasn't a problem if William demanded to be friends, Thomas was going to ensure he didn't put on airs and graces. And besides, Alistair was just as intrigued about William as he seemed to be about Alistair. William was infuriating, that was very true, but some part of him liked him as well. He wanted to see him laugh again, and he wanted to look into those star blazing eyes and get to know him better.

"Oh, Carlisle, I thought you had better taste than this lot," Eleanor again.

Thomas's arm tightened around Alistair's shoulder and then he let go of him. William looked up at Eleanor, who had come to stand by their table with Eulalia and the boy from the entranceway Alistair had noticed them talking to before. The three of them placed their dirty plates on the table.

"I don't see that it's any concern of yours who I speak to," William said. His voice was beautifully dry, Alistair envied him.

"It should be," the boy said. His voice was dry as well, although he drew his words out with a strange accent. Alistair thought perhaps it was American. "Lennox here is a walking disaster, everyone knows that."

William rolled his eyes. "Alistair is fine, Everett."

"Alistair is going now," Alistair said. He stood up abruptly and glared at the three students. "I don't know what your problem is with my being here, but I am here, and you'd better bloody get used to it."

Everett chuckled darkly and folded his arms. "You'd better

clean those plates off the table, Lennox, or you'll get into trouble."

Alistair glanced at the plates the three of them had set down. "Those are yours."

Eleanor and Eulalia linked arms and walked off, laughing.

"Are they?" Everett said. "Well who's to say? They're on the table you use after all."

Alistair glared at Everett, and wished he knew how to hex someone, because his anger had flared up high again.

Everett looked back at him with a casual smile, as if he hadn't a care in the world.

"Leave it, Lennox," William said, softly. "Bullies like this, you can never win. Just ignore him."

"Fine." Alistair turned and delivered his plate to the kitchen window.

Thomas appeared beside him, a stack of plates teetering as he set them down. "Thomas you didn't have to do that..."

He looked back to see that Everett had joined Eleanor and Eulalia by the dining hall door, where they were laughing.

"It's all right," Thomas said. He didn't meet Alistair's eyes. "I was bringing mine over anyway. And they were right, if we leave dishes on the tables it gets reported."

Alistair's cheeks flared. "It's wrong of them," he said. "They can't just go around bossing people about like that."

Thomas smiled sadly at Alistair. "It's what they're used to, and look, no harm done."

Alistair sighed and the two of them waited for William, who bussed his plates over to the kitchen window as well.

"How about we have a nice cup of tea in one of our rooms?" William said, bright as a summer morning. It was as if nothing at all had happened. "Let's get to know each other better."

CHAPTER 23

They ended up in Alistair's room. William didn't want to offer his room because it was so far out of the way and probably full of all sorts of things to mitigate his curse. Thomas said his room was on the small side, so Alistair opened the door and let both of them in.

The fire had recently been stoked, and although there weren't really a lot of chairs, they pulled cushions off the bed and sat on the rug around the fire. Cups of tea in hand.

"Monday tomorrow," Thomas said. "I wish they didn't schedule so many classes on a Monday, it's such a bore after the weekend."

Alistair tried to remember what his schedule said, but yes, he had rather a lot of classes on a Monday as well. "Is it to start off our week right?"

"I think it's to train us to expect a full day's work on a Monday," William said. "Once we've graduated and taken up our careers that is. If we do manage to graduate. If we do need careers."

Even though the room itself felt quite cosy with the three of them in there, William's countenance had become drawn and gloomy. Alistair wanted to roll his eyes and toss a scone at him, but they hadn't brought any scones up with them.

"Of course you're going to graduate," Alistair said, not minding the huffiness in his tone.

Thomas looked between them with a knowing expression and looked pointedly over at the stack of books Alistair had piled on his desk.

"Perhaps, since we're all here..." Thomas said, slowly, gently, as if he was talking to a deer that might take fright and bolt at any moment. "We might take a look at these books about curses you found?"

Alistair smiled a little, it was a very good idea of Thomas's. "Yes, might as well." He pulled himself up from the cushion and retrieved the stack of books and his notebook. "Let's all take one and see what we can find. That might be a start. You can mark the pages off of things which look interesting."

William instantly picked up the one he'd been interested in back inside the library. "Fine. Have you anything to use as a bookmark?"

Alistair looked around for some notepaper, saw his journal and hurriedly pushed it under his satchel so it wasn't obvious, and tore up his map of the school instead. "We can use this. I've been finding my way around by feel more than anything else."

Thomas picked the next book off the top of the stack and took a strip of paper from the pile Alistair made as he sat down.

"I do wonder if there's not something in the gardens which might help," Alistair said. He decided to try and get information from William then, something about the origin of the Secret Garden, or the source of the Wellspring. Surely, as it was his family's estate, there must be some stories or something he'd been told. "William, do you know anything about the gardens?"

William peered at him over the lip of the book he was holding up. "What about the gardens?"

"I mean," Alistair struggled for the correct words. "This is a magical place, a magical house, and that means, surely there must be magical gardens as well, surely."

He'd tripped over his own tongue, distracted by the arch of William's eyebrow.

"Of course, you've been in the greenhouses by now, I assume," William said.

"Yes, I mean, other than that," Alistair set the book he had picked up on his lap and leaned forward. "There are a lot of walled gardens, which we don't seem to be allowed into, and I was wondering if you knew why not? I mean, there must be something inside there, mustn't there? Things growing wild and maybe overgrowing... perhaps there are even magical places that no one has looked at for years and years."

William looked away and his expression darkened further. Alistair glanced at Thomas, uncertain, but Thomas nodded and made a 'go on' gesture.

"Do you know of any place like that?" Alistair asked, his voice a little lower.

"There's... well, I suppose there's my mother's garden," William said. His voice was faraway. "But my father locked it up long ago. No one's allowed in there at all, now."

"How long ago did he lock it up?" Thomas asked, his expression all innocent interest.

"Must be two hundred years," William said. His voice was so soft and faraway that Alistair couldn't exactly be sure of what he'd heard.

"I beg your pardon?" Thomas asked, his voice louder, surprised. William looked up and a quick smile came over his face and then died away.

"Uh, twenty years," he said. "It must be twenty years since he locked it up, when my mother died. He couldn't bear to visit it, or to think of anyone going there. She loved that place so much."

Alistair felt disquieted. *Had* he said twenty years the first time? It had sounded like he'd said two hundred... but then, that couldn't be possible could it? No one could live that long, and besides William couldn't be much older than Alistair himself, and he was only twenty.

Had the garden looked like it had been shut up for more than twenty years? Alistair had no idea. He had no frame of reference, except to know that it was overgrown.

Thomas had tilted his head to one side, like a dog uncertain about something, but when he met Alistair's eyes he shrugged and Alistair thought it meant they shouldn't press him right that moment.

"What was she like?" Alistair asked, instead. "Your mother?"

"I don't remember her," William said. "I was so young. But I think Father doesn't like looking at me because I have her eyes and he misses her so dearly."

"She looks cheerful, in the portrait in your father's study," Alistair said.

"I'm sure she was cheerful, up until the Carlisle family curse got her," William said. His voice was all doom and gloom again, and not knowing what else to do, Alistair patted his knee and then picked up the book of curses to get to work.

Perhaps after all, William had every right to be gloomy about things.

"So the curse affects not just blooded Carlisles, but those who marry into the family?" Alistair made a quick note.

"The ones we love, as I understand it," William said. His voice was dry.

An hour passed and then Alistair started to yawn. He looked up from his book and his notes to see that Thomas had sprawled out on the rug in front of the fire and was dozing, his cheek propped on a book of spells.

He looked delightfully soft and warm, and Alistair felt the sudden urge to crawl over and curl up beside him. But of course, he couldn't do such a thing.

William sat up straight and stretched his neck to one side, groaning when there was a soft click from his spine.

"I ought be to going," he said. "It's almost the time of night when..."

He didn't finish, and Alistair didn't need him to finish. "Of course. Thanks for uh, for helping," he said. He scrambled to his feet as William elegantly unfolded himself.

"Come along, Thomas," William said. Thomas twitched once and then sat up.

"I'm awake!"

Alistair wanted to bundle Thomas into his arms and hold him. He flushed, and busied himself with tidying up the books instead.

"We should leave Alistair to go to bed, we've all got classes in the morning after all." William offered Thomas his hand, and Thomas, astonished, took it and was helped up.

They bustled out with a call of goodnight, and Alistair was struck by how quiet and empty the room felt now. He went to lock his door and felt unaccountably sad as he did it.

He hadn't even been at Misselthwaite for a month yet, but he'd already formed attachments for those two men, and the gardens... What would the next week bring?

CHAPTER 24

*M*onday morning Alistair was woken by a strange feeling of promise. As soon as he opened his eyes, he was aware that something was different in the world.

There was a different smell, an energy in the air which hadn't been present the day before. He felt it thrumming through his veins and muscles, and it was all saying the same thing. *Get to the Garden!*

He threw his bed clothes aside and pulled on the nearest clothes he had, shoved his feet into his boots and fairly flew out of his room and down the hallway. It was early, only the servants were up and the dining hall hadn't yet opened for students and the sun was only just cresting the horizon.

Alistair sidled past the scullery maid as she brought in a bucket of milk, and made his way as fast as he could down the pathway and to the ivy-covered wall.

He was pulling the ivy aside when someone cleared his throat right behind him, startling him so badly that he dropped the key and it clattered on the cobbles.

Alistair whipped his head around and found himself face to face with Samal, whose wings were in the process of folding along his back.

"Sam! Er, Samal, what are you about, following me and startling me?" Alistair snapped. He ducked down to grab the key.

"You shouldn't be sneaking about on your own," Samal said. "Eleanor, Everett and Eulalia were up last night with some scheme and I'm sure they're aiming to target you."

Alistair straightened up and gripped the key to the garden. "They wouldn't do anything this early in the day, surely."

Samal shrugged. "I don't know, but I didn't want to risk it."

"How do you know what they've been scheming, anyway?" Alistair asked. "And how did you know I'd come down here?"

"I..." Samal had the good grace to look a little ashamed. "I put a charm on your room door, so that I'd know when you came out."

"And why, precisely, would you do a thing like that?"

"Because I'm afraid for you," Samal said. He had been looking down but he met Alistair's eyes now. "You are so beautiful and so strange, and I hate to think of them trying to take advantage of their superior knowledge to hurt you."

Alistair opened his mouth to argue but Samal had called him beautiful. Strange too, but beautiful? That dried his mouth out. He pushed a hand back through his hair - he'd forgotten to comb it or tie it back in his haste, and it was falling around his shoulders. He tried to decide what to say to Samal.

"I... that's very kind of you, to be concerned, but I'll be quite safe out here." Yes, that would do.

"No, you won't. You'd probably forget where you were and let your guard down and then those awful people would seize their chance." Samal folded his arms. "But I'll protect you."

"I don't need your protection," Alistair said, although it didn't sound convincing even to him.

"You have it, whether you need it or not," Samal said, shrugging. "I've never felt the urge to protect as much as I do with you, and I think it's a guardian angel thing and I don't understand it but I can't fight it either. So. I'm here, and I'm going to make sure you get to breakfast safely."

Alistair blinked at him. Perhaps he should have found it annoying, or even frightening that Samal had been keeping tabs on him magically. If it had been William, he certainly would have. But Samal... he was an angel. And he was so open, and honest, and Alistair was so drawn to him as well. He found he wasn't upset in the slightest.

Now that the initial shock of being surprised had worn off, Alistair found he didn't mind the company. Something about Samal gave him a calm feeling.

"All right, uh, well, if you're determined to accompany me..."

"I am."

"Right, then you might as well come into the Secret Garden I suppose," Alistair said. He turned, pulled the ivy aside and unlocked the door.

Samal didn't ask any questions, he just followed Alistair through the door and into the Garden. Alistair was again struck by the energy of the morning, the way the earth under his feet seemed to thrum with life and potential.

Once the door to the garden was closed, Alistair paused to take a deep breath, inhaling the sweet dew and the crispness of the new morning.

"Spring is coming," Alistair said. The realisation breaking on him at the same time he spoke "That's what it is. I can feel the change in the seasons, and the flowers waking up... they've been asleep for such a long time."

Samal touched a drooping branch. "Well, I guess it's that time of year."

"Of course it is." Alistair made his way down the path and under the archway Thomas had done such a good job of pruning back and made his way to the flowerbed where he'd left off work. There was still so much to be done, but the green spikes had certainly grown since he'd last seen them, an inch or two more, most of them.

Alistair knelt in the soil and placed his hand beside one of the spikes. Instantly he felt the flow of energy and sighed, happily. He had all but forgotten Samal was there, he was so lost in the tingling way the green light flowed from the ground, into the roots of the plant and then up his fingers.

He felt a joy unlike any he had yet felt. The energy of Spring, of the Earth herself waking up and stretching her arms, filling him so that his cheeks ached with smiling and he felt nothing inside himself but lightness.

He let the magic flow into the plant, accelerating its growth until it had several long leaves and several shoots of flowering heads. Soft, white flowers, the most beautiful Alistair had ever seen bloomed as Alistair watched, as he nurtured them. Snowdrops, he thought, recognising them from the book of botany. They were much lovelier in real life than they had been in the sketch. Alistair caressed one tiny white bloom with his fingers and marvelled at how simple it seemed, but how complex it was. This little flower had pushed its way out of the cold, hard ground and found the light. Alistair had helped it of course, but if he hadn't the flower still would have bloomed. It had so much power in it, and it seemed so fragile.

He looked back at Samal. "Isn't it wondrous?"

Samal's smile was lop-sided, as if he didn't really want to smile but found he couldn't help it.

"Wondrous indeed," he said. He wasn't looking at the flower, and Alistair started to blush again.

What was it about these men, what did they see in him, that they would smile at him like that?

Samal was such a mystery, and Alistair wanted... he wanted something from him. Friendship? It didn't seem like a strong enough word.

Alistair got to his feet and took Samal's hand. He felt as

full of potential as the garden itself. The energy inside him pulsing with light and promise, filling him with a frivolous need to laugh and run. "Let me show you the rest of the garden."

He didn't wait for Samal to reply, just started tugging him up and down paths, showing off the things he'd found, and finally bringing him to the fountain. "This is where I unlocked my magic."

Alistair felt in his pocket for the black stone, he had been placing it in his pocket every day along with the garden key. He couldn't imagine being without either one.

"You see? I was cursed. I don't know who by, or why, but I was, and here, the fountain broke it for me."

Samal's eyes were wide, and full of awe. He had been laughing softly, as Alistair showed him the garden, but now he matched the sombre mood.

"That's incredible," Samal said. "What... what will you do now?"

Alistair looked around himself, and one tree, across the meadow seemed to stand out. The green of its leaves seemed brighter to his eyes than the rest of the plants. It was a willow, its branches arching gracefully and laden with long trailing leaves. Beautiful and strange, it seemed to call for him, but to what purpose?

"I have my magic now," Alistair said, slowly. Puzzling it out loud. "I have my magic which means I'll be able to participate in class and learn things properly. But to do that I need a wand..."

"Oh," Samal said. "You seem to be staring at the tree. Is there... is that tree calling to you? They say it can happen that way, with wands."

"Yes, I believe it is."

Alistair pocketed the stone again and picked his way across the meadow to the tree. He laid a palm on the bark and sighed, feeling the immense and ancient power of it. This tree had stood in this place for centuries. He could feel it, not an intelligence exactly, but a sentience, an awareness.

Alistair pressed his forehead to the tree, trying to open a pathway of communication with it. "I should like to know you better," he whispered.

He could hear movement behind him. Samal, watching from a respectful distance.

Alistair felt the tree sending its own essence into him. He stroked a hand up the tree's trunk, to the nearest branch, where something pressed back against his hand.

Worthy?

Alistair's eyes were closed, but they squeezed shut now. The voice of the tree, such as it was, had delivered a word to him. Worthy. What a magnificent and valuable word. It filled Alistair from the crown of his head to the tips of his toes.

Worthy.

His own magic flowed back into the tree and for a moment he felt as if he perhaps *was* the tree. That the two of them had come to an understanding and had joined in some mystical manner.

Then he became aware of the thing pressing against his hand. A branch from the tree, fitting itself to his palm. He smiled. His wand.

He moved his fingers, turning his head so he could watch as a slender branch of willow formed itself, fuelled by his own magic, into a workable wand in his hand. He could see the essence of the willow, twisting around his own bright magic, the wood of the branch slimming and twisting to fit his hand perfectly. The bark stripped itself off and the wood underneath gleamed pale and pure.

Alistair felt the magical energy from the tree peak and then started to ebb, as if the wind were dying down. He peeled himself back from the willow, his eyes on the wand in his hand. It was his. A magical wand that he had made, just for him.

He was filled with light, happiness giving him a buoyancy which led him to turn around, beaming to Samal, bouncing on the balls of his feet

"Did you see what I did?" Alistair asked. To his ears his voice sounded like it came from far away and he didn't care at all.

Samal had some of his angelic seeming over him, brushed with golden light and his eyes wide and beautiful. Alistair rushed towards him, thoughtless of nothing but the magic. The Garden had given him more magic, and this time Samal had been there to witness it.

Samal's arms lifted as Alistair approached, and before either of them knew what was happening they were embracing. Alistair crashed somewhat into Samal's arms. There was a brief moment, Alistair's hand grasping Samal's lapel as Samal's arms curled around his waist.

They gazed into each other's eyes for the span of a breath. Whatever it was between them, Alistair felt it was inevitable. That something inside him had recognised Samal and it reached out to him. He felt a yearning deep within, which didn't care that he didn't know much about Samal, it just *wanted*.

Alistair tilted his jaw, and Samal leaned down to press his lips on his.

Alistair's mind was still full of magic, and now he could feel Samal's energy against him.

The essence of Samal's divine power, so different to the magic of the Garden and the Earth. It flooded Alistair's senses and he felt an incredible *rightness*.

Samal's hands tightened on his waist and pulled him still closer. Alistair's entire being flushed with happiness. This was surely the magic of the Secret Garden again.

Breathless, Alistair opened his mouth against Samal's and a moan escaped him. "Sam…"

Samal pulled back, his expression soft but wary.

"We shouldn't have done that…" Samal said.

Alistair wound his arms around Samal's neck and held him in place. "Yes, I'm rather certain that we should have."

Samal laughed, surprised, and Alistair laughed too because he was so full of joy it simply bubbled out. His eyes were warm, dancing with golden light and a familiarity which assured Alistair that Samal was feeling that same sense of recognition.

Samal's hand moved to the small of his back, rubbing gently, and Alistair wanted to stay there forever with him. Just pressed against him and gazing into his eyes.

Then a thought struck him. "Oh, is it because we're two men? Is that why we shouldn't be kissing?"

Samal shook his head and his glorious pale blond hair caught the morning sun. Alistair's breath caught in his throat, dazzled all over again.

"Ah, no. The magical society doesn't mind so much about who you kiss. I meant, because you already have Thomas. And... er, possibly William."

Alistair blinked, trying to parse what Samal's objections were actually about.

"I'm afraid I don't follow. Thomas and William?"

Samal loosened his hold on Alistair a little. "Didn't you have both of them in your room last night?"

"To read books! And have tea!" Alistair protested. But his voice cracked a little. He had definitely entertained thoughts of getting to know both of them as something other than friends, but that didn't mean he wanted to kiss them too, did it?

Samal tilted his head. "I think Thomas at the least, would like to do more than read books and have tea with you."

Alistair looked at his hand, which was still clutching Samal's lapel and he tugged on it, confused about what he wanted and what he should do.

Except that he didn't at all regret the kiss he'd shared with Samal, and being in his arms felt so absolutely right. He looked up at him and smiled softly. "I liked kissing you, I know that much."

"I liked it too," Samal said.

"And some part of me... it knows you. Are soulmates a thing?" Alistair asked. He was astounded he was being so bold, but at the same time, he knew Samal wouldn't laugh at him, or take offence.

"I've never looked into it," Samal said. "But I feel the same about you, as if I know you, and I need to be near you."

They gazed at each other a moment longer, and then Alistair's stomach rumbled audibly. He flushed as Samal laughed softly.

"We should head in, or we'll be late for breakfast."

Alistair nodded and on impulse, went up on his toes to kiss Samal's cheek softly. A promise to figure things out later, perhaps.

CHAPTER 25

*S*amal walked Alistair back to the Manor, and Alistair wasn't at all sure what to say. The moment he'd closed the door to the Secret Garden a silence fell over them both.

The blissful feeling of being immersed in the magic of the Garden, of the tree, of the Earth itself was gone. Alistair felt bereft, wrung out and far more uncertain of himself. He felt all elbows and knees, too awkward in his clothes which were starting to feel too tight, or too short, or something.

Inside his mind he kept replaying the moment of their kiss, trying to recapture the surety he'd felt, and failing miserably with each step they took back to the University building.

Samal looked like an ordinary human again, albeit a very handsome one, and he didn't seem inclined to break the silence either. Instead he loped beside Alistair, his long legs eating up the distance quickly, so that Alistair had to hurry to keep up.

They walked into the dining hall together, and Alistair piled his plate with fried eggs, bacon, sausages and thick buttered toast before going to join Thomas.

Samal was over the other end of the buffet, fussing around with the porridge urn, but Alistair saw Martha was at their usual table so he didn't assume Samal would want to sit with him.

He turned his attention to Thomas, fresh faced and bright.

"Good morning," Thomas said. He waved a buttery knife at him, and then resumed spreading butter on his split English muffin. "You been out in the garden?"

"Yes, and you won't believe what happened." Alistair set his plate down and retrieved his newly minted wand from his jacket pocket, displaying it on his palm for Thomas to admire.

"You found this? Or?"

"I made it," Alistair said. He didn't bother to conceal his pride, because he was so thrilled with the event itself. "The magic called me. This one willow tree, across from the fountain. I could feel it, like it was asking me to... to commune with it, I suppose. So I did, and then this happened."

Thomas gazed at it reverently and then beamed up at Alistair. "I'm happy for you, Alistair. That's marvellous."

"It is." Alistair rubbed his thumb up the handle of the wand and then stowed it safely again in his inner jacket pocket. He was about to tell Thomas a little of what had happened with Samal as well, when the chair opposite him screeched on the flagstones and William sat down. His plate held only bacon and blood pudding.

"I had a thought," William said, with no preamble. "Perhaps the reason that you're the only person who can hear me at night is because we're fated."

"I beg your pardon?" Alistair asked.

William looked a little wild that morning. His hair hadn't been combed and the curls were unruly, falling about his shoulders. His waistcoat was unbuttoned and the sleeves of his shirt rolled up to his elbows.

Alistair took in his appearance, and his bizarre statement and shook his head. He saw again the black swirling vines and sigils on his arm.

Alistair didn't know enough to identify what they meant, only that they were magical. He pointed at William's wrist.

"What do these mean?"

"What does what mean?" William, deflated as if the wind had suddenly gone out of his sails, slumped on the chair, looking at his hands.

"These symbols."

"What symbols, Alistair?" Thomas asked, gently. Alistair looked between them, uncertain if they were teasing him or if there really was something that only he could see.

"These symbols here." Alistair tapped one with the tip of his index finger and instantly regretted it, his vision going white for a second, and his stomach roiling as if he had been poisoned. He whipped his hand back and cradled it against his chest.

"What on Earth...." Alistair started to curse but his voice died away as he caught his breath.

"Alistair, are you all right?" Thomas had half stood up and was whipping his head side to side, eyes wide and concerned.

"I..." Alistair took stock of himself. His vision had cleared, and with a grumble his stomach settled down again. His headache was back though, and with a new intensity. He realised he hadn't had a headache of this strength since he'd first gone into the Garden, and he hadn't missed it at all.

"There are symbols there," William said slowly. "But they're ... they're usually only visible at night, when the curse is tormenting me. I didn't think...Alistair it has to mean something that you can see them. That's right," he snapped his fingers. "You saw them once before too, didn't you? No one is supposed to... I didn't think anything of it at the time as I was so sore from the curse."

Alistair breathed out heavily and rested his forehead in one hand, trying to convince the headache to ease off a little. He'd been so happy just a half hour ago, why did these things have to keep on happening to him?

"Alistair, drink some tea," Thomas said. He slid his teacup closer to Alistair. "Steady your nerves, like."

"Thank you," Alistair rasped and picked up the cup. His hands were trembling slightly, but he got the cup to his lips for a life-restoring sip. "Why did ... is the curse the symbols? They hurt me."

William shrugged hopelessly, and when Alistair looked into his face he could see he was genuinely distressed at what had happened. His lips and jaw worked, but he didn't say anything else.

"Perhaps some of the curse was stored there?" Thomas asked. He slipped an arm around Alistair's shoulders, and Alistair felt restored again. Nothing bad could happen to him while Thomas was there, touching him.

As if summoned, Samal was also by his side. He stood at the head of the table looking between the three of them, before settling a glare on William.

"What did you do to him, Carlisle?" he demanded. He didn't have any of his angelic magic on him, but his voice was still darkly commanding and there was no doubt that if William had hurt Alistair intentionally, Samal would challenge him in some way. Alistair felt a pleased stirring in his chest at the thought of it.

"Nothing," William said. He stood up so abruptly that his chair tipped over and clattered to the ground. "I'm not feeling well. I'll be in my rooms."

His face grey and drawn, William stalked out of the dining hall. Alistair took a breath, wanting to call him back but not sure why exactly. He had no idea what he could possibly say which would make things right.

Instead, Alistair looked miserably at William's plate of breakfast, which had barely been touched. A part of him was sad, wanting William to eat and build up his strength.

The headache thudded in his temples. "I'm all right, Sam," he said, finally. He looked up at Samal, who had moved closer, standing almost close enough to touch on the other side of him to Thomas.

"Sam?" Thomas echoed, confused.

"If you're sure," Samal said. He met Thomas's eyes and something passed between them that Alistair had no idea how to read. There was something like an energy crackle in the air, the promise of lightning. Thomas's grip on Alistair's shoulders tightened.

Alistair was torn between telling them both to grow up and stop fussing and from leaning into Thomas and accepting his comfort. Maybe he could do that while also reaching out to Sam?

He closed his eyes and breathed out, leaning against Thomas. When he opened his eyes, his hand already lifting to find Samal's hand, but Sam had turned and was walking back to his own table with Martha.

"Better eat up, if you think your stomach can handle it," Thomas said, softly. "We're due in the greenhouse shortly."

"Thanks, Tom," Alistair said. He took another breath. "I think I'm all right, I can eat."

"Good man." Thomas placed a soft kiss on the top of Alistair's head and let go of him. Now he had another thing to be utterly confused about.

Had Samal been right in the Garden? Did William and Thomas both want more than friendship from him?

And come to that, what did Alistair want?

He suddenly yearned for the end of the day, so he could sit down with his journal and try and puzzle it all out.

CHAPTER 26

*C*lasses were far easier for Alistair that day.

For a start, his headache cleared from the moment he inhaled the good air of the greenhouse. The scent of soil and growing things acted instantly to clear his mind and ease the pain.

When he brought out his wand, he was quietly pleased about the surprised looks on the faces of the other students. But he was most proud about impressing Professor Weatherstaff by quickly copying the charm against parasites and casting over his and Thomas's tray of sage seedlings.

The willow wand was like an extension of his hand, feeling as natural and simple to operate as his foot was. Professor Weatherstaff leaned over the seedlings and nodded slowly.

"Aye, very nice work, Lennox. I'd wager not as much as a mealy bug will come near these leaves for the next six weeks."

Alistair fairly shone from the praise. He grinned at Thomas, who nudged him with one elbow. "I reckon you've found your talent, Alistair."

Alistair nodded, satisfied that was the truth as well. And what a glorious magical talent to have! To connect oneself to the Earth and all the things which grew from her. To be the one to

167

make flowers bloom. It was as if the most delightful dream he had never dared to actually dream was coming true.

"Aye, looks like," Professor Weatherstaff said. He straightened up from examining their seedlings and stuck his hands in the pockets of his coveralls. "If you'd be interested in some extra-curricular work in the gardens, just come and find me. There's plenty of gardens on these grounds and not enough of us with the talent for it."

If Alistair hadn't found the Secret Garden he'd certainly have said yes on the spot, but as it was he was uncertain. He didn't want to spend less time in the Secret Garden, but at the same time there were sure to be things the professor could teach him.

"I'll think about it, sir," he said, finally. He swiftly accompanied it with a smile so the professor didn't feel like he was being rejected outright, which was something he would never have worried about mere weeks before, when his parents were still alive.

There was barely a half hour to get lunch, and then it was onto afternoon classes.

Afternoon classes were similarly successful to his morning ones. Although there was still a lot to learn about magical history, the runes in Spells and Hexes were beginning to make sense to him.

The day was a breeze, and his success at spellwork gave Alistair a break from worrying about curses and handsome boys.

By the end of the Magical Theory class he felt impatient to do something proactive. He wanted to talk to Samal about what they had shared that morning. He wanted to check that William was all right, after he'd missed all the day's classes. He wanted to go back to the Secret Garden and feel that sublime connection to the world again.

He dithered in the hallway, trying to think of where he could find Samal, or Thomas... William was likely in his rooms, but it felt sort of presumptuous to go and knock on his door.

He went to his room, deciding that perhaps if he washed up and changed his clothes he might have a better idea of what to do.

There was a note pinned to his door again. This time the handwriting was different, very precise and neat. He unfolded it.

Meet me in my room at nine tonight. We need to talk. William

Alistair sighed and pocketed the note. He went to unlock his door and frowned, finding his door was off the latch and ever so slightly ajar. He hadn't left it that way, he knew for certain.

His heart thundered in his chest, although he hoped wildly that it was simply a servant who had been careless. He pushed the door open and found his room had been turned inside out. The bedclothes were strewn over the floor, his clothes a crumpled mess heaped by the washstand, the water jug had been turned over, soaking the clothes.

His books were in disarray, although thankfully none of them seemed to be torn. Whoever had done this had apparently cared enough about the sanctity of library books to not go entirely overboard there.

The notebooks and things on his desk had been stained with spilled ink, and even the trunk which stood empty in the corner of the room had been opened, and looked inside.

The horror of it sank in slowly, as he walked around the room, surveying the damage. He had no doubt who was responsible for such an act, but he was too overwhelmed to deal with that just then. He felt like he'd been punched in the gut, violated in a way he'd never expected.

He remembered his journal, with a flash of terror, and went to his desk. The drawer was still closed, and when he opened it there was his journal, untouched and apparently safe from invaders.

How had they missed this drawer when everything else had been ruined?

He didn't know, but he clutched his journal to his chest and thanked the stars.

"Alistair? Are you read to go to dinner?"

Samal's voice at the door. Alistair swiped at his eyes, turned reluctantly to see Samal standing in the doorway, surveying the damage. "What happened?"

"I have a guess," Alistair said. "While they knew I was in class..."

"But for what purpose?" Samal moved into the room, stooping to pick up one of Alistair's jackets and shaking it out.

"They've said I don't belong, beyond that I couldn't really guess. Perhaps they simply don't like the look of my face." Alistair sat heavily on his bare mattress and looked hopelessly up at Samal.

"Impossible, you're adorable." Samal hung the jacket in his wardrobe and then crossed the room to stand before Alistair, whose cheeks were warming. "You're just something new, and people don't like new things."

"That's..." Alistair sighed and set his journal down beside him, gazing at the worn leather cover and thinking back over his own self in the last while. He was exactly the same. He hadn't come to the university full of joy for the new, he hadn't embraced the things he didn't know about immediately, it had taken time.

"I don't know what to say to help," Samal said.

"I don't know either," Alistair said.

Samal suddenly went to his knees and took Alistair's hands in his. Alistair, startled and wondering, looked up to meet his eyes.

"Sam..."

Samal's face brightened into a lopsided smile and his eyes sparkled. "I like it when you call me that, you know."

"I'm glad," Alistair said. He remembered with clarity the kiss they'd shared just that moment, and he was considering leaning in to kiss him again when there was a knock on the doorframe and Thomas's voice exclaimed.

"Alistair! Your room! What happened?"

Samal sat back on his heels, and his hands slipped from Alistair. Alistair flushed and pushed his hand through his hair. "Thomas, I think... I think it was Everett and Eleanor and Eulalia, I don't... really know why but I can't think who else would have done it."

"Well, that's awful of them, we must report them," Thomas said.

Samal ticked his tongue against his teeth. "It's sort of against the honour code to do something like that."

"Honour code?" Alistair laughed, a harsh sound. "What kind of honour code allows actions like this?"

Samal had no answer.

Instead, the three of them started the slow process of setting the room to rights. "I'll take all the clothes and sheets down to get washed," Thomas said, gathering things into his arms. "Can you please hand me those?"

Alistair stood and piled the crumpled sheets onto Thomas's pile of damp clothes. "Thank you Thomas, that's very kind of you."

"Make sure you get fresh bedclothes while you're down there," Samal said. Then quickly added. "Please."

"Have either of you had dinner?" Thomas asked. He peaked out from behind the pile.

"No." Alistair's stomach rumbled. "I suppose I thought I'd go down and get something after I changed, but then this had happened."

"Neither, I was coming to collect Alistair for dinner..." Samal said.

"I'll bring up some sandwiches then."

Alistair went to stack the library books carefully in a pile, and Samal waved the palm of his hand over the desk, and spoke a soft series of runes. The ink rose off the surface of the desk, and seemed to suck itself out of the pages of Alistair's notes. The ink formed a strange, shifting black ball in the air, and with a twist of his fingers, Samal syphoned it back into the inkpot.

"That's very useful magic," Alistair said.

"Cleaning magic," Samal said. He carefully replaced the stopper on the inkwell and set it to one side. "It's very useful, all household magics are, but they're not exactly looked on as respectable or impressive by the likes of the university."

Alistair frowned. "I suppose because people like Lord Carlisle would use servants for cleaning?"

"Exactly." Samal set Alistair's schoolwork and notebooks into neat stacks. "But my mother taught me, right from when I was small, and I've never regretted learning it all."

Alistair realised he knew very little about Samal's home life, and he wondered if it would be polite to ask, just then. But it didn't feel quite right.

"Could you show me?" Alistair asked instead. "There's still water on the floor from the jug."

Samal straightened up and gave Alistair a soft smile. "Of course. You'll need your wand."

Alistair drew his wand and held it at the ready. Samal moved slightly behind him and took hold of his elbow. "Just wave it like this, and then the runes you need sound like…"

Alistair could feel Samal's presence behind him, solid and reliable, a protective force of nature. His hand gently directed Alistair's forearm and his breath brushed the hairs behind Alistair's ear.

It was all terribly distracting, and Alistair stumbled over the pronunciation of the runes the first three times.

Samal laughed softly. "Are you concentrating?"

"Yes," Alistair said. Before he could stop himself he kept

speaking. "I'm concentrating very hard on how warm you feel at my back and how sweet your voice sounds."

Then he blushed hard because he had never in a million years meant to say those words out loud but now he had and Samal was laughing again.

"Just try once more," he said. His other hand found Alistair's hip, and he moved in closer, gently pressing his chest against Alistair's back. Alistair couldn't suppress the soft, approving moan that came out of his mouth.

"Go on."

Alistair, although distraction was still very much present, felt his magic centre itself inside him, and flowed down into the wand. This time he said the runes well enough that the magic worked and the water pulled itself up off the wooden floors, sucked itself out of the rug and formed a shifting blob in midair.

"Now just point it at the jug," Samal said. His lips were so close to Alistair's ear that they brushed the soft skin of them, and gasping, Alistair jerked his hand.

The water went in the direction of the jug, but overshot it and splashed into the wallpaper.

"Oh dear," Alistair said.

"Could happen to anyone," Thomas said, cheerfully from the door. Alistair, feeling suddenly guilty, moved swiftly out of Samal's embrace and flushed again. Thomas didn't seem surprised or upset in the least, simply moved into the room and set about making up Alistair's bed.

Samal busied himself coaxing the water out of the wallpaper with a practised hand.

Alistair went to help Thomas, feeling very aware of the intimate nature of what they were doing. Setting up the bed where he was going to sleep that night. He kept stealing glances at Thomas and then Samal, his heart and stomach awhirl with longing. How could it be that he wanted to kiss both of them?

Thomas was so sweet and kind, his presence such a comfort.

But Samal's presence was warm and comforting as well, just in a protective way. And why did William's face also appear in his mind's eye? He was usually more frustrated at William than anything else. But he couldn't deny there was a connection there.

Thomas straightened up once they'd finished tucking the bedclothes in and looked around the room. "I say, I don't feel entirely good about leaving you alone tonight after that break in," he said.

Samal hummed his agreement. "Neither. If they decide to escalate and do something worse to you, while you're asleep, I'd never forgive myself."

"Well," Thomas said. He eyed Samal cautiously. "It's easy enough for me to sleep over in your room, Alistair. I could change into a dog and sleep at the end of the bed."

Alistair nodded.

"I don't mind staying as well," Samal said. "Although I can't change shape, I could just... sleep in the chair."

"That sounds dreadfully uncomfortable," Alistair said. "I don't mind if Thomas wants to stay, but I'd feel awful sleeping comfortably while you were suffering in the hard chair, Sam."

Samal chewed his lower lip and folded his arms. "I'm not going to be able to sleep worrying about you though."

"I know!" Thomas clapped his hands together. "We can drag your mattress in here, Sam...Samal. It will be just like one of those boarding school sleepovers."

"I used to read about those in books," Alistair said, a little wistfully. He had often dreamed of having friends to share such experiences with, and perhaps, now he did? A tentative butterfly of excitement fluttered in his chest.

"If it's all right with Alistair," Samal said. "I think the both of us staying would be the safest."

"Yes, I'd like it very much," Alistair said.

Samal nodded once and made for the door, then paused and

looked back at Thomas. "I don't mind if you call me Sam. It's... allowed."

Then he left the room.

Thomas beamed at Alistair. "He's quite nice once you get to know him isn't he?"

"He is." Alistair's head was full of dreams of his childhood readings. Should he go down to the kitchens and get some bread and sausages to toast over the fire? Some sweets of some kind? Pots of tea to sustain them?

Then with a start he remembered the note from William. He checked the time - he was already late.

"Oh, blast it all, I have to go and see what William wanted," he said, standing up. "You'd better wait here and let Sam in when he comes back. Then maybe you two could run and get some tea and things from the kitchen?"

Alistair pulled his jacket back on and went to the door.

"Is it quite safe? You wandering about on your own when this has just happened?" Thomas said. "I could come with you?"

"I'll just be up the hall, I won't dawdle," Alistair said. "William's room up the far end of the corridor, lots of twists and turns but I know the way quite well. No one goes there but him, and I'll come straight back after." He hesitated, because he didn't want to worry Thomas or Samal. "It just feels wrong to not show up at all."

"I understand," Thomas said. He was so sweet and agreeable that Alistair crossed the room in two strides and placed a kiss on top of his rust-coloured hair. He knew he was allowed to do that, because Thomas had done it for him that morning.

"You're wonderful," Alistair said. "I'll be back soon."

CHAPTER 27

*A*listair made his way down the darkened hallways to William's room. Despite the reassurances he'd given Thomas, he found the walk to the sigil-covered door was rather frightening. There were plenty of dark shadows and doors where someone might be lurking, ready to leap out and hex him. He was still far too new at all this to be able to defend himself but his hand sneaked into the inside pocket of his jacket and he curled his fingers around the handle of his wand just in case. Some defence was better than none at all, after all.

He tried to walk as silently as possible, down the hall, candle in his free hand as he passed the various portraits and tapestries. Finally, he came to the door covered in sigils, and for the first time it sat ajar.

He hesitated, looked behind him and then knocked twice on the door - softly, since he had been as quiet as a mouse the entire way there.

"Come in," William said.

Alistair pushed the door open by the handle, carefully avoiding touching any of the sigils where they were carved into the door.

William's room was large, much larger than Alistair's, and he saw that this wing of the house had obviously been meant for grander guests. There was a large, impressive wrought iron four poster bed visible through an open connecting door, and the room William sat in was a pleasant, if somewhat dourly decorated sitting room. There was a long chaise before the fire and this was where William had arranged himself, half reclining. His waistcoat was unbuttoned and his jacket hung up nearby. He had no shoes or socks on, and the sight of his pale feet struck Alistair as far more intimate than he had expected. His black trousers clung to his thighs, and one leg was hitched up. His cheek rested against his hand, and he looked at once careless and casual and extremely intent. The firelight caught the lights in William's eyes, and his expression was a sly smile, his eyes fixed on Alistair.

"Good evening."

Alistair felt his cheeks burning. It felt as if he had somehow stumbled into the scene in a Gothic romance where the hapless lead is seduced by the monster.

And worse, he didn't hate the feeling at all.

He moved closer to the fire and to William. "You uh, you wanted to speak with me?"

William nodded and gestured to the armchair positioned just across from the chaise. "Please, take a seat. I want to ask you something. Help yourself to tea."

Alistair prayed silently that he wasn't about to get in over his head, but had come to the conclusion that he likely already had. He took a teacup and poured for himself, just so he didn't have to look directly at William for a moment.

"So," he said, slowly. "What was it you wanted to ask?"

William gazed at Alistair with a look of bemused wonder. "Why are you so special, Alistair Lennox?"

"I'm really not," Alistair said, quickly. "I'm half convinced I shouldn't even be here. I don't know why anyone noticed me at all, let alone you or your father." Or Eleanor, Eulalia and Everett, he added silently.

"But you *are* special," William said. "You can hear me at night when the wards should prevent that. You can see my sigils when almost no one else can." He straightened up, and rolled his sleeves up to demonstrate.

"Yes, I can see those," Alistair said. He found it hard to catch his breath. When had he forgotten how to breathe? Perhaps he was too hot so close to the fire.

"You're different, and you fascinate me," William said. It was starting to sound like an accusation. His brows drew down and together, staring into Alistair's face until he felt pinned in place. "When I first met you, I thought you were some kind of buffoon. Do you remember what you said to me that night?"

Alistair nodded. "I told you I wasn't drunk, and that... that you were astoundingly pretty." If William was trying to intimidate him, he wouldn't let him. He lifted his chin and caught sight of the portrait on the wall behind William. The same woman that Lord Carlisle had in his study, and it was clear from this portrait that she was the same lady rendered in marble sculpture in the Secret Garden.

Utterly distracted, Alistair stood and walked over to examine her closer. "This is your mother is it?"

"Yes," William said.

"She's the same as the woman there's a statue of in the Secret Garden."

"What Secret Garden?" William's voice moved closer, he had got up off the chaise and was approaching him.

Alistair hesitated but then realised he really didn't have a right to keep the garden from William. It had been his mother's garden, and he wanted to take him there anyway to see what the fountain might do to help him.

"I've found your mother's garden," Alistair said. There was

something off about the painting, and he couldn't entirely place the cause of the feeling. He stared and stared at it.

"You can't have," William said. "Father locked it up and hid the key away. He forbade everyone from entering it."

Alistair shrugged, he wondered if he ought to feel guilty, but he didn't at all. "Well, I found the key, and let myself in, and I've been visiting it for a few days. There's a fountain there with a statue of your mother, and it ... unlocked something in me. Broke the curse that had kept my magic from me."

He felt in his pocket and produced the key and the black stone, offering them to William to examine. "You see? That stone was inside me."

William eyed it uncertainly. "That's... disgusting."

"I suppose," Alistair said. He hadn't thought of it that way. "But I was thinking if it could do that for me, maybe you should see if it can help you too."

Alistair turned back to the portrait. Something wasn't quite right. Her clothes looked sort of old fashioned, but that was normal enough for formal portraits. His eye landed on the artist's signature. It was dated... that was it, that was the anomaly.

"This portrait is dated 1696."

William said nothing.

"It's your mother, though?"

"Yes, that's my mother."

"But how can that be? The garden has been locked up for ... well, we don't know how long, if she died before it was locked... that means.... Is the date a forgery?"

William sighed heavily and put a heavy hand on Alistair's shoulder. "Perhaps we ought to sit back down. It's... complicated."

"I should say that it is," Alistair said. "So are you going to explain it?"

William directed Alistair back towards the armchair, and he

went, although his heart was pounding now. Eager to hear the explanation.

"I don't know that I should," William said. His expression was one of extreme world weariness, and he looked tireder than Alistair thought a twenty two year old ought to. Or however old he was. It changed as Alistair watched him, easing into something more like despair. "Father has always closely guarded the secrets of our family."

Alistair folded his arms.

"And what good has that ever done you?"

William blinked, his expression changing to one of astonishment. "I beg your pardon."

"Well, your condition, whatever that actually entails, is tormenting you, and you're clearly miserable. So why keep on with all this secretive business just because your father said so?"

William blinked again, owlish in the dim light. He leaned forward over his knees. "I ... I don't think I've ever deliberately disobeyed him."

Alistair regarded William doubtfully. "If you don't want to tell me, that's fine. You keep your secrets and I'll head back to my room." He remembered with a start that Thomas and Samal would both be waiting for him, and felt like that was by far the superior idea to pursue. He gathered himself to get up.

"No, wait, don't go," William said. "I want to talk to you so much more."

"Then talk, tell me why your mother's portrait is dated over two hundred years ago." Alistair sat back against the chair.

William sighed. He relented, leaning back on the raised part of the chaise and looking weary all over again. "Because she died two hundred years ago, that's why."

Alistair bit down on the obvious retort of 'how could that be?', some instinct of his telling him that he needed to be patient while William gathered his thoughts together.

"The family curse took my father when he was thirty."

"But he's still alive," Alistair said. William's eyes cut to the side.

"In a manner of speaking, yes. But because he was infected when he and my mother had me, I inherited some of it."

"I still feel like you're talking around something," Alistair said. "Please just be plain."

"Right, sorry." William sighed and looked at the fire for a moment and then back at Alistair. "Have you heard of vampires?"

Alistair shrank back against the armchair, a chill racing up his spine. "Yes?"

"Well, that's... more or less what my father is. It was caused by a magical curse and not by, uh, a vampire attack, but there it is. When Mother had me she gave birth to a hybrid child, half vampire and half human."

"So, what is the curse doing?" Alistair said.

"It's trying to turn me all the way," William said. He looked at his forearms and sighed again. "These are slowing it down, considerably, but they can't stop the process. And I would rather die than live as my father does, forever lonely for the woman he loved. I don't wish to drink blood, or hide from the sunlight the way he does. I know I have no particular love for the sun but even still..."

Alistair felt awful on William's behalf. What a sad and terrible life he must have led. He pushed himself off the armchair and went to his knees before William, taking his hands in his. His fingers felt cold, and Alistair wrapped them in his warm ones.

"I'm sorry," he said, softly. "That must be constant torment."

"It's worse, too," William said. "Regularly I fall into a sort of prolonged sleep. It's an unconsciousness where I am not aware of anything at all, I cannot respond or defend myself. I simply exist in a waking death. Sometimes for months at a time."

That seemed to go some way to explaining how William

could look and act so young even though he was apparently...
"How old are you?" Alistair asked.

"My mother died very shortly after my birth," William said.
"But as I said, a lot of my time I am not well. I wouldn't call my
spells of sleep living. Sometimes a whole year will pass before I
wake again."

Alistair pressed one of William's cool hands to his cheek,
trying to warm it. "I want to help," he said. "I'm not really
convinced that I can help, but I want to."

"I think you can." William's voice turned soft and his fingers
curled to cup Alistair's jaw and lift his face so they were gazing
into each other's eyes. Alistair's breath caught in his chest. "I
think there really is something special about you, Alistair. You're
interesting, blunt and clever. You see through things to the truth
inside, and you're handsome and yes, infuriating, but you
intrigue me in a way that no one else ever has."

Alistair felt like his cheeks would never be a normal shade
again. He wanted, wildly, to disagree with William, to claim that
he was none of those things. But the want clashed violently with
the happiness and desire that William had awakened in him. He
wanted to hear William say those things about him. He wanted
to be handsome and intriguing, and he wanted to help William.
William's eyes crinkled in a sad smile.

"I think that the stars brought you here to Misselthwaite to
bring it back to life. To bring me to life."

"Oh," Alistair breathed. Then William tugged him closer
and kissed him on the mouth.

It was different to kissing Sam. This kiss felt dangerous,
wildly exciting and dangerous. His initial thought coming into
the room that evening had been that William was a monster of
some kind, and he had confirmed that, in fact. A half vampire,
cursed to live a tormented life.

The kiss reflected all that. William nipped at Alistair's lip,
and he moaned from the sweet sting of it. He pushed his tongue

into Alistair's mouth and lashed at his tongue, and Alistair's body responded very positively. Heat flashed through him and Alistair was consumed with a desire for more. More of William, especially his tongue and more of his teeth.

Without thinking, he surged upwards, landing in William's lap, William's arms circled his waist and pulled him closer still, and he felt the telltale hardness in his lap, pushing against the seat of his trousers and moaned into William's mouth. A wanton and needy sound that Alistair hadn't known himself capable of making. William responded to the sound by grabbing Alistair tighter against him, trapping him between his arms and kissing him so hard Alistair's head tipped back somewhat.

This was so much more raw than it had been with Samal, so much more... well, violent. Perhaps it was the vampire side of William which made him this way, or perhaps it was just who he was. Either way, Alistair loved it, and wanted more.

Only he couldn't have more, could he?

He turned his face to one side, trying to catch his breath and remember what he was supposed to be doing. William kissed Alistair's jaw and found a sensitive place on his throat which he grazed his teeth over, moaning. Alistair's eyes flickered closed again and he tipped his head, wanting to give William access.

For a moment, William's mouth lingered over Alistair's throat, kissing, his teeth teasing here and there in tiny bites.

Then without warning he let go of Alistair and shoved him off his lap onto the end of the chaise. Alistair looked up to see him covering his mouth with one hand, his eyes wide and frightened. He shook his head.

"You have to leave," William said, his voice hoarse. "I can't... the curse... it's too much, it's coming on. Please."

Alistair was breathing heavily, his own hands reaching for a body which wasn't there. He cleared his throat.

"Uh, if ... if you're quite sure?" Alistair said, his own voice was strained, a little too high.

William nodded emphatically and turned away, going to stare into the fire. "Please understand that I don't regret what just happened...but it's night time, and the pain is coming on... The smell of you, the press of your body, it's too much, I want you too much... For your own safety, go now."

Alistair dragged his hands through his hair, it had come loose at some point, his ribbon lost, and swallowed any further objections. He could deal with William tomorrow, when the curse had eased some more.

He hesitated at the door and turned back. William was sitting on the floor before the fireplace, his head in his hands. He felt a wave of affection for the poor, tormented boy.

"Good night, William," he said.

He closed the door behind him and made his way quickly back to his room, the earlier fears completely replaced by the confusion of feelings still washing through him, entirely caused by William.

CHAPTER 28

*H*e met Samal on the walk back, he looked relieved to see Alistair. "There you are. I was beginning to get worried."

He stopped walking and Alistair met him in the corridor. Samal looked him up and down. "Are you all right? You look rather... dishevelled. Upset. Did William do something to you?" He took Alistair by the upper arm and moved him aside. "I'll kill him."

Alistair caught him by the hand and pulled, although he got the feeling that if Samal wanted to do something there was very little Alistair could do to stop him.

"No, it was nothing like that. Please stop threatening to kill people," he said, quickly.

Samal looked back at him, his forehead furrowed. "If you're sure."

"I'm sure, he's... having one of his spells now," Alistair said. "Let's just go."

Alistair realised they were stopped rather close to the tapestry that had so frightened him the first night he'd seen it. Alistair had forgotten his candle back in William's room, but Samal held one.

"Would you take a look at that tapestry?" Alistair said, slowly. "I don't know if it's just me, but I thought the figure in it looked rather..." he didn't want to lead Samal to any particular confusion so he didn't finish the sentence.

Samal raised his hand up with the candle and the tapestry was bathed in light. "The fountain and the garden, it could be the Secret Garden," Samal said slowly. He leaned in to examine the figure. Alistair wasn't sure now, if he'd been right and the figure did resemble him, or if it was just a fancy of his imagination.

"His hair looks sort of like yours," Samal said. "But it's always hard to tell with tapestries. Perhaps the hair is your colour but then, lots of people have your hair colour." He shrugged and turned back to Alistair. "Was that what you meant?"

"Yes, it gave me rather a fright," Alistair said, abashed. "But then, it was the first night I'd heard William crying out and I thought perhaps there were ghosts or monsters or something."

Samal nodded and didn't let go of his hand, so they walked back to Alistair's room like that.

Thomas was in his pyjamas when Alistair opened the door, he was seated on Alistair's bed and looking slightly anxious, which melted into relief when Alistair and Samal walked in.

"Oh, there you are, everything all right?"

"Yeah, just fine." Alistair had done more than kiss with William, and his blood had got up from it. Now the sight of Thomas in his pyjamas, the top few buttons undone to show a promisingly brown and muscular chest stirred him again. To say nothing of Samal's hand in his, his body gently ushering him into the room.

"Oh, thank you Tom. Yes, I'm quite alright."

Two men, in his bedroom... for the entire night?

There was a time when Alistair had believed himself to never be in such a situation. But hadn't they agreed to sleep over to keep him safe? Not to... to kiss him and so on.

He silently mourned for the time he had hoped to sit and write in his journal, but he wouldn't feel comfortable at all doing that with these two in the room.

Instead he let go of Samal's hand, picked his way over the mattress which had been set up on the floor and changed into his own pyjamas behind the folding wooden screen in the corner.

Samal used it after him, and soon Alistair and Thomas were seated side by side on his bed, and Samal was sitting cross legged on the mattress, and no one seemed to know what to say.

"I should change form," Thomas said, after the silence had dragged on rather too long. He looked between them, apparently tense for any objections. Samal waved his hand to say go ahead and Alistair nodded.

Alistair in all honesty, very much wanted to see how one could change shape, so he sat back on the pillows to watch.

Thomas swallowed, a little nervous perhaps, and then something came over him. The air around him started to glow with magic. It was a warm orangey brown colour, which set Alistair in mind of sunsets staining the clouds.

The magic made the edges of Thomas seem to blur. He had his eyes on Alistair, looking pleased and shy at the same time as he leaned back on the bed and absorbed the magic into himself. In a blink, instead of Thomas there was a large, beautifully groomed and silky furred golden retriever. The pyjamas were quite gone, leaving a perfect specimen of canine beauty in their place.

Alistair had never had a pet, but as a child he had longed for a dog. The kind of friendly dog who would sleep on his bed and play chase with him and be his best friend. The kind of friend who was real and not imaginary, like the boy he used to fancy he could talk to.

Alistair didn't hesitate, he moved onto his knees and ruffled the fur on Thomas's neck. It was softer than it looked. Thomas's tail thumped happily on the bedclothes.

"Is that good?" Alistair cooed.

Samal got up and scratched Thomas's ears, his face softening into a gentle smile as Thomas yipped and butted his head first against Samal's hand and then Alistair's.

It was just the tonic that Alistair needed to let go of the stresses of the day and start to yawn. Samal and Alistair both rubbed Thomas's belly, for as a dog he proved to be rather shameless, rolling onto his back and waving his paws in the air. His doggy smile and wagging tail were too much to resist.

But finally Alistair yawned so loudly that Samal pulled back and looked at the both of them. "It's quite late, we should probably turn in."

"Right." Alistair moved back up towards the pillows as Thomas got right way up again. Alistair shuffled under the covers, and Thomas watched from the end of the bed, his eyes huge and pleading. Alistair smiled and patted the covers beside him. "There's plenty of room, you could sleep up here."

From the ground Samal responded. "Thank you for the invitation but then we would have brought the mattress in for nothing."

Alistair quickly extinguished the lamp so that no one could see his blush.

Thomas flopped down beside him with a 'wuff', and Alistair, unable to resist, put his arm around the dog's neck, and buried his fingers into the thick fur of his ruff.

"Good night Alistair, good night Thomas," Samal said, from the floor.

Alistair wished, briefly, that his bed really was big enough for all three of them... or maybe four... before he fell asleep, lulled by the deep breathing of Thomas in his dog form and his warmth against his side.

CHAPTER 29

*A*listair woke up on Tuesday morning feeling warm and safe and absolutely delightful. He was facing the wall and there were arms around him, and a warm body pressed against his back. A warm body with something rather insistent and hard pressing against his lower back.

His eyes flew open.

Hadn't Thomas been a dog?

The hand on his chest was most definitely a human hand. Alistair swallowed and slowly turned his head to see Thomas's face beside him on the pillow. He must have shifted back into human form at some time during the night, and... started cuddling Alistair? Although Alistair had to admit that he had cuddled Thomas first. But that had been when he was a dog...

Alistair closed his eyes and pretended he was still asleep. He was, after all, deliciously warm. What would it be like to wake up like this every day? To have someone who cared about him enough to cuddle him?

He had that now. He had Tom and Sam, and maybe even Will. Was he being terribly wicked to want all three of them to like him?

They all did care about him in their own ways, Alistair

couldn't deny it.

It was a strange thing to realise. Overwhelming really. He'd come from nothing, two parents who didn't seem to be able to tolerate him, and living as a ghost in a house empty but for the servants… to this.

Now he was a man in bed with another man and there was a third man snoozing nearby. Part of him wondered if he deserved all this, if he was allowed to have it… and part of him wanted it too badly to care about that.

He shifted a little, pushed himself harder against Thomas's chest and Thomas stirred, mumbling something soft.

Alistair smiled and started to roll, trying to see more of Thomas. Thomas's grip on him loosened and he smiled softly, his eyes fluttering open. The beauty of his eyelashes, slowly revealing his warm brown eyes, in the early morning light was enough to take Alistair's breath away.

"G'morning," Thomas whispered.

Alistair grinned and whispered back. "Weren't you a dog?"

"Maybe," Thomas suppressed a yawn. "But sometimes in my dreams I change back."

Alistair, feeling daring, stroked his hand up Thomas's arm, feeling the hard muscles under the soft flannel of his pyjamas. His mouth started to water.

"Alistair…" his voice was barely audible, a soft murmur that Alistair took as an invitation. He stroked his fingers over Thomas's chest and hummed, appreciating the muscles there too.

"Might I kiss you?" Alistair asked. Part of him was shocked at his own brashness, but he ignored it entirely, instead embracing the unexpected boldness.

Thomas answered by closing the distance and kissing Alistair. He was struck by how different it was from the kisses he'd shared with Samal and William. It was just kissing, surely there couldn't be *that* much variety in it?

And yet, Thomas's kiss felt like acceptance. It felt like coming home to a place that you loved and finding a warm fire, tea brewing, and someone who was happy to see your return. Thomas tasted faintly of butterscotch, and Alistair wanted to kiss him forever.

Thomas's hand moved to Alistair's hair, his fingers stroking through it, gently tugging the strands and heightening the kiss to something more urgent.

Alistair moaned softly into his mouth, then pulled back. "Is this all right?" he whispered. "Sam is … he's right there…"

Thomas opened his eyes and shook his head. "I don't mind."

Alistair hesitated for a moment and then kissed Thomas again. If Thomas didn't mind, and Alistair didn't mind… Well, they just had to be mindful of if Sam was going to wake up or not.

Alistair's upturned ear felt acutely tuned to any possible sound as he sunk into the rightness of his kiss with Thomas. Thomas's hand tugged on his hair again, and then settled on the back of his neck, as if holding him in place. Alistair didn't mind this at all.

Almost of its own volition, his hand was sliding down Thomas's back to run over his pert rear, feeling the swell of it against his palm. His touching Thomas there seemed to spur Thomas on, and he rolled so he was on top of Alistair, who was now on his back. He ground his hips down against Alistair's morning hardness and both of them gasped.

There was a noise which neither of them was the source of.

"Sam," Alistair whispered. Thomas pulled back from Alistair so quickly and violently that he toppled out of the bed and landed half on top of Samal.

Samal groaned. "Good morning to you too."

"Sorry Sam," Thomas said, laughing a little.

Alistair poked his head over the edge of the bed to see Sam

looking more confused than annoyed, although it can't have been a pleasant wake up.

"Good morning Sam," Alistair said. "Shall we dress and go down for breakfast?"

He felt a very pressing need for some kind of distraction from his arousal and the presence of two handsome men in his bedroom. Their all being in underclothes and pyjamas wasn't helping matters at all.

"You use the screen first," Samal said to Thomas, pushing him off him playfully. "You're the most out of bed."

Thomas hurried behind it, clutching the folded pile of clothes which was his outfit for the day.

Alistair watched him go, and clenched his hand, remembering how nice and firm Thomas's bottom had felt to him.

He rubbed his face, he had to at least try not to be quite so shameless.

And he'd kissed William the night before as well. How ridiculous of him, to be so liberal with his affections. They would certainly need to have a conversation about all this. He could apologise to them all at once, and explain that after a lifetime of sitting alone in a house he was clearly overwhelmed by the presence of handsome people and couldn't be trusted.

Samal sat up, his hair adorably mussed from sleep and his eyes not all the way open yet. He swung his head to look at Alistair.

"You all right? You look ...pink."

"Yes, it's just... warm in here," Alistair said. "And I'm not used to company first thing in the morning."

Samal grunted by way of response and ran a hand through his hair, making it even more dishevelled. He nodded.

Alistair wasn't sure what else to say, so he sat up as well, pushed the bedclothes back and went to start picking out his own clothes for the day.

CHAPTER 30

$\mathcal{A}$lthough it was clear that Samal wasn't at his best in the mornings, they had a pleasant breakfast together. Samal seemed to take a long time to wake up, and although they were all sitting at the breakfast table with food in front of him, he would let his eyelids droop and fall asleep every so often. This lasted until he'd had a cup of tea, to Thomas and Alistair's amusement.

Martha waved at them as she collected some muffins and toast and then hurried out again.

"She looked busy," Thomas remarked.

"Mm." Samal lifted his head and looked at the door and then back at his tablemates. "She's doing a special research project on the transformational properties of unicorn hair."

"Unicorn?" Alistair asked. Something tightened and then loosened in his chest. "They're real?"

"Yeah, dragons too, although they're very rare now," Thomas said. "Mam said most of them have gone where there's less humans to bother them."

Alistair could relate, although just at the moment he felt he wanted more people around him than he'd ever wanted before he was sure it wouldn't last and soon enough he'd want to be alone more often. "Well, fancy that."

"So, what do you have on today, Sam?" Thomas asked.

"Two and a half hour healing training with Madame Waxleaf," he said. Then he yawned so wide Alistair saw every one of his perfectly straight teeth.

"We've got Greenhouse," Thomas said. "But we could all meet up again for dinner?"

"I'd like to go into the Garden this afternoon," Alistair said. It felt wrong to go even one day without visiting it. "If either of you would like to join me, I'd be happy to have you along."

"I'll see," Samal said. He stretched his arms over his head and yawned. "Waxleaf's training can be quite draining, although the garden is rather restorative."

"I'll come," Thomas said. "It feels like there's so much more to discover there."

The morning's class in the Greenhouse was another revelation for Alistair.

Written on the blackboard was a large admonishment. "Do NOT touch the flowers!"

Professor Weatherstaff had set a strange looking potted plant on each table. It had small rounded leaves, but the flowers, if that's what they could be described as, were very peculiar. They were shaped almost like opened seashells, with lines of spiked green fibre lining them. Each little flower was a brilliant green on the outside but sapphire blue inside.

"Venus fly traps?" Thomas exclaimed.

Weatherstaff smiled and shook his head. "A little rarer, but good work recognising the family."

"Fly traps?" Alistair asked, softly, just to Thomas.

"Yes, these must be the magical version, but the mundane sorts, they're from the swamps of America. You can grow them here in a hothouse, but you don't see many of them." Thomas smiled. "They have these little hairs inside and if a fly lands on them they snap closed."

Curious, Alistair leaned in and looked inside one of the flowers. Sure enough, right at the hinge of what was surely its mouth, he could see some little threads of white. Those must be the triggers.

"Don't touch it!" Weatherstaff roared. Alistair, startled, straightened up quickly. But his roar had been directed across the room at Eleanor, who whipped her hand back from the potted plant before her.

"I wasn't going to," she said and sniffed.

"Before you can touch the Meridian Trap plant, you must first learn how to lull it to sleep," he said. "Wands out and I'll show you the charm. If you don't do this just right they'll pretend to sleep and then nip off your finger, and once they get the taste of human blood they'll never get enough."

Thomas grimaced and Alistair folded his hands on top of the table, far from their Meridian Trap's reach.

Professor Weatherstaff spent fifteen minutes of the two hour class ensuring everyone had mastered the charm and put their Meridian Trap to sleep. Once he was satisfied that no one would be bitten, he led the class in the handling of the plants, repotting them into far more generously sized containers.

"They grow a lot in spring, and we're coming up to the vernal equinox. They'll want to stretch their roots and put out larger flowers."

Once all the plants were successfully replanted, he had them make detailed sketches of them in their notebooks and advised them on how to label all the parts.

The time flew past, Alistair's sketch of the plant was perhaps a little clumsy, but he at least could recognise it when he looked over it at the end.

Soon enough Weatherstaff was directing them to set their Meridian Traps in the back rooms of the Greenhouse.

Alistair and Thomas carried theirs in together, a little gingerly because the plant was stirring and Alistair didn't want to be bitten.

They'd set it down and were turning to go back in when Eulalia walked in, preceded by the Meridian Trap she and Eleanor had been working with. She was levitating it with her wand, and, narrowing her eyes, she sent it straight for Alistair.

Without thinking, Alistair drew his wand and tried to catch the plant with his magic. He had no idea how to do such a thing, it hadn't been covered in any of his classes, but on instinct he felt the energy from the Earth under his feet, and the energy within him, and then the energy of the Meridian itself and somehow slowed it's trajectory enough that he could guide it onto the shelf, instead of letting it crash into him.

"You ought to be careful with that," Alistair said. "It's rare, valuable, the Professor said."

"I was just putting it away," Eulalia said with false innocence. She made her eyes all wide and fluttered her eyelashes. "Thanks for helping, Lennox."

She turned on her heel and stalked off, not even acknowledging Thomas's presence.

Alistair turned to ensure there was no damage to the plant and then took Thomas's hand, leading him back to the table with his chin held high.

"I don't know what her problem is," he said. "But she ought to know better than to try and use plants against me."

Thomas chuckled and rested his chin on Alistair's shoulder. "If she knew better she wouldn't be doing anything like this at all."

"You're probably right."

Before they left the greenhouse, Alistair asked Weatherstaff if he might borrow some gardening tools, explaining that he'd like to help the professor out soon with the gardens, but he'd like to get a feel for them first.

Weatherstaff gave him a curious look, his eyes sparkling with something before he nodded. Alistair had the horrible sudden feeling that Weatherstaff knew what he was up to, but it didn't seem to be a bad thing. Weatherstaff gave him protective gloves, and a selection of tools and told him to come back if he needed anything else, and didn't ask him any questions at all.

CHAPTER 31

*T*he session in the greenhouse had been very illuminating, and Alistair felt more excited than ever to head to the Secret Garden and do some work there.

Thomas and Alistair had a quick lunch of sandwiches and lemon slice, washed down with lemonade before they headed back outside to the Secret Garden. He had stashed the gardening tools from Weatherstaff down one of the pathways, and intended to pick them up as they walked past.

"I have an idea," Thomas said. "Just to be sure that no one's following us when we go out."

They hadn't seen Samal at lunch, although his insistence that Alistair never walk anywhere alone was forefront in Alistair's mind. It was almost exactly as if he could hear Sam's voice in his head, loud and clear and it was saying "Be careful!"

Eleanor, Eulalia and Everett certainly didn't seem deterred, and if the attack on his room wasn't the worst of it, it would be best to be a little paranoid.

"Go ahead," Alistair said. "Whatever you've got."

Thomas shifted into dog form as soon as they were outside, and Alistair walked slowly, watching Thomas with unbridled joy. How lovely it must be to be able to walk on four legs. To smell so many more things in the wind, to be able to run free and easy without anyone watching and judging you…

"I wish I could change form," he said, once they were out of sight of the manor.

Thomas butted his head against Alistair's hand and he rubbed behind his ears. Then Thomas doubled back as Alistair fished out his key and opened the door to the Secret Garden.

He watched as Thomas-the-dog ran to the end of the path, looked up and down and then ran back tail wagging. That felt like the all-clear, so Alistair unlocked the door and held the ivy aside for Thomas to trot through. He followed and locked the door behind him.

Thomas shifted back into human form and grinned at him.

"It feels even nicer today, don't you think?"

Alistair nodded. "I think you're right." He paused at the gate, bending to unlace and remove his shoes and then his socks, balling them up together and stashing them in one shoe. Then he went ahead and rolled the cuffs of his trousers up as well.

The ground was cold under his feet, but not unbearably so. The connection to the Earth was more than worth it. For a moment he had the sensation of his blood flowing down, into the Earth straight from his veins, and pure energy returning up through the soles of his feet. It wasn't entirely a comfortable feeling, but it wasn't as alien as it probably should have felt.

Thomas followed his lead and undid his boots, leaving them beside Alistair's. Alistair shrugged off his jacket and rolled up his shirt sleeves. It was time to get to work.

Removing weeds was hard work, when they were as well established as these ones were. Soon, Alistair and Thomas were both sweating from the hard work, but rather than feel repulsed or tired out, Alistair felt exhilarated. Looking over the planting bed that they'd freed from dandelion plants as high as his waist and seeing the promise of bare soil filled his soul with happiness.

"What do you think used to be planted here?" he asked Thomas.

Thomas looked at the bed, and then around at the surroundings of the garden and shook his head. "No idea. But you're the one with the knack for plants. Why don't you see if you can sense it? The soil must have some memory of it, don't you think?"

What an idea.

Alistair was shy at the thought of even trying to ask the soil itself what it knew. "Is there a spell for that?"

"Might be," Thomas said. "But I never bothered too much about whether there was a spell for the particular thing I wanted to do. I just tried to see a way to do it with my magic."

Alistair frowned. Well, he was still new at magic, and he saw no reason that he could *only* do it the way Professor Bernard had instructed. He'd broken the curse by accident, and the creation of his wand was largely coincidence, and following his instincts. Why not try it again now?

He knelt down beside the soil, which was fluffy and soft from weeding, and sunk his fingers in as deeply as he could manage.

He closed his eyes and summoned up his magic, which was always easy to do in the Garden, and let it flow through him. Once again he felt that ineffable connection to the ground, the feeling that he was somehow part of it. Perhaps this is what trees feel like, he mused. Taking the energy from the sun, the water from the earth and drawing it into themselves to make it into sap and leaves.

He let himself adjust to the feeling for a long minute, and then started to form the question in his mind. Once he'd embellished the words with his magic a few times, he spoke them out loud, the hairs on the back of his neck rising with the crackle of his magic.

"What grew here when Lady Carlisle was in charge of the

garden?"

It was two hundred years ago... Alistair had no idea if soil had any memory at all, let alone a two hundred years memory.

But after a moment, an image came into his mind.

The bed he was looking at, flourishing with soft purple bluebells in the front and tall pink foxgloves behind. Here and there were red poppies as well.

He could see it in his mind's eye and when he opened his eyes he could see just how it was laid out. "Foxgloves and bluebells," he said. "With poppies."

"It might be too late for those," Thomas said. "But we can plant them for next year?"

Alistair shook his head, dug his fingers deeper into the ground. He could feel it. The bulbs were still there. The soil... the soil wanted him to know they were there. The Garden was telling him that he could make it happen, right now. He could make all the flowers bloom just as they had for Lady Carlisle.

He concentrated hard, letting his magic flow out of him and into the soil, then with a gasp, he felt it. The bulbs were responding, they were reaching up towards him as he reached down. They were pushing their long buried green hearts up as stalks. The tips of them pushing through the soil to find the light.

Alistair sat back, pulling his hands out of the soil to give the plants space to grow. His magic had given them what they needed, and as he watched the spikes erupted from the ground, put out leaves and grew a few inches. Not quite enough to flower, but that was all right. They were there now, and soon they would be a riot of colour.

"Oh, I felt that," Thomas said. He had been somewhere nearby, and Alistair wanted to turn to him and converse, but he wasn't quite done watching the plants he'd just summoned. He dusted off his hands on his trousers and gazed over all the new seedlings with a sort of paternal pride.

"You did?"

"Mm, that was fairly big magic, whatever you did," Thomas said. His voice was soft, awed. "I could feel it reaching up through the ground and touching me."

"Touching you?" Alistair turned to Thomas then, feeling a sudden anticipation although he couldn't have said why.

Thomas was smiling at him, his smile wide, and showing some slightly too sharp teeth. From his brown hair poked two bright red fox ears. Alistair's laugh burst out of him, surprising them both.

"What's so funny?"

"Your ears!" Alistair pointed. Thomas tilted his head to one side.

"What?"

"I think..." Alistair bit his lip, hardly daring to believe what he was about to say. "Is it possible that what I did with the bulbs brought some more magic into you?"

Thomas raised a hand tentatively to feel where his human ears weren't any more. Then his hand moved up and he touched the twitchy fox ears and beamed even wider. "Oh stars above, what do they look like Alistair? They're pointy like..."

"A fox! See if you can turn into a fox!" Alistair said, laughing again.

Thomas jumped to his feet and once again Alistair got to witness the strange magic of shapeshifting. It seemed even faster this time, only a blink for the light to settle down around Thomas and then he was there, a russet orange fox with the thickest, fluffiest tail.

Thomas yipped, a curious high sound and jumped into the air and then raced around Alistair. His long black legs nimble as he jumped here and there, and finally climbed into Alistair's lap to lick his face.

"All right, all right," Alistair said. He'd been laughing the entire time, and now his cheeks ached. "I'm glad you can change into a fox now, too."

Thomas changed back, and then he was a human person, sitting in Alistair's lap, his arms around Alistair's neck and his face close enough to kiss again.

"I love it," Thomas said. He rubbed his cheek against Alistair's cheek and hugged him close. "Thank you."

"I'm sure... you would have found out how to do this on your own, in time," Alistair said. He was flustered by Thomas's proximity, but also by his gratitude. His magic had been wonderful, but surely he couldn't be credited with this?

"Probably," Thomas said. "But it'd have taken me years, there's usually a lot of study, and practice before new forms are learned. Because of you finding this garden and then the Wellspring, you've saved me so much time. I wonder if you could do it again?"

Alistair gazed at his surprising, wonderful friend and wanted to give him the world. He wanted to immediately dig his hands into the Earth and summon up more magic, but then he'd have to let go of Thomas's waist.

"I..." Alistair started, listening to his heart and ready to promise him all the forms that Alistair could summon, but instead he yawned hugely. His mind became muzzy and dull and he wanted to curl up on Thomas's chest and sleep.

Thomas chuckled and climbed out of his lap. "Come on, get under the tree here and have a rest. Big magic always takes its toll and you're not at all used to it."

"Thank... you..." was all Alistair could manage as he staggered after Thomas, who was insistently tugging his arm. Thomas sat under the tree and pulled Alistair down, pillowing his head on his lap.

"You're incredible," Thomas said softly. "I'm so glad you came to Misselthwaite, Alistair. So, so glad."

Then Alistair slept.

CHAPTER 32

When Alistair woke up, the sun was dropping behind the wall, and Thomas was playing with his hair. "Awake again?" he asked, his voice soft and warm.

Alistair yawned and stretched his arms and legs as far as they'd go and then sighed. "Yes, for the minute anyway."

"Good. It's almost time for dinner, we should head back up to the Manor."

"Gosh," Alistair sat up, feeling suddenly guilty. "I'm sorry for just trapping you here while I snoozed."

"You didn't trap me," Thomas said, chuckling. "I was happy to give you a pillow."

He seemed on the verge of saying something else, and Alistair's heart leapt into his throat, but Thomas seemed to decide not to in the end.

They both got up, brushed the grass off their trousers and made their way up to the Manor.

When Thomas and Alistair entered the dining hall it was to find Samal and Martha already seated at their table with heaping plates of food.

Alistair filled his plate, his stomach ached as if he'd never eaten in his life, and he felt like he'd eat his weight in cottage pie and dinner rolls. He sat down at their table and nodded at Samal and Martha.

"Good evening."

"Hello Alistair," Martha said, giving him a warm smile from in between sips of hearty corn soup. "I hope you don't mind us barging in like this, but as Sam's so keen on you it just made sense. No more yearning from across the room, eh? I was just saying - Ow! That hurt Sam." She gave Samal a wounded look but he just glared back at her. He must have kicked her under the table, Alistair thought. His mind was whirling with the phrasing Martha had used.

"Martha, please be quiet," he said through clenched teeth. Then he looked over at Alistair with a much softer expression. "Forgive her, she was born on the summer solstice and has no tact whatsoever."

"It's fine," Alistair said. "It's nice to have you here." And what surprised him was that he genuinely meant it.

Will sat down at the head of the table. His plate had a generous helping of cottage pie and two pieces of blood pudding. Alistair hadn't even seen blood pudding on the buffet table, but then again he'd been rather intent on the rolls.

"Good evening, all," Will said. He looked paler than usual, his eyes sunken into his face and his cheeks gaunter. It must have been a terribly hard night on him.

Alistair reached over to pat the back of his hand. "It's good to see you," he said, stiffly.

There was a silent moment where no one said anything. Will looked at Alistair's hand on his as if he couldn't comprehend what it could mean. Thomas watched the both of them, and Samal stared determinedly at his plate.

"Well," Martha said, finally. "You won't believe what happened in illusions class today, we were meant to be conjuring a part of a labyrinth, dead tricky stuff, of course, and the Professor was in one of her foul moods, I swear she's part werewolf."

"Werewolves are real?" Alistair asked, somehow surprised and not at all sure how he could still be surprised by revelations of the magical world at this point.

"Oh yes," Martha said. She waved her hand. "They're not usually as frightening as they are in the stories. Anyway, as I was saying..."

Alistair picked up his fork and began to eat. Grateful to Martha for cutting the strange tension, but also intrigued by her story of magic illusions gone wrong. Her story reminded Will of something funny which had happened a few weeks back in Spells and Hexes, before Alistair had arrived at Misselthwaite, so he told that story, and soon enough all six of them were laughing.

A cosy feeling settled over Alistair as he buttered his third roll. He felt at home.

He looked between the faces of his friends. All of them had seen him at terrible moments, crying or raging or complaining, but all of them were here with him at the table now. They were his friends, and he had longed for them. Missed them before he knew anything about them.

"What is so amusing, Alistair?" William asked, his voice mock-stern.

Alistair shook his head. "Nothing, I'm just... I think I'm genuinely happy, and it's been an awfully long time since I could say that."

Thomas leaned against his shoulder briefly. Across the table Sam gave him an uncharacteristically goofy grin and a wink, and when he turned back to William, his cheeks flushed, William winked at him as well.

Alistair's heart fluttered in his chest and he felt drunk off his own joy.

"Well, I'm very happy for you," William said. His expression went from sardonic to almost shy. "The stars only know I've hardly got a wealth of friends, myself."

"You have us now," Alistair said.

"I'm going to get us some pudding," Samal said. "Who wants some?"

"Oh yes, please."

The evening wore on with pleasant company, cups of tea and two helpings of pudding, until they were chivvied along by Medlock to tidy up their dinner plates and go to their rooms.

"I suppose I'll do some reading on curse breaking," Alistair said as they tidied up. "If anyone wants to join me."

"Of course," Thomas said. William nodded.

Martha looked between them all and slowly nodded. "You all have fun, I have some illusion work to read up on and it's best if I practice alone."

Sam smiled at Alistair and slung his arm around his shoulders. "Well I was intending on sleeping in your room again, so I might as well join in."

William blanched at that but didn't say anything as they all made their way up to Alistair's room.

CHAPTER 33

*A*listair's room wasn't quite large enough for everyone to sit comfortably and study. He half wished William had suggested his rooms as a venue, but perhaps he needed those empty in case he had another attack and needed to quickly withdraw.

The room was cosy enough, the fire crackled merrily, although Alistair thought that soon it might be warm enough not to need one. Possibly. Unless Misselthwaite was this cold year round, which felt very possible.

Thomas sprawled on his front on the rug by the fire, his book propped up on the edge of Samal's mattress. Samal sat on his mattress, his back braced against the frame of Alistair's bed. Alistair sat up on his bed, propped against the pillows, and William was at the desk, the chair of which barely had room to pull out with the mattress taking up so much of the floor.

Thomas shifted to his fox ears, and after a moment a long fluffy fox tail poked out over the waistband of his trousers. He looked so warm and cuddly, but Alistair resisted every urge to go and flop on top of him.

Samal was much as he always was, quiet and mysterious, a reassuring presence who didn't dominate the room with his personality, although Alistair knew he was capable of it if he let his angelic form come out.

Really, Alistair was most distracted from reading by the way William looked. The dinner had put a little more colour into his cheeks, but he still looked rather ghastly. Especially in contrast to Thomas who seemed full of life.

Alistair wondered if this was a precursor to one of the terrible sleeps that William was prone to, and he felt bereft at the thought of it. He didn't want a whole day to go by without seeing William, let alone weeks or even months. What had this curse done for William to be so poorly so much of the time? He should be full of life.

The thought spurred him into more diligent research, but everything he read seemed wrong for their circumstance. It was frustrating, feeling like the answer to their problems must be close, but finding nothing of use.

꙳

The rest of the week passed in the blink of an eye. The very last of winter made itself known with torrential rain, dark afternoons and dismal, misty mornings.

Alistair couldn't go down to the Garden in such weather, he had no wet-weather gear at all.

With his wand, and his growing understanding of runes and how magic worked, Alistair's course loads increased. Professors gave him make-up work for the early part of term that he had missed, and he had more readings for his courses as well. He was improving though, which was gratifying.

The research over William's curse took precedence over the Garden, much as Alistair missed it, and the miserable evenings were very well suited to gathering his friends together in his room by the merry fire and reading their way through the library books. There were frequent trips to the library to return and borrow more volumes, and Alistair was impressed to see that the supply seemed to be endless. He decided that it made sense for a Magical library.

Thomas and Samal insisted on sleeping over in his room for his own protection, but William would excuse himself around ten or eleven, and retire to his own rooms.

It was the next Tuesday that Alistair had something of a breakthrough in his readings. He was in his room, in his customary place on the bed. The others had all made a habit of sitting in the same places as well, and indeed, Alistair was so used to looking to his right and seeing William, looking to the fireplace and seeing Thomas, and having Samal closest, leaning against the bed, that he had come to find it quite normal.

He picked up the next book from the stack beside him. It was titled *Curses Moste Evile* and Alistair ran his finger down the page of contents. Idly, he flipped to the chapter which detailed the kinds of people who typically had the most success in curse breaking. For such potentially exciting subject matter the book was written in a terribly dry academic tone, and Alistair felt his eyelids start to droop. It was rather warm in the room, and he was quite comfortable up against the pillows. Outside there was an extra heavy downpour of rain and it was all so cosy and soothing, he could easily have fallen asleep.

Instead, he forced himself to read the words.

There are some family lines which are particularly gifted. One might see for example, a Walton or a Stanley with a prodigious talent for the breaking of curses. However even in a family without curse-breaking in the bloodline any magically inclined person may show an aptitude for the talent. In particular it seems to occur when a magical family has an instance of twins.

Much is written about the particular magical powers between twins. One might refer to such texts as...

Alistair read the paragraph again.

"Twins," he said, softly. He couldn't say why exactly, but that the sentence about twins had struck him as important. There were no twins at the University that he knew of, and of course, none of them in the room were twins. Were they?

No, he thought hard and concluded they weren't. William and Samal were both only children like Alistair himself, and Thomas's siblings were all younger. Oh, but Thomas's family had twins in it!

"Thomas!" he exclaimed.

Samal dropped his book and Thomas looked up. "What?"

"Twins, your siblings are twins, didn't you say?"

"Esther and Madrigal are, yes," he said. He sat up, folding his legs below him and wrapping his tail around his feet. "What about it?"

"This book says twins are more likely to be able to break curses, so... so maybe that's a lead?"

"They're five," Thomas said. His left ear twitched and Alistair wondered if it was an amused tic, or if he'd heard something.

William snorted. "I hope that's not the best plan we can come up with."

Samal tipped his head to the side, considering, tapping one finger on his knee. "You do hear things about twins, though, don't you? The two who graduated five years ago were incredible healers, Madame Waxleaf still talks about them, how they made a burn salve even better than hers. She teaches their recipe for it, now."

"Hmm," Alistair said. "So their talents were in the healing arts? Not curses..."

"That's right."

"I'm sure if there was anything in the twins thing Father would have already recruited them to help," William said. "Although perhaps he did, I was asleep much of the time they attended."

"The book says it," Alistair said. "I'm sure we can't just dismiss the theory altogether."

"I wasn't," William said quickly. He got up and poured tea from the pot he'd had sent up to Alistair's room. "I just don't think five-year-olds can help, although I'm certain, Thomas, that they are lovely children."

"They're all right," Thomas said. "But they don't know what their talents are yet, and I don't think they'd be up to something like curse-breaking, not until they're a lot older."

"Curse breaking takes a lot out of someone," Alistair said. "It must do, mustn't it? Because magic does drain me, and I know I haven't been practising long but... after the Garden, for example..."

He looked quickly at William, who returned his gaze. "My mother's garden you mean?"

"I did something there, and I had to sleep right after," Alistair said.

"I expect so," Samal said. "Healing comes easily enough to me due to my blood, but casting hexes or anything complicated wears me out. I always have to eat more at dinner after a class that challenges me."

Alistair wondered if Thomas or William would prod Samal about what he meant by his blood, but apparently they were too polite.

William brought the cup of tea he'd made over to Alistair's bed and handed it to him.

Alistair took it, surprised. "Oh, thank you."

"You looked sleepy," William said, his voice surprisingly soft. "Perhaps this will revive you?"

"I don't feel as sleepy now," Alistair said. "Something about this twins thing is catching at me and I'm not sure why. Perhaps because of that strange tapestry..."

"What tapestry?" Thomas asked.

"There's a tapestry in the hall that leads to William's room," Alistair said. "It looks sort of like me."

"There's a lot of strange artwork in this place," William said. "And a lot of it has traces of magic in it." He sat down on the bed by Alistair's feet.

"What do you mean traces of magic?" Alistair tried to focus on the topic of conversation and not the fact that William was now on his bed with him. He could stretch out his leg and touch him with his toe. He wouldn't, of course, but he *could*.

"It's a consequence of the house being a school of magic, and of course, from my family living here so long. Magic, it leaves traces… think of say, how if you dipped your fingers in ink and then touched my shirt." he brushed his own fingers over the dark grey cotton of his shirt where it covered his chest. "The stain would remain, even if I washed the shirt, there would be a faint mark."

William talking about Alistair touching his chest wasn't helping Alistair concentrate at all. "So, the thing giving me a strange feeling might just be because of some strange leftover magic someone did a century ago?"

"Precisely."

"Perhaps we should all go look at the tapestry all the same?" Thomas suggested. "I know Alistair is new at this, but he has good instincts for where the mystery is and the solution, if you ask me."

"Might be nice to stretch my legs for a moment," Samal said.

But before anyone could make any moves, there was a sharp knock at the door.

CHAPTER 34

*A*listair got up to open the door. Medlock stood on the other side, her expression severe and her hair pulled back in its signature tight bun.

"Mister Lennox." Her voice sounded flustered. "I know the hour is late but Lord Carlisle requests a word with you."

"Oh," Alistair said. He reached for his jacket and pulled it on. "Of course, although I don't really have any news for him."

Medlock looked over Alistair's shoulder at the cluster of boys and the mattress on the floor. "Goodness me, it seems I am interrupting a party. Boys, it's a bit late for a Monday evening isn't it? I would strongly suggest you make your way back to your own rooms. Lord Carlisle may be talking to your host for some time."

"If it's quite alright," William said, getting up. "I should like to accompany Alistair and speak with my father myself."

"My orders were quite clear," Medlock said. Her tone was crisp and brooked no argument and William actually seemed cowed by her. Alistair was a little impressed at Medlock. "I'm sure you can visit with your father in the morning, Mister Carlisle."

Thomas got up, uncertain. "Perhaps I could... ?

Medlock cleared her throat. "You boys should all go back to your own rooms. This is a university not some kind of..." she paused, apparently struggling to come up with a comparison that was suitable enough. "Dosshouse for wayward young men."

"I'm staying," Thomas said. Alistair realised he'd hidden his fox ears and tail again and looked totally normal. "I'll wait here for Alistair."

Medlock pursed her lips and turned on her heel, apparently giving up on this particular battle. "Come along Lennox."

"If you're staying I won't bother to lock the door," Alistair said. He waved awkwardly at his friends. Thomas nodded and settled down on the bed where Alistair had been sitting.

Samal had stood up and was staring hard after Medlock.

"It's fine," Alistair said. "I'll be back as soon as I can. Lord Carlisle has never wanted to talk for long before."

He turned and hurried to follow Medlock, whose heels tapped against the wooden floorboards with rapidity, encouraging him to walk faster just to catch up.

She held a small lantern with glowing light inside it - some kind of witch light, which was brighter and steadier than the candles Alistair was used to carrying around. He made a mental note to find out how to make such a light for himself. Although, he did hope that his late night wanderings around the halls of the Manor were largely over, now that William was talking to him about everything going on.

She led him up the stairs, holding her skirts up primly to one side.

There was something strange about how she was walking, and Alistair examined her as he walked a few feet behind. What could it be?

He slowed at the top of the stairs, trying to remember the last time he'd walked behind her to compare, but there was nothing he could put his finger on.

If he was going to be paranoid, at least he could protect

himself better now. He had his wand, after all, and he'd connected his power to that of the Earth itself.

Alistair's pulse thrummed as he reached the top of the stairs and turned to follow Medlock towards Lord Carlisle's study. He could feel his heartbeat in his wrists and in his throat. Remembering his spell from the Secret Garden, Alistair felt a reassuring knowledge that he had the potential to do or achieve anything at all. With the magic in his soul, and his logical brain, and his friends, he could overcome any obstacle at all.

His friends, who were waiting for him in his room, he was sure about. He almost laughed at his concern about how Medlock was walking. What did it matter what she did or said, when he had the world at the tips of his fingers?

He felt ten feet tall.

Naturally, that was when he walked directly into an invisible web formed of strange magic. One moment, he was striding down the corridor, following Medlock, and the next he was held in place.

It felt as if a thousand ice cold threads had caught him up as securely as a fly in a spider's web. He swallowed, trying to reach for his wand, but the threads had wound around his arms and torso as well as his legs, holding him so tightly he could barely move.

"There's the fool, followed just like you said he would," Medlock said. She turned and folded her arms, a self-satisfied smile on her face.

"Listen, Lennox, we gave you numerous warnings. I don't know why you felt it was all right to ignore them," this voice he knew. It was the slow, upper-class drone of Eleanor as she stepped out of the shadows.

Alistair swallowed, squirming. The threads were even across his face, chilling his skin and threatening to cut if they got even a little bit tighter.

He turned his gaze back to Medlock, confused more than

anything else about why she would be working with Eleanor. He opened his mouth, but the threads moved closer to his lips and he quickly closed it again, not wanting the magical web to get into his mouth.

He had to do something.

He knew he had to do something.

The last time Eleanor and Eulalia had caught him they might have killed him if it wasn't for Samal. And they'd overturned his room since then, warning him away. He had no doubts that they meant to seriously hurt him now, possibly even kill him.

And what could he do about that?

He couldn't move. He couldn't feel the energy of the Earth, he was on the third floor of a building. He couldn't feel anything at all.

Alistair tried to think, tried to shake his head to loosen the threads but there was nothing he could do. His heart thundered in his ears and his chest got tighter still, aching in need of a deep breath that he was too afraid to take.

"There's absolutely no point in struggling, Lennox," Medlock said. She moved closer to him. He watched her, yearning to ask why she was doing this, beg her to let him go. "The spell will hold you tighter if you do."

She cocked her head to one side as Eleanor and Eulalia moved into the small pool of light cast by Medlock's candle.

"Well then," Eleanor said. "Shall we get started?"

"We don't want to rush things," Eulalia said. She raised her wand and pointed it at Alistair's nose. "We have him where we want him after all."

"It's time for us to set some things to rights," Medlock said. She started a spell, filling the air with cold grey lights - magic. Not unlike what Thomas did. It settled around Medlock like an aura. Alistair watched in horror as her face began to blur. Her voice deepened and changed as she spoke. "The Lennoxes with their money and their talent, you make me sick."

Medlock had melted away and in her place stood Everett. That made more sense, at least. Alistair had no inkling that Everett's magical gift had been for this - some form of shape changing. Why did they look down on Thomas for shape changing if it was something Everett did as well?

"Even you, who we were certain was a dunce," Eleanor said. "You were picked specially by Lord Carlisle. And why do you think that is?"

Alistair swallowed. They seemed to be waiting for an answer from him. He shook his head infinitesimally. He had no idea why he had caught anyone's eye at all, for any purpose.

"They say the Lennox name is charmed," Eulalia said, she walked slowly around him, a cat circling its prey. "Even though the Lennoxes all but vanished from the magical world sixteen years ago."

"I don't understand!" Alistair blurted. Then he felt the ice cold threads tease at the corner of his mouth and snapped his lips shut again.

"Doesn't matter." Everett shrugged and cast a sudden spell at Alistair's feet, lighting a curiously grey fire which lapped at Alistair's feet - it wasn't quite as hot as a real fire, but it was plenty hot enough to put a new wave of fear through him. This was it, they were going to kill him, and there was nothing he could do about it. He closed his eyes. Of all the ways to die, burned alive seemed like the most horrible.

"The Lennoxes did everything they could to show up the Birches, back before they vanished," Eulalia said. "Everyone who matters knows that."

"Your parents didn't care who they hurt," Eleanor said. She aimed her wand at Alistair's chest and cast a sequence of runes he didn't recognise.

With a slow, agonising movement, something inside Alistair

broke. Perhaps it was his collarbone, or the bone in his left shoulder, he had no idea, but his vision went white and he cried out, unable to stop himself from making the noise.

The threads pushed into his mouth, holding it open and reaching for the back of his throat.

He was vaguely aware of Eleanor talking, but his ears were ringing and he was fighting his body's urge to pass out and spare him the suffering.

Maybe he shouldn't fight that, he thought, somewhere in the back of his mind.

They've already won haven't they? And there was nothing Alistair could do about it.

CHAPTER 35

*A*listair must have passed out for a moment. He came back to wakefulness groggy and confused. His entire left side was hot with pain. His legs from the knees down hurt as well. His head was pounding with agony and he couldn't close his mouth, he could even feel the saliva dripping out his lower lip. Humiliation adding to his woes.

But there was something else - something which had woken him. He forced his eyes open and saw that Eleanor, Eulalia and Everett were pointing their wands, but it wasn't at him this time. They had turned, and were looking down the corridor towards the staircase. Had they turned Alistair around at some point? He groaned as another wave of pain threatened to overwhelm him.

There were shouts and the thundering of footsteps and suddenly Everett stumbled back and crashed to the ground, a fox on his chest wrestled the wand out of his hand, growling ferociously.

William wielded his wand as if it were a rapier, blasts of energy shooting out the end of it and aiming for Eleanor, who was busy flicking her wand back and forth to deflect his attacks. Samal strode towards Eulalia, fists raised, and between steps revealed his angelic form. The soft golden glow of him set the corridor into sudden relief. Eulalia let out a string of curses, runes which Alistair was passingly familiar with from all the reading, although he'd never heard them cast in such a way. Samal raised his glowing hand and deflected the curses as easily as swatting a fly.

"Curses don't work on angels," Samal said, his voice clear even over the grunts and growls of Everett and Thomas wrestling on the floor.

Eulalia's wand dropped from her hand and the clatter of it distracted Eleanor long enough for William to land one of his energy bolts on his chest; she crashed into the wall with a dull thud.

Alistair swallowed, finding it increasingly difficult to breathe. The grey flames of Everett's fire continued to climb and were at his mid-thighs now. He cried out, deep in his throat, all he was capable of.

"Will, check Alistair," Samal said. He raised his hand, placed it on Eulalia's head and she fell instantly asleep.

"I surrender, please don't kill me!" Everett cried. Thomas had his jaws clamped around his throat.

William approached Alistair, banishing the spells on him as he walked.

First the magical fire went out - which was a distinct relief. Then the icy threads, which to some extent, appeared to have been holding Alistair up. His knees gave way and he stumbled. William grabbed his left arm to steady him and Alistair howled with pain. His vision went white again.

"Sam! We need you! He's in a bad way!" Alistair was vaguely aware of William shouting as he crumpled to the floor, blacking out again.

When he was once again aware of his surroundings, things were a lot less dire.

He was sitting, propped between William's knees and leaning back on William's chest as Samal's hands moved slowly over his body. The pain in his left side was waning. There was nothing of the intense pain he'd felt before.

Samal glanced up and met his eyes. "Welcome back, Alistair."

"Did I die?" Alistair croaked.

William's hands were on his sides, holding him steady, and he felt them tense, squeezing him a little at the question.

"No," Samal said. "But you might have if we'd been any later."

Alistair shuddered bodily. "How did you know? Know to follow?"

"Ssh, just, quiet for a moment more," Samal said. He placed the palm of his hand on Alistair's chest and the last shreds of pain vanished from his body.

Alistair sighed with relief.

"What's going on here?" The voice of Medlock rang out.

"Is it the real one?" Alistair asked, suddenly panicking that perhaps there never had been a real Medlock and it had somehow been Everett all along.

"Of course I'm real," Medlock said, tutting. "What in the blazes are you all doing in the corridor to Lord Carlisle's rooms?"

Thomas, who had been sitting on Alistair's lap in fox form, shifted back into human form, causing Alistair to gasp at the sudden extra weight on him. "Miss Medlock they were trying to kill Alistair," he said.

Medlock looked between them. She didn't seem at all surprised to see Samal glowing, and with wings. Or surprised at Thomas shapeshifting from a fox. In fact, she didn't look surprised at all.

"Well, you'd better explain it all, Lennox," she said. "Then I'll hear from Everett and the others. Come along, we'd better do this in the infirmary."

She lifted a chain of her chatelaine and flicked the key at the end of it. A door appeared in the corridor, standing on its own in the middle of the space. She opened it onto a dimly lit room with rows of white sheeted beds. "Come on through. I'll bring these three."

"I can help," Thomas said. Alistair was helped to his feet by both William and Samal, which he wasn't sure he needed.

"I'm fine," he said. Then his knees buckled again and Samal slipped his arm around his waist.

"You're not fine. I've healed the breaks and your wounds, but you've still had the shock of those injuries, and healings are exhausting as well. Please just... let us help you."

Alistair gazed into Samal's eyes and saw genuine fear there. What did Samal have to be afraid of? He was a magical being with the ability to heal.. He shouldn't be afraid of anything. But he was. He had been afraid for Alistair. He was afraid now that Alistair might hurt himself.

Alistair, flushing from the knowledge, nodded quickly. "Thank you." He leaned his weight on Samal and then William, who had slid in under his other arm.

In the infirmary, Medlock put some magical wards over Eleanor, Eulalia and Everett and confiscated their wands.

"We're innocent, Miss Medlock," Eleanor said, her eyes huge and round. "We were just minding our own business when Lennox and the others set on us for no reason."

Medlock's mouth was a thin, determined line. "I can see the traces of the spells you put on Lennox before Carlisle removed them, there's no use lying to me."

The actual course of events was laid out by Alistair once he'd downed most of a warm, honeyed drink from the head of the infirmary, who was also the professor of healing, Madame Waxleaf. It was delicious, and it brought him back to himself. He hadn't even realised he'd been confused still, until he'd drunk the elixir.

Medlock sent Thomas to run for Professor Barlow and Lord

Carlisle; they would make the final decisions on what was to happen with the three who had attacked Alistair.

"You're welcome to stay here for the rest of the night," Professor Waxleaf said. "But Samal's healing is more than sufficient. You just need to sleep now, and take it very easy tomorrow. No classes, or anything strenuous."

"I'd like to go back to my room," Alistair said.

"Of course." Professor Waxleaf said. "And if anything worsens, let Samal know and he will tell me."

Sam and Will had been taking turns holding Alistair's hand as she had checked him over, and Thomas, in dog form, had curled up on Alistair's feet.

"Will you three come back to my room with me?"

The real Medlock had nothing at all to say about Alistair opening his room to Thomas, Samal and now William. She escorted them back through the magical door and ensured they were safely ensconced before leaving them to it.

Alistair pulled off his outer layers and collapsed into bed.

CHAPTER 36

"*P*erhaps we ought to have a conversation," William said, slowly. Alistair had climbed under the covers and was sitting looking at them all. Thomas, Samal and William all looked sort of awkward. There was a tension there that hadn't been present in the infirmary.

"A conversation?" Alistair said.

"Well, there are four of us in the room and..." William cleared his throat. "After what just happened I want to stay here with Alistair. I feel the need to protect him."

Samal grunted and crossed his arms. "I've been feeling that way since I met him. I'm staying. Besides, my mattress is here."

"I'm not going either," Thomas said. He sat decisively down on the end of Alistair's bed.

"I want all of you to stay," Alistair said. "There's no argument about that."

William shifted his weight from one foot to the other. "Well, perhaps the argument then is about who is going to court Alistair."

Alistair blushed and pulled the bedclothes up to cover his face. "Do we have to talk about that right now?"

"Perhaps we should let him rest?" Thomas said.

"Alistair and I shared a kiss," Samal said, suddenly. His cheeks flushed red but his eyes were blazing with determination. "I don't go around kissing people lightly."

Alistair pulled the bedclothes down, horrified that they were all going to talk about how he'd kissed them, and when and where. He had to take control of the conversation right then. William was right, they did need to clear things up.

"I've kissed all of you," he said. He looked between them and then dropped his eyes. "I'm sure it was wicked of me, and I'm sorry for that. But I like all of you, and I'm... I'm drawn to you all in very different ways."

Samal took a step towards Alistair, his expression confused but not angry or hurt.

"No arrangements were made," he said, slowly. "I suppose I didn't consider the possibility of more than one..." he looked at Thomas.

Thomas shrugged and smiled softly. "I won't give up what I have with Alistair, and to be honest, I kind of... the idea of sharing him, and myself, with the both of you is quite, well, fun. Exciting, even."

The three of them looked at William. He considered for a moment and then grinned. "Thomas is right. I don't mind sharing at all. In fact..." he moved closer to the bed as well. "It is rather thrilling to consider."

Alistair blushed again. "People won't think we're, I don't know... odd?"

"People already think we're odd." Thomas moved up the bed a little, and rested his chin on Alistair's knee where he had it propped up. "But even still, not entirely. Same gender lovers are more accepted in our society than in the mundane world."

"And... multiple... partners?" Alistair asked, not quite able yet to say the word 'lovers' even though his mind was happily singing it. Lovers! Not just friends, but people who loved him! He had never dreamed he could be so lucky as that.

William shook his head. "It's not common to be sure, but it's certainly not unheard of."

Alistair's heart thumped again, but this time it was with hope. He looked between them. Warm, sweet Thomas, intense, infuriating William and wonderful, mysterious Samal. He really did want all three of them in his life, and as more than friends. He wanted three lovers... and they were all saying that they were all right with that.

He cleared his throat and decided to try and make a joke. If he didn't make a joke, he might get overwhelmed and cry.

"Well, then, I suppose it's a pity that the bed isn't any bigger."

Thomas laughed, a sort of yip of a laugh that Alistair found endearing.

"Luckily this is a *magical* university," William said.

He moved to the doorway and gestured for Samal to get out of the way, then waved his wand. The mattress levitated off the floor and he leaned it against the wall. Then he pointed his wand at Alistair's bed and said some words of power. The bedframe creaked, and then slowly expanded. The mattress and bedclothes also seemed to stretch as the bedframe elongated and slowly crept across the floor. Alistair and Thomas were suddenly in the middle of a very large bed, one with plenty of room for two more.

Alistair flushed again, but his joy at this development overcame his embarrassment. He pulled back the covers and patted the mattress. "Come on in, then. Can't sleep standing up, can you?"

Thomas chuckled and went up on his knees, pulling his shirt and then trousers off, and climbing into bed beside Alistair with a bare chest. He lay back on the pillows and slipped his arm around Alistair. If Alistair hadn't been quite so worn out and shaken, he might have thought something truly salacious was about to happen, but as it was he was just comforted. Overjoyed, somewhere in the back of his mind about the promise of salacious things in the future, perhaps, but for now this was enough.

Thomas pulled him closer as William and Samal undressed and climbed into the bed as well, jostling for a moment about who got to be next to Alistair and then laughing. William cuddled in next to Alistair and Samal next to him.

Samal extinguished the light and for a moment the only sounds in the room were the rustling of bedclothes as each of them got comfortable, and four sets of breathing.

"This is..." Alistair said, sleepily, feeling the need to address the strangeness of the situation. "Not how I imagined today would end."

Thomas chuckled into his ear. "Neither."

"It... sort of feels right to me," Samal said. He was closer than Alistair had anticipated, perhaps he was cuddling William as well. Alistair felt William's hand on his chest and smiled softly.

"It feels right to me as well."

CHAPTER 37

*A*listair woke because someone's hand was on his arse and that wasn't a feeling he was familiar with. It wasn't a bad feeling at all, in fact, he felt the urge to press back against the hand and demand it do more, but shyness overtook him and he settled for opening his eyes instead.

Beside him, William lay curled on his side, his fists against his chest and his knees pulled up under his elbows. So, it wasn't his hand, Alistair thought. He looked so calm in his sleep, the intensity of worry smoothed out of his forehead. His cheek was cushioned on Samal's bicep and Samal's hand had curled around him, and was holding him by the chest.

Samal, on the other side of William was sprawled carelessly on his back, the blankets kicked off his legs and his breathing was a soft, snore, so faint it would never bother anyone. He too looked softer in sleep, more approachable. His walls had come down, Alistair thought. Well, it wasn't Samal's hands either, which meant...

Alistair was lying on his side but partially leaning against Thomas's chest. He turned his head slowly, reaching up to brush the hair out of his own eyes as he saw that Thomas, whatever he was groping, was doing it in his sleep. He moved slightly, as if dreaming, but his breathing was steady and his eyes were closed.

Alistair turned more, withdrawing his bottom from the affectionate hand, and snuggling against Thomas's chest, planting a kiss here and there without even really thinking about it. He dropped back to sleep for a little while longer.

He woke again when the mattress moved under him. Groggily, he opened his eyes and turned to see Samal had gotten up and was stretching his arms over his head as he yawned. Every muscle in his back moved under his golden skin, gilded by the sun filtering through the crack in the curtains. He looked like a painting of Adonis.

Alistair suddenly became very aware of his own hardness, and the proximity of both William and Thomas as they too woke up.

William grinned at him, a cheeky sort of expression, although his eyes were bleary. "Morning, Allie."

Alistair stuck his tongue out, seizing the opportunity to tease and pick a fight - it would distract him from his body's request to rub himself all over each of the boys.

"My name is Alistair," Alistair said.

William reached up to tweak his nose. "You have nicknames for us, why can't I give you one?"

"Allie is actually really cute," Thomas said, through a yawn. He turned on his side, moulding his chest to Alistair's back. Positioned like that he could very clearly feel Thomas's own morning hardness and he was startled to find he wanted to rub himself against that as well.

"Agreed," Sam said. He was washing himself at Alistair's basin now and the dampness of his skin did nothing but enhance his beauty. Alistair closed his eyes and tried to think only the purest of thoughts. "I like Allie for you."

"Fine," Alistair said. He shook his head.

"Aw, Allie's blushing," William teased.

Unbidden, the events of the night before came rushing back to Alistair. Eleanor, Eulalia and Everett had meant to kill him, he was certain of it, and his heart thumped with the knowledge.

"I don't know if I..." Alistair couldn't say this with Thomas distracting him the way he was, so he hauled himself reluctantly into a sitting position, which forced Thomas to move and William as well. As they made distance between them, Alistair felt his head clear somewhat. "I don't know if I thanked you all last night, for coming to my aid."

"No thanks necessary," Samal said.

"Even still," Alistair said. "I'd be dead now if you hadn't intervened, I have no idea how to defend myself against attacks like that."

"I'll teach you," Samal said. "There are some basic wards and defences we all learn as teenagers, and you ought to know them too."

Thomas hopped out of bed and went to use the basin as Samal dried himself off. Alistair's mind was still on the things that Eleanor and the others had said though. "I don't understand why she kept saying things about the Lennoxes though," he said. "I have no real idea of what my parents did, or why, but she said they vanished from the world of magic sixteen years ago."

William paused in raking his fingers through his hair and shrugged. "I have no idea. Oh, except I had a particularly bad spell around that time."

"A bad spell? How bad?" Samal asked.

"I think that was one of the times I was unconscious for two years," William said, matter-of-factly.

There was silence in the room as they all considered that.

"I think I need the library," Alistair said. He rubbed his eyes. "What day is it?"

"Wednesday," Samal said. "And we're about to miss breakfast, so you'd better all hurry up."

They made it down to breakfast in time to grab the last of the pastries and porridge. There was no sign of Eleanor, Eulalia or Everett, and Alistair wondered if they'd been expelled or simply reprimanded. Surely an attempt on another's life was grounds for expulsion, wasn't it? But he knew that the rules in the magical society were different in a few ways, so he couldn't be sure.

"I'm going straight to the library after this," Alistair said. Medlock had said he shouldn't have his usual classes so he had time to research.

Something about his parents' past had angered Eleanor enough to seek revenge. What had happened sixteen years before? It seemed like if he discovered the answer to this it would be the key to everything. Or at least, he hoped it would.

"I'll come with you," Samal said.

"I'll go to Spells and Hexes class and get notes you can copy," William said.

Thomas chewed his lip. "I'd probably better go to Shapeshifting too, show off my new form and let the Professor know what happened, with the Garden and everything."

"Maybe it's best if you don't mention the Garden specifically," Alistair said. "Not until we know more."

"I'll just say it was your magic in a garden, then," Thomas said.

"I still need to visit the garden," William said.

Alistair crammed the last of his cherry Danish into his mouth and nodded. "We can go soon, assuming the weather clears up, but I need answers today. The library is my best bet."

Samal and Alistair walked into the library together.

Kincade looked up with a smile. "Alistair, I wasn't sure when I'd be seeing you again. I thought you'd be in the infirmary after last night. Professor Barlow told all us staff that there'd been some trouble."

"I'm all right, Sam's a very good healer," Alistair said.

"Well, I'm glad you have him then," Kincade said. "How can I help?"

"Have you got any uh, I suppose, old newspapers about the magical society? From more than ten years ago? Like, news from sixteen years ago?" He asked, utterly unsure if such a thing even existed.

Kincade raised an eyebrow. "Uh, not exactly no. Although I'm sure the magical archives hold things like that, we simply don't have the space. There are some history books, though. Perhaps you'd like to start there?"

"Right," Alistair said. He bit his lip, wondering if he looked in those books they would only have news of the Carlisles and the most rich and influential people. "I suppose so, yes, do you think - do the history books cover all the different families? Or just the most important ones?"

"Any magical family's doings, if they are considered newsworthy, will be recorded somewhere," Kincade said. They were clearly confused by his line of questioning and Alistair didn't blame them at all. He was barely sure what he was asking for.

"All right, where's the history section then?"

The history section was on the ground floor of the library, the furthest side of the room from the mezzanine, and situated beside a tall window which let in sunlight, although it was filtered through a thin net curtain. There were a pair of leather armchairs and a generous coffee table, so that's where Alistair set himself up with his notebook and pen.

Soon enough Alistair and Samal were making a big pile of books to look through. Samal was useful in reaching the higher shelves and lifting down the particularly giant books.

"This one looks promising," Samal said, bringing down a burgundy linen-bound book from the very topmost shelf. He had gone to the very top of the ladder to retrieve it, and if Alistair hadn't known that Samal had wings he might have been nervous about him being up there. As it was, he simply enjoyed watching him.

The book was very dusty, as if it had been sitting undisturbed for many years. Alistair brushed off the dust to reveal the title on the cover: *The British Wizarding Families.*

Many of the history books he'd been reading were simply books, but this one had a buzz of energy to it. He could feel it humming in the spine, and it filled him with anticipation perhaps this was the book which would hold the answers?

He sat on the armchair and laid the book in his lap, opening it carefully, reverently. Books had always been his friends, but this one, with the positive energy buzzing softly in his hands, was even more welcoming. He held his breath as he looked over the table of contents.

"The Lennox family tree…" he murmured as he read the words. Samal settled on the arm of the chair, balancing as lightly as a bird as he leaned close to read over Alistair's shoulder.

Alistair turned the thin, delicate pages of the book to the Lennox page. It seemed the book was full of articles and sketches of family trees, all using the same basic design, and filled with identical handwriting. It was up to date, from what he could see in the pages he skipped over, including new babies from that very year. When he opened the page to the Lennoxes, he saw that it had the death dates for his parents written in.

He stroked a fingertip over their names, feeling as if he ought to miss them but instead only longing to better understand who they had been.

"The book was covered in dust, it hadn't been moved," Alistair said. "How has it got dates from a couple of weeks ago?"

"Magic," Samal said, not unkindly. "I could feel it as soon as I touched it. The author must have cast a spell to keep it updated as things changed."

Alistair pulled his hand back and frowned, his name was there under his parent's, but his wasn't the only name.

The tree branch sprouted two identical leaves, one with his name and one which read Ambrose. The birth dates were the same, but under Ambrose there was a death date. The year of the death was sixteen years ago.

"What?" Alistair blinked. He read it again. Ambrose Lennox... and there was a little connecting line between the name and Alistair's. Twins. Alistair had been born a twin.

Alistair's vision clouded with sparkles and he felt on the verge of passing out, his mind clouded with the enormity of the news.

Samal put his hand on Alistair's shoulder and the sparkles cleared. "You need to breathe," Samal said. "I know this is a shock but just... breathe in please."

Alistair did as he said, and his head cleared somewhat.

"That's it," Samal said, his voice soothing. He took the book from Alistair and set it on the coffee table, open to the Lennox family tree. He slid into Alistair's lap and put his arms around him. "Just breathe. For right now, that's all you have to do."

Alistair felt tears welling inside him and buried his face in Samal's shoulder. "I don't know what to do," he wailed, muffling his volume in Samal's pale blue shirt.

"You don't have to do anything," he said, softly. "Just breathe, love."

Love? Alistair's head swam with confusion. No, one thing at a time, that was how he was going to deal with this. He could mourn his lost twin later on. He clung to Samal until his breathing was back to normal and he felt a bit more able to cope.

"I'm all right," he said, although his voice sounded strained. "We need to puzzle this out."

Samal planted a warm kiss on Alistair's forehead and climbed out of his lap. But he settled on the floor at his feet, leaning an arm on Alistair's knee. It was very comforting to have him so close, and Alistair was glad of it. He picked up the book again, gazed at the name of his twin a moment longer, and then flipped to the articles about the Lennox family.

"Here," he said. "It says my parents were... My parents were investigators into magical mysteries. They would travel the land, banishing demons and ridding folks of dangerous ghosts. Then, there's one about them having twins and then... nothing until the report of their death."

"If they left magical society then there can't have been much to report, I suppose."

"But why isn't my brother's death reported?"

They gazed at each other as Alistair chewed his lip. He felt strange saying 'my brother', but it wasn't in a bad way. It felt right. If they'd been four when he died, then Alistair must have known him. He couldn't remember him, but he had to have known him.

All at once Alistair remembered his imaginary friend.

He'd been named Ambrose.

He did remember, or at least, he remembered something of his brother. He had told Ambrose everything, everything that mattered they had shared. And then he'd been gone.

Alistair shook his head, overwhelmed with grief for someone he could hardly remember. He closed his eyes and tried to see Ambrose's face. The face from the tapestry was all he could see. Himself but younger, more innocent. "How could this have happened? Why didn't my parents ever..."

But he could guess the answer to that. Surely the trauma of losing a small child would affect anyone. They had left the magical world and thrown themselves into frivolity. If you never cared about anything too deeply, then you could never get hurt. Alistair's mother had never said that to him, of course, but she had shown it in a thousand different ways.

He felt tears wetting his cheeks, dripping onto his shirt front.

Samal murmured and pulled him to the edge of the seat so he could wrap his arms around him. "We'll get to the bottom of this, somehow," Samal said. A promise that Alistair had no idea if he could keep. He nodded against Samal's shoulder and clung to him.

"The Garden," Alistair whispered, after a while. "I think we need to take Will to the Garden."

CHAPTER 38

Thomas and William both met them at the dining hall, although Alistair was feeling too much of a sense of urgency about getting to the Secret Garden to feel hungry. Thomas pressed him to at least eat a sandwich, and he managed that, before hurrying them all up and chivvying them down the pathway towards the Secret Garden.

Thomas shifted into fox form once they were outside and ran circles around the other three as they walked. Alistair had told William and Thomas what he'd discovered as they'd eaten, speaking in hushed tones although Eleanor, Eulalia and Everett were also absent from the lunch service.

"I wish I could remember what happened," William said. He pursed his lips, furrowed his brow and looked up at the sky.

"You were…" Alistair had been about to say very young, the way Alistair himself had been, but William was almost two hundred years old. He had no idea how young William had been. "…very sick," he said.

"I suppose," William said. "Father would know, but when I went to see him this morning Medlock said he was busy dealing with Baron Birch and what was going to happen to Eleanor and her cronies."

Alistair's soul felt in turmoil, but the closer they got to the door of the Secret Garden the more he started to feel like he'd be able to make sense of things.

It was also a relief to know that there would be consequences for the people who had attacked him. Samal pulled aside the ivy so that Alistair could get to the door and unlock it. The key felt like an old friend at this point and as Alistair turned it, the familiar click of the lock warmed his heart.

There were still a lot of unanswered questions, but this was the right place to be. He was bringing William to his mother's garden. He pushed the door open and gestured for William to step through.

Although Thomas and Alistair had done several hours of hard work in the garden, it was still largely overgrown. One part of Alistair wished he had worked harder, made it look perfect, before showing it to William, but he dismissed the thought almost as soon as he'd had it. Part of the appeal of the Secret Garden was the overgrown wilderness of it.

William went through the door and Alistair heard him gasp. Thomas the fox streaked past his legs and disappeared into the Garden. Alistair followed and Samal came through last, locking the door behind him.

Alistair loved to look around with new eyes. Each time he showed someone the Garden he saw new things as well. It was a lesson, he thought to himself. He must never take anything for granted. What his eyes saw might be misled, or he might overlook important details. The trick was to always look upon things as if they were brand new, and to let the wonder of it all wash over him.

Yes, this was certainly the right place to be.

William had stopped walking at the small crossroads, and was standing quite tensely from the set of his shoulders. Alistair went to him, and gently, a little shyly, slipped his arm around William's waist. "This way, I think," Alistair said. He pointed towards the meadow, and the fountain. "That's where the statue of your mother is."

William nodded and half turned to Alistair. His eyes were misty, and Alistair thought *I've never seen him overwhelmed like this. Speechless.* He felt a mighty and all-encompassing need to protect William and keep him safe through whatever was about to happen. He leaned in and kissed him on the cheek.

"It's alright. I'm here, and Sam and Tom are here too. We're all going to work this out together."

William nodded again, quicker this time and Alistair could see his throat working as he swallowed.

He took William by the hand and led him down the path. As they walked the path and the meadow was revealed, Alistair laughed out loud. Thomas was jumping around in the meadow, capering and yipping for pure joy.

Beside him, William laughed as well. Samal jogged ahead to join Thomas, letting his wings unfurl from his back and his golden aura come out in the midday sunshine. It was a scene of pure joy, and Alistair was glad once more that he had all three men in his life. If it had just been William and himself, the approach to the fountain certainly wouldn't have involved laughter.

All four made their way to the fountain, Thomas changing back into human form as he stepped onto the paving stones.

"I can feel something," William said, softly. "A presence." He tipped his head up to look at the face of the statue and took a deep, heaving breath. "She's here."

Alistair felt his arm prickle with goosebumps. He felt the same awe and wonder that he always did at the fountain, but William's deeper connection was evident.

"Try touching the fountain," Alistair said, his voice hushed.

William stepped forward, stepped into the dry pool of the fountain and placed his hand on the carved fawn statue at his mother's feet.

He laughed, tears streaming down his face, and started to speak, a one-sided conversation to Alistair's ears, but clearly William could hear the other half of it.

"Thank you... I'm sorry... I miss you so much... I had no idea... he's all right but he doesn't come out much. I don't know why he locked up this place... maybe you're right." Then a long pause, as he listened.

Samal and Thomas pressed closer to Alistair on each side, perhaps comforting and perhaps protecting him. It didn't really matter which. They watched William, and stayed quiet. After a few more minutes William nodded and said "I love you too" and then turned to face them.

"She's here, in this garden. She was so happy when you unlocked it, Alistair, she asked me to thank you."

"I should like to thank her just the same," Alistair said. "I expect it was she who removed the curse for me, not just the Wellspring itself."

William listened for a moment and then nodded. "It was."

"Thank you..." Alistair paused, trying to think of what her name was. William supplied it.

"Melusine Carlisle."

"Thank you Melusine," Alistair said. "You've changed my entire world."

William made his way back out of the pool and embraced Alistair tight. "Thank you for bringing me here."

"I'm sorry I didn't do it sooner," Alistair said. "Things just seemed to get in the way of it..."

William shook his head. "It's fine, we're all here now."

Alistair was at a loss for what they should do next. William, Samal and Thomas were all looking at him with a certain amount of expectant anticipation and he didn't know how to answer them.

"I suppose," Alistair said. "If your mother is here, perhaps she can tell us what happened, or how we can start something?"

William shook his head. "She said it was up to us to use the power of the Garden, but she couldn't give instructions. Some of what she said was very clear, and some was less so. I think.... I think she's here in a sense, but not all the time. She has a connection to the garden, but perhaps she's in heaven at the same time?"

Alistair sighed. He was the least educated in magic of all of them, and now they all wanted him to come up with a plan?

He looked around himself at the Garden, up at the statue of Melusine and then at the three men looking back at him. He realised he didn't need to have a plan, he could just listen to his instincts, feel the flow of energy between him and the Earth and go from there.

He sat on the edge of the fountain and removed his shoes and socks, rolled up the hem of his trousers and walked into the meadow, feeling the energy flow up and down as he had become accustomed to.

"Here's what I think," he said, after a while feeling the magic and thinking things through. "To get to the heart of all of this, we need to understand William's curse. And to do that, well, we need to all put our gifts together and make a ritual. A ritual to draw out the magic and reveal the truth."

"That makes sense, I guess," Thomas said. "But my gift is for shapeshifting, I'm not sure if it will help. Sam's a healer, which does seem a bit more relevant."

"No, you're needed," Alistair said. He tried to put words to the certainty inside him. "You have a connection to nature itself that none of us share. You are the wildness of the moors and the moon at night."

Thomas flushed pink and smiled. "Thank you Alistair, except I think you have a connection to nature too."

"Mine's different, it feels different. Here's what I think. We all draw our wands, stand in a circle, or, well, square, around the fountain since it's the Wellspring. We each channel our magic as best we can, and then we'll see what feels right from there."

"Sounds like a very good, classic approach," William said. "There are certain runes we can speak for protection, and for summoning up visions of the past."

Samal walked to the far side of the fountain and flapped his wings so they stretched out as wide as they could go. Alistair estimated it must be a six or seven foot wingspan of gloriously beautiful soft brown wings, tinged with sparkling gold. Alistair would never get sick of seeing those.

Thomas stood directly opposite Samal, and William and Alistair stood opposite each other, each instinctively taking one of the cardinal points on the compass. It felt right, and good to Alistair. He licked his lips, feeling the energy of the Wellspring powering him and fuelling his confidence that he was doing the right thing. Each of them drew their wands, and Alistair weighed the willow wand in his hand, appreciating once again the comforting feel of it.

He drew his magic up and let it flow out his hands. Around him, long hibernating flowers and plants pushed their way up from the ground. Samal seemed to glow as if the light of heaven was shining directly on him as he summoned up his magic. Alistair could feel it, humming through the air and teasing at the corners of Alistair's magic. On the other side he felt Thomas's magic, wild and optimistic, full of life and potential and instinct.

William, the furthest away and only just visible on the other side of the statue of his mother, his magic felt different again. It was so precise, so ordered and organised. Alistair could feel how strong he was after years and years of study and practice. The arcane bloodline, tinged with a curse, which had informed his magic so much.

He wondered how his magic felt to them.

But he couldn't be distracted with that. They had to press on.

This was a ritual with a purpose after all. Alistair reached invisible tendrils of magic out towards the Wellspring.

"Samal please speak the runes of protection," he said. "William, you summon the visions of the past, and Thomas..." he paused for a moment before Thomas's obvious role sprung into his mind. "Please keep us grounded in the present, don't let us lose ourselves in the magic."

The other three began to speak, words of power which Alistair could feel as solid objects, weaving around the diamond the four of them had made. Tapping into the power of the Wellspring and the ghost of the woman who lingered there, powered further by their intentions and their passion for each other. He could sense all of this, visualise it as a series of fleeting images, and he looked past them.

Alistair imagined himself looking deep into the Wellspring. It looked like a golden and green tree, but it was upside down, its roots in the air waiting to be caught, and the branches and foliage spreading in the ground beneath their feet.

He felt as if he was slipping into a dream, his eyes flickering as he started to see a different kind of reality.

The spell was working.

They had all done their parts, and now the spell drew him deeper. Alistair could see the Wellspring fading and something else in its place. He was watching people move in a room. A Misselthwaite room, William's bedroom, he recognised the drapes.

Lord Carlisle was the first he recognised, standing next to the bed.

Alistair's mother and father were there, but younger than Alistair could remember seeing them. They wore sombre grey robes over sensible clothing, and they looked very serious. Each of them held the hand of one of the twins. Two small children. Alistair couldn't tell which was him and which was Ambrose.

In the bed lay William, drawn and pale, looking perhaps a

year or two younger than he did now. He seemed to be dreaming, troubled, mumbling and twitching.

Lord Carlisle gestured them forwards and Alistair's mother led one of the twins to the bedside, lifted him up.

"Go on Ambrose, just like you did with the little girl."

The little boy, Ambrose, Alistair thought. His brother. They were probably four years old. Ambrose laid his hand on William's shoulder. There was a scream, jolting Alistair back out of the vision as he gasped. His chest was on fire, aching with tension.

"Keep breathing Ally!" Thomas shouted. Alistair could feel Thomas's magic winding around him like a warm blanket on the shoulders. He drew in a shaky breath and felt his body relax.

"Thank you."

"I think there's another vision coming," William said. He was grasping the air as if there were things there to manipulate, his fingers moving in intricate patterns as if pulling threads and weaving them together. "Keep breathing everyone."

This time there was no strange play in the room to watch. This time, as Alistair felt his eyelids flicker and the sensation of falling into a dream, he felt his eyes drawn to watch William.

For a moment there were two of him. The one which was moving, casting the spell and holding onto the roots of it so the others could see, his hands moving through the air. The other was standing still, superimposed over the moving one. This one's skin was a pale grey and his eyes were closed, his head tilted back and his arms spread out to each side.

There was something in his chest. Something Alistair was supposed to see, to understand. And a part of him did.

There was a voice in his ear. A new voice, curiously familiar. "You need to puzzle it out," the voice said, faint as a breeze through the grass.

With a jolt, Alistair realised he knew this voice. It was Ambrose.

CHAPTER 39

"This is our gift," Ambrose said.

Alistair looked around, trying to see Ambrose, but there was nothing to see. He could feel his presence, feel him standing just behind him, but there was nothing there. A ghost, just as William had felt. His knees wobbled, threatening to give out on him.

He felt a chill, raising goosebumps over his skin, and his breath caught again. His chest ached as he forgot once more to breathe. He sucked a breath in noisily between his teeth. He had to focus, he had to keep it together - they were in the middle of a magic ritual and he couldn't fall apart. He had to keep leading it, solve the mystery.

The ghost of his dead twin was a shock, but he had to focus for the moment and deal with the emotions later on.

Alistair closed his eyes, drew a steadying breath and focused on the flow of magic. Ambrose had said it was their gift.

He needed more information.

"What is our gift?" he said, his voice wavering just a little.

Ambrose breathed in his ear, he could feel it - the faintest breeze. "Curse breaking."

Alistair swallowed. "But the plants, the energy of the Earth... I can feel them so clearly, this is where my gift is."

"It's the same..." Ambrose's voice faded to nothingness and then came back into hearing. "...Wellspring is linked. You are a cursebreaker, just as I was."

Alistair swallowed the lump in his throat. Was this what it was to truly understand oneself? He felt like he wanted to cry, to fall onto the ground and howl out his feelings. But he couldn't. Must keep on focusing.

"Look at him," Ambrose whispered. "You can puzzle it out..."

Alistair didn't want to open his eyes again. But he had to. He opened his eyes and looked back at William.

More accurately, the two Williams.

One was the ordinary William, the one he knew and loved. The one manipulating the spell.

The other William stood still with a black symbol carved into his chest, into the blackened heart within him. Because that's what Alistair saw now. His skin was grey, and his arms spread to show his chest cracked open and his heart beating slowly inside his chest, looking black as if it had been burned.

The curse.... It was on his heart. It was wrapped around his heart and squeezing the life out of him.

Sweat broke out on Alistair's forehead. *It's too much,* he thought wildly. *This is too much for me and I don't know what to do.*

He felt his hold on the magic ritual waver, like he was holding a rope taut but now someone was pulling hard on the other side of it. Threatening to pull him over, plunge him forward into something utterly unknown.

He cried out, feeling a sudden yank on the centre of him. He was going to fall, he couldn't hold on. He was going to fall into the abyss of the curse, perhaps, or the magic itself, and lose himself somehow.

But then magic nudged against him from either side. Samal's warm, healing magic propping itself against his side, bearing him up. Thomas's magic, free and airy, taking some of the weight off what he was holding.

He wasn't alone.

He had his friends. Even William himself, although he was the subject of the vision, Alistair could feel his magic under everything else, a strong foundation for all that he was doing.

Alistair memorised the shape of what he could see. The runes which appeared on William's cursed heart. The way that the magic seemed to be leaking from his heart and into his body, and the pattern it made.

He swallowed, lifted his head and spoke as loudly as he could.

"I have seen what I needed. It's time to end the ritual."

He'd said that aloud because he hoped one of the others would be able to end the thing properly. Alistair was suddenly, painfully aware of all that he didn't know about magic. All the things he should be studying, all the variations of spells, runes and the use of intent.

He was in over his head, but he had Thomas, Samal and William to buoy him up.

Samal spoke some words, and the magic connecting them all slowly ebbed. Each taking their own essence back into themselves, and the Wellspring's magic flowed back into the fountain. Alistair felt a sudden release, and now his knees did give in, and he fell onto all fours, panting heavily.

This is our gift.

Alistair felt less like he'd been given a gift and more like he'd been handed an extra burden... but then if he was really a cursebreaker, if that was the gift that Ambrose and he had shared, then it did explain why he could hear William in the night, didn't it?

It explained how he could see the symbols on William's arms, because he was supposed to be able to remove them, or augment them. To take the curse off William and rescue him.

He liked the idea of rescuing him. He had never been a hero before.

"But there's so much I haven't learned," Alistair breathed. He sat back on his heels and looked up at the sky. His mind was a whirl of new information and the horror at how *much* it all was.

"Are you all right?" Thomas was at his elbow, touching his shoulder.

"I think so?" Alistair said. "But I don't know. There's a lot."

William approached at a jog. "What did you see?"

"And hear?" Samal asked, going to his knees to sit beside Alistair. "It sounded as if you were speaking to someone." His hand found Alistair's forehead and a dull pain Alistair had barely been aware of vanished under his ministrations.

"My twin was here, I saw him, and then I saw...Wait, did you all see the visions too?"

Thomas shook his head. "No, I think that was just for you."

Alistair took a deep breath and related what he'd seen as best he could, ignoring the crack in his voice when he told them how he'd heard Ambrose's voice. He got to the end of what happened and thought for a moment longer.

"Ambrose's voice, only it wasn't a child's voice," he said, remembering. "It was older, he sounded as old as I am."

"Ghosts in the garden," William said. His tone was bleak. "I suppose it's a side effect of the Wellspring being here."

"So what does it all mean, do you think?" Samal asked gently.

"Lord Carlisle asked my parents for help. Twin curse breakers, there was a good chance we could help, right? But something bad happened instead. Maybe the curse," he looked at William uncertainly. "Maybe the curse was too strong for a four-year-old? I don't know why they didn't have us both try at the same time."

"A four-year-old, even a twin, is too young to attempt something like that," William said. He had taken a seat on the edge of the fountain and was tapping his fingers on his chin. "I don't know what my father, or your parents could have been thinking."

"Maybe they wanted to prove themselves, prove that their twins were truly gifted," Thomas said, slowly. "I know there have been people coming to call on mam, asking for her to show off Esther and Madrigal. She tells them to bugger off," he chuckled a little and then sobered. "But she's not in high society, trying to look good for the other mages and witches."

"They always did put a lot of stock in what others thought," Alistair said. "Although when I knew them it was just the party set, not magical people. I'm sure..." he stopped then, thinking it through. "And they lost one of their sons. Maybe they were so afraid of it happening again, that's why they left the magical world and put the curse on me?"

It made a certain amount of sense, but of course it was all just theoretical. They couldn't confirm any of this without the input of someone who had been there. Lord Carlisle. They'd have to talk to him.

William suddenly went to his knees in front of Alistair, clasped his hands together and bowed his head. "Please forgive me!"

"Err..." Alistair said. "For what, for being cursed?"

"I killed your brother," William said. He was staring at the ground, and his voice was dull, heavy. "I'm so sorry. I know it was the curse, but still. If it hadn't been for me, he would still be alive."

Alistair shuffled closer to William and put his hands on William's clasped fists. "It's not your doing. If I'm going to blame anyone, it will be my parents."

Sniffling, William looked up at Alistair, his face even paler than before. He looked as if the spell or perhaps the revelation about Ambrose had taken a lot of strength out of him. "Are you sure you're not angry with me?"

Alistair considered this, wanted William to know he had really given it thought before he answered. "No, I'm not angry with you. You are the victim of this curse. And there's an opportunity before us. Maybe I can succeed where Ambrose failed, because I have you three and the power of the garden's Wellspring. I don't know a lot about any of this, but I can learn. I've learned a lot already, and I want to help you. I'm not angry. I've been angry with you before, and you'll know when I'm angry again. Mostly I'm worried. You look like you're on death's door."

William licked his lips. "I do feel rather ill. I should probably get back inside as soon as possible."

"But I'll want to use the Wellspring for any spells I do..." Alistair said, slowly. Then shook his head. "No, it's fine, I don't know yet what to do, so I'll need to research anyway."

"Do you think you can puzzle things inside?" Samal asked.

Alistair nodded. "Although I'm feeling rather tired as well."

"Come on, some tea and an afternoon snack will revive the both of you, I'm sure." Thomas got up and offered his hand to William, who took it and got to his feet. Samal did the same for Alistair, who smiled wanly at him.

"Between the four of us, we'll get to the bottom of all of this," Samal said. "I'm certain of it."

CHAPTER 40

*A*listair and William went straight up to Alistair's room, Thomas went to get the tea and snacks and Samal went to ask if Lord Carlisle had a free moment.

Alistair and William sat on the side of the newly giant bed and were silent for a moment. Alistair needed some time to process everything, so he looked around his room. Wondering how things would have been different if Ambrose had survived. Perhaps they would have gone to a magical school together, then graduated to Misselthwaite.

Perhaps he would have been a very different person with his twin by his side, his magic freely available and understood.

Alistair wasn't at all sure he liked the idea of being a different person. He dragged his gaze from the bright rectangle of the window back to William.

"Thank you for all this," William said. His expression was downcast. "I feel perfectly beastly for how I've been acting, demanding your attention and saying we're soulmates and all of that, so I'm truly sorry."

Alistair took William's hand and squeezed it in his own. "You don't need to keep on apologising," he said. "I forgive you. And I hope you'll forgive me for being obstinate and sour when I didn't need to be. I feel like a different person to who I was when I first arrived here."

"Maybe you're the same, but better," William said. He gave Alistair a watery smile. "You're still as sure of yourself, as blunt with your words as you were before. But you're... I don't know, more at home in your skin."

"I've learned so much, and heard Ambrose too," Alistair sighed. "I was just imagining what my life would have been like if he hadn't died." They were both silent for a moment. Alistair sighed. "I expect there's no point wondering about things like that, I can't change it after all, and I'll just make myself sadder, or more confused."

William squeezed his hand this time and chuckled. "It's human nature, I think, to consider the what ifs."

Alistair thought about that word 'humans', and half turned to look at William. "I'm not sure if I can stop you turning into... into a vampire," he said. "I could see the blackness of the curse and it was pumping through your veins, it wasn't contained to the heart."

William shrugged. "I just don't want to die. If I have to do that by being vampire kind, well, it's better than being dead. Or falling into a coma at any given moment."

He fell dramatically back on the bed as if he were a fainting maiden.

For a moment Alistair was concerned, but then William tugged him by the hand until Alistair was practically on top of him. They stared at each other for a moment. His heart thumping, Alistair dipped his head down and kissed him.

Alistair's woes were temporarily forgotten, the proximity of William overwhelming his senses entirely as he pressed against him.

They looked into each other's eyes, and William seemed on the verge of asking something else, his hand firm on the small of Alistair's back, holding him close. The door to Alistair's room opened and they both looked up to Thomas walking in with a tray of tea things, including a plate stacked high with steaming hot scones, jam and cream.

Alistair rolled off William, trying his best not to be embarrassed at being found lying on top of him, although Thomas was smiling as he set down the tray.

William's hand trailed up Alistair's back as he moved away, and tugged gently at his hair. It was a pleasant feeling, and Alistair wanted more of it at some point.

"This should keep us going," Thomas said. "Although I'm feeling dashed tired after that ritual."

"Mm," William said. "I am too."

Just hearing the other two talk about it made Alistair yawn, but although he did feel worn out he also felt like he was too close to answers to stop now. He wanted to keep reading, to find the answers, to speak to Ambrose again, if he could.

Samal came in as Alistair was stirring sugar into his cup of tea. "Lord Carlisle has gone to London to speak with the Birches," he said, frowning. "William, perhaps you ought to send him a letter? That way he'd at least know that you want to speak with him."

William nodded. "I can do that."

Samal slipped his arm around Alistair's waist. Alistair looked up and Samal leaned in to kiss him softly on the lips. Alistair felt giddy and warm, full of joy. Was this going to be what his life was like from now on?

So that no one was left out, once Sam let him go, Alistair gave Thomas a kiss as well and was rewarded with a happy smile and a quick hug.

Alistair sat down at his desk and pulled his notebook towards him, setting a scone on his saucer and looking through the notes he'd made from the book. Twins. He'd left it at twins. Perhaps he could try and summon Ambrose to him here, in this room?

"How can we help?" Thomas asked. He was looking over Alistair's shoulder and stifling another yawn.

"I don't know," Alistair said, earnestly. "I suppose we'll all just have to keep reading and see if there's a way to undo what I saw."

Thomas nodded and picked up one of the library books. William and Samal did the same.

Thomas soon fell asleep, curled into Samal's side on the bed where they sat propped against the pillows. Alistair was distracted from the book he was reading when he noticed this. Samal had a book held in his left hand, which he was reading, but his other arm was around Thomas. Thomas had curled his knees up, and was pressing them against Samal's side, his face pillowed on Samal's chest, and his fox ears twitched as he dreamed. His fluffy fox tail lay straight out on the bed and Samal's hand slowly moved up and down his back, soothing him. It seemed as if Thomas's preferred form now included the fox ears and tail, and Alistair was glad of it.

Alistair watched, feeling the love he had for both of them washing over him. He would have got up to slot in under Samal's other arm, or perhaps to press himself against Thomas's back, but the curse kept on nagging at him. He glanced over to William, who was sitting close to the door, and saw that he was also gazing affectionately at Samal and Thomas.

Maybe this really was his life now?

Alistair turned back to his notes and shook his head. It would only be his life if he could fix the curse.

He looked into the light of the candle which he had on his desk and tried to connect to the power which had linked him to Ambrose.

Under his breath he murmured his name. "Are you there? Or are you only... are you close to the Wellspring?"

He held his breath and waited. Ambrose's voice sounded in his ear, soft as a whisper.

"I'm here. I'm with you if you need me, Alistair."

Alistair's eyes welled up with relief. He was comforted beyond measure to know that Ambrose could be spoken to, even if he wasn't at the Wellspring.

"What should I do? What happened there?" Alistair murmured.

"Are you talking to Ambrose again?" William asked, his hand on Alistair's shoulder. Alistair would have startled on any day previously, but now, apparently, even William's silent crossing of the room was something he had become accustomed to.

Alistair nodded. William placed a kiss on Alistair's head. "Don't worry about keeping it down, you won't bother me, and I expect Tommy here can sleep through anything." He paused, looking at Samal, who raised an eyebrow in return. "And Sam will cope."

Samal rolled his eyes at William but smiled at Alistair. "Of course, don't mind me, Allie."

"I was too young," Ambrose said, softly. Alistair wondered if he could hear the others, or if he could only hear and understand Alistair himself.

"You *were* too young," he repeated, louder, so the others could hear. "I'm so sorry."

"Mother and Father had seen me, seen us, break other curses, little things. A hex on a doorway, one on a fencepost which caused all who touched it to stub their toes."

Alistair chuckled a little. "Who would make such a curse?"

Ambrose continued without answering. "We were only four, but I was the strongest, and so they asked me to look first, to see the man with the curse in his heart."

Goosebumps rose on Alistair's arm and he swallowed. "William Carlisle."

"That's right," Ambrose said. "The curse... it fought back. We'd never seen a curse that defended itself, we were so young..."

Alistair swiped at his eyes with the back of his sleeve. "Go on, please, whatever you can recall."

"The curse didn't want to leave his heart... lashed out, I was too little, I had no defences, had never needed them."

Alistair picked up one of the curse books and scanned the index for defences built into curses. Nothing in that book. He set it aside and looked up the index of the next one.

There was a reference, he quickly flipped to the page. "Defences," he said, so the others could hear. "The curse has defences on it."

That was something that they could research.

CHAPTER 41

*T*he next few days passed in a blur for Alistair.

He attended classes and made cursory notes. In between and after classes were a flurry of referencing, note taking and reading interspersed with short naps. He made frequent trips to the library to return books and borrow different ones, assisted by some or all of his friends depending on their schedules.

Thomas had taken to insisting Alistair attend meals, because otherwise he would ignore his rumbling belly and skip them. Even so, he would take a book to the dining table and continue reading.

At dinner time each night Samal brought him a plate of food and William gently and firmly removed the book from Alistair's clutches so he would actually eat and talk to them about what he was discovering.

Alistair found it hard to make small talk, his mind too full of sentences and runes and possibilities. He felt he was doing a jigsaw puzzle but he didn't have enough of the pieces to complete the picture. It was infuriating.

Once they'd eaten, they would escort him back upstairs and

one by one they would go to bed, until Alistair was the only one still awake.

Each night Alistair's eyes would start to blur from reading. Then he would stand up from his desk, stoke up the fire and climb into bed where three warm forms waited for him.

Every day he was filled with a determination he had never before known. He couldn't give up. William, Lord Carlisle, Thomas and Samal, they'd all put their hopes on him. Alistair was aware with each new morsel of information that he still had so much to learn. The pressure of it, of saving William and removing the curse, settled over him like a heavy mantle, weighing his shoulders down.

Through the days and the nights Ambrose came and went, sometimes nudging him towards a particular bit of information, sometimes simply repeating that he had been too young and inexperienced. Alistair wasn't young anymore, not like Ambrose had been, but his inexperience was clear.

It had been almost a week of furious research, when Alistair went to his desk after dinner.

He replaced the almost burnt out candle with a fresh one. The smell of beeswax filled his nostrils and for a moment he was distracted, wondering if they could attract a swarm of bees to the Secret Garden. It would be pleasant to tend the hive and collect honey from it...

He shook his head and bent back over the many pages of notes he had been making. He read and reread them, trying to pull each thread together into something he could understand.

It was all well and good, he thought, *to say that I am a natural born cursebreaker. For my dead twin to confirm it, but it doesn't mean that I know instinctively what to do, which honestly, is a pity. Surely my talent should come with direction.*

On the contrary, what he had was a distinct feeling of being lost. As if he was in the middle of a huge hedge maze and there was no apparent way out, but everyone was waiting for him on the outside.

He rested his head on his hands and sighed. The books on curse breaking all seemed to assume previous knowledge of runes and glyphs, a foundational knowledge of spell-working from years of schooling and practice. None of the books seemed to indicate that it was something people brand new to magic could just pick up and do.

Alistair knew a mere handful of runes and he wasn't confident in his use of them at all. The vision had shown him the place of the curse. With his friends... lovers... by his side, he had done something extraordinary there.

Perhaps he would need to continue to lean on their strengths. William certainly had the strongest foundational knowledge of magic, and Samal and Thomas also, although they didn't have as many years of practice.

He looked around the room. Samal and Thomas were hard at work on homework, and William was trying to solve a puzzle box Barlow had given him as a test. He knew if he asked for something one of them would retrieve it, or give him an answer, or do whatever he could to help.

But for the moment it felt like what he had to do was study harder, see if there was anything the professors could do to help, and keep on learning as much as he could. Maybe...

He leaned back in his seat and gazed at the ceiling, trying to grasp at the idea which had just nudged him.

They needed time for Alistair to learn and grow as a mage. They didn't have time as the curse was wearing William down.

Maybe there was something small they could try in the meantime. Something which would buy them time to solve the larger problem?

He smiled, scribbled a few notes of his idea. It might work, although he expected they would need to be in the Garden to work the ritual.

He turned to the others

"I can't break the curse," Alistair said, abruptly, once they were all looking at him. "I'm not good enough yet, I don't have the training or anything. This new idea I've had, I think it will work like a stopgap. The curse is hurting you, which means we don't have much time," Alistair said. "But I think we can, all of us, remove the time problem." He swallowed, feeling suddenly nervous. Thomas, Samal and William looked at him, expectant, waiting for him to go on. "I think I can create a ward inside you. Like the curse which was on me."

He pulled out the black stone from his pocket and held it up between thumb and forefinger. "I think we could even reuse this to do it. Although we may not need it."

"A ward," William looked stunned,

"Right, a magical barrier which gets in between the curse and you," Alistair said. "It would buy us time. You'd stop having the symptoms, and theoretically, you'd be able to live without the comas. It would give me time to learn more, to grow into my powers." He looked around at their faces. "I'm just the same as the garden, you see. I need tending, I need help, then I'll be able to really break the curse." He swallowed, feeling vulnerable. "Well, what do you all think?"

Samal was nodding slowly. "I think it might work, it should be easy enough to guide the magic to the correct position with my knowledge of human anatomy."

Thomas tilted his head to the side and then smiled wide. "Yeah, hey, it worked on you right, it stands to reason we could do a similar thing for William."

William pursed his lips, squinting up at the ceiling as he thought it through. "It seems sort of obvious, but at the same time, I don't think anyone's ever tried it before...curious."

"Well, I'd never heard of a ward inside someone before Alistair's," Samal said. "It's not exactly common magic."

William shrugged and spread his hands. "Well, I trust all

three of you, for some reason, so we may as well try it. I'm willing and I'll help however I can."

Alistair felt a flush of pride that he had come up with a solution that no one thought was ridiculous. He ran a hand over his face and smiled to himself, finally relaxing, knowing there was a possible solution to the puzzle.

Then the hard work and intense mental strain of the last few days hit him. He yawned and suddenly couldn't keep his eyes open.

"Come on, you've been working too hard for five days," Samal said. He took Alistair's elbow and helped him up off the chair. "You need to sleep."

"But I could further refine the plan," Alistair said.

"No, I insist," Samal said. "Your brain is liable to give up altogether and then you'll have migraines or start passing out."

"Don't disagree with Doctor Bancroft-Dalton," William teased.

Samal, with perfect dignity, stuck his tongue out at William.

Alistair allowed himself to be led to bed. Samal gently undressed him and he pulled on his pyjamas.

Thomas hopped up onto the bed in fox form and curled up against his side as Samal tucked him in. "Now sleep. You've done enough for today."

Alistair was asleep in seconds.

CHAPTER 42

*A*listair woke in a jumble of limbs. He had fallen asleep next to Thomas. Now he had William's arm around him and he was crushed against Samal on the other side, whose wings were out, pillowing Alistair and Williams' heads on one side. Thomas was sprawled half on top of Alistair and half on William, and their legs were tangled in the sheets. It was a bit too warm, but Alistair allowed himself a long moment of enjoying the closeness of them all. His fingertips tingled, and he realised that he could feel magical energy flowing between them as well.

It was gentle, soft, as natural as breathing in and out, but it connected them all together. He wondered if that was why Samal's wings had emerged while he slept?

Alistair stretched his arms up over his head and groaned. He hadn't slept enough, he knew that but it had been deep, the sleep he had got.

He could see the hint of sunlight through the gaps in the curtains and he knew he would need to get out to the Garden as soon as possible. There was something calling him, something filling him with energy to get things done, to solve what he could. To dig his toes into the soil and enjoy the world as it was, coming back to life after the freeze of winter. He hadn't had time to visit the garden since the ritual, he'd been so busy with research.

The idea he'd come up with the night before hummed in his brain, encouraging him to act. His movements woke the others.

Samal, smiling with a distinctly embarrassed air, waited until Thomas, then William and Alistair had moved before folding his wings away. Thomas sat up and yawned, showing teeth slightly too pointy to be human.

"We need to get down to the Garden," Alistair said.

"After breakfast," Thomas said. He reached over to gently brush his fingertips against Alistair's cheek. "You need to keep your strength up."

Alistair rolled his eyes and nodded. "Fine, that's fine, but right after breakfast?"

"Yes," Samal said. After they'd all washed up and dressed they trooped down to the dining hall. Alistair's nerve endings were all on fire, fizzing with the promise of what would happen once they were in the garden once more.

"Why can't you sit still?" William asked, looking at him askance.

"I want to try out my new idea," Alistair said. "I can't wait, and I can feel the Garden calling to me."

William nodded and sat back, sipping at his tea slowly. Alistair wished they'd all eat faster. He'd made very short work of his French toast and bacon.

Finally, finally, they were walking down to the Secret Garden. The weather was bleak, the hint of sunlight Alistair had seen previously replaced with heavy-looking grey rain clouds. There was a brisk breeze, which nipped at Alistair's fingers and reminded him winter was still lingering barely, although it served to stir the energy inside him up even more.

Alistair could barely stand still as he unlocked the door, so eager he was to get inside, and once in, he led the way down to the fountain.

"Right-oh, we are going to make a ward inside of William," he said. He opened his mouth to continue but he wasn't exactly sure what the next step should be. He swallowed and looked between each of their faces.

"Shall I set up a protective circle?" Thomas said, kindly. Alistair could have kissed him just for that. He held himself back for a moment before remembering he was allowed to do that. So he darted in and gave Thomas a quick kiss before moving back.

"Yes, please, that would be good. Then William and I can start with the basics of a warding ritual. Mostly William," Alistair said quickly. "Because I don't really know-"

"What you're doing," William said. He sounded impatient. "Alistair whatever else you are, you're clearly very talented at magic and your instincts have all proven themselves to be good. We know you don't have all the training but we trust you, otherwise we wouldn't be here."

"That's right," Samal said. "You may not feel confident, but we are confident in you."

Alistair very much wanted to argue this point, but a quick look at his boyfriends changed his mind. Samal and William wore matching stern expressions, daring him to contradict them, and Thomas's smile was guileless and utterly trusting.

Alistair swallowed down the argument and nodded. "Fine. All right. Let's begin, I'll call on you if I feel that you are needed, otherwise just follow my lead."

Thomas put the finishing touches on the protective circle, which he had drawn with his wand, demarcating the grass invisibly. When it was completed, Alistair could see the shimmering bright green lights which indicated Thomas's magic.

The quality of the air around them shifted a little. Alistair could still feel the breeze but it was muted somehow. As if feeling the wind inside from an open window, rather than being out in it.

"I just want to..." Alistair said, and bent to remove his shoes and socks. He flexed his toes in the grass of the meadow and felt the cool of the soil beneath the soles of his feet. The energy of the Earth immediately sought him out and he felt his magic respond in kind.

"Wand out," William said, with something of the air of a school teacher.

Alistair did as he said, and produced his willow wand, smiling as it hummed in his hand, apparently as eager to do magic as Alistair himself. This is it, the wand seemed to be saying to him. This is the day! He pulled out the black stone as well, and held it in the palm of his hand.

"I'm ready."

"We start like this..." William waved his wand and began speaking runes. He paused, nodded at Alistair. "You say them too."

"Right." Alistair copied William's movements and repeated the runes, feeling a pleasant buzzing in his chest as his magic welled inside him. Below him, the essence of the Earth pulsed into his bloodstream and he smiled as he wove the spell. Before him, in the air, he thought he could make out the magic as a slight sparkle against the sky, woven together from magic of William's and his own.

This felt good, it felt right.

"We'll hold it here," William said once enough of the runes had been cast that they could both sense the ward coming together.

Alistair inhaled. It was as if he could reach out and touch the ward, although he knew that it wasn't at all a physical object, he had the sense of it so clearly in his mind that he felt he could have.

"Sam, we have the ward," Alistair said. "Can you please... work out how to get it inside Will?"

Without words, Samal moved closer. He had, whether consciously or not, put on his angelic guise, and the glow of it seemed to light up the circle Thomas had enclosed. Samal put out a hand, his fingers softly curled and holding his wand loosely, and raised both hands over his head. Then, with movements as if he were pulling threads from the air, Samal drew the ward towards William.

Alistair held the black stone out to William, who blinked at it then took it. He curled his fingers around it, and held it against his chest.

Alistair could feel the movement of all the magic. The essences of both men and his own, and his body responded with excitement of two kinds - one the excitement that this was working, that the spell, and his idea, might actually work, and the other rather more carnal. He tried to ignore the second excitement as it wasn't the time to be distracted in such a way, but he could feel a distinct tightness in his trousers.

"Maintain your focus," said Ambrose, his voice a cool reassurance. "You are needed for this part."

Samal moved closer to William and Alistair did too. He could feel how Samal's magic was working on William's body, opening him up in a metaphysical sense, in order to receive the ward. The black stone seemed to work as a gateway of sorts, channelling the ward into him.

It was difficult work, and Alistair could see how to assist. With gentle movements of his wand, he wove his own magic between William's and Samal's, feeling something pulse between them like a heartbeat.

They were playing with William's life force, he realised, and the thing which might very well save him. He would have to be very careful indeed. He took a deep steadying breath.

Ambrose was there, whispering instructions in his ear, how

to metaphorically hold the magical ward in one hand while disentangling parts of the curse with the other. How to lean into Samal's powers to ensure that he wasn't doing any harm as he worked.

The world fell away as he did the complicated magic, barely breathing for fear he might inadvertently unravel something.

William's breathing was heavy, laboured, and Alistair knew that he couldn't spend too much longer doing this or William would be in danger.

Although his body hadn't been touched at all, Alistair knew on a spiritual level it was as if they had cracked open his rib cage and were fiddling with his heart. They had to be as precise and swift as possible.

The pressure that came from that knowledge mounted fast and the blissful state he had achieved with the world falling away, shattered. He was suddenly all too aware of the world around him. The hum of a grasshopper, the wind which had picked up to snatch at his hair. William's breathing became a rasp, and the sweat formed on Alistair's own forehead, threatening to drip into his eyes.

What am I doing? Alistair's thoughts fractured into a thousand doubts. *I could kill him doing this. And I love him, I should be protecting him not putting him at risk.*

Alistair caught his breath, almost sobbing, and the ward moved suddenly, listing to one side, although it was somehow half inside William's chest. The black stone flared with a magic of its own, holding the ward precariously in place. Alistair was in danger of dropping the magic entirely and he had no idea what would happen to William if he did.

Samal's sharp intake of breath cut through his panicking mind. "Hold it steady," Samal said.

A warm hand touched the base of Alistair's spine. Thomas.

Thomas's hand poured power into Alistair directly, filling him with new energy and confidence. A small part of Alistair's mind wondered if Thomas didn't need a wand as much as the rest of them did.

"Try to change it," Thomas said. His voice sounded curiously distant to Alistair's ears. "What you're doing is correct but it can't be a fixed form, let it change, let it shapeshift into what the curse cannot get through."

A shapeshifting spell? Was such a thing possible?

Alistair's eyebrows drew together as Ambrose breathed the word 'genius' into his ear. Of course, the curse would continue to change and to reach out into more of William, so the ward he had built with him would have to change as well.

If he could use some of Thomas's shapeshifting magic to introduce that quality to it, then the ward would be more robust, it wouldn't simply shatter and break at the first instance of the curse pushing out in a new one.

It made sense, if Alistair could somehow just make it work.

Alistair used the energy that Thomas had poured into him to weave the strands of magic of ward and healing together, to bring the fluidity of what Thomas was capable of into the spell and thereby make it stronger.

Alistair breathed out slowly. It was still difficult work, forming disparate threads into something more whole, something which could hold together and do the job he needed it to do.

The sweat on his forehead beaded and formed drops which fell onto the ground. Somewhere along the way Alistair had begun to stoop over, and when he opened his eyes he could see William's feet and the green grass below it.

The grass, the Garden, his friends, his brother, his magic, even the residual curse magic echoing in the black stone, something of his parents...

Alistair felt his lips pull into a smile as he saw the spell's threads woven together in the way he had hoped for.

"Nearly there," he said. His voice sounded strained, as if he were carrying a great weight on his shoulders.

Samal placed a hand on his shoulder and warm light filled him, relieving the weight somewhat. Thomas's hand was still on the small of his back, and he felt stronger than ever.

Alistair straightened his back, looked William in the eye and pressed his hand to his chest, right over his heart and the black stone. He felt the magic within him surge as he pushed the ward and the stone into place, surrounding William's heart and protecting him from the curse.

Around them, inside and outside the protective circle, plants burst into life. The seedlings Alistair had nurtured rapidly grew to full size, then larger still, blooms larger than Alistair's hand popping up all around them. The flowerbeds were full with luscious, healthy plants in the blink of an eye as Alistair's magic, boosted by the ritual and by his friends, flowed into the ground and into the roots.

Hollyhocks and foxgloves shot into the sky, only stopping their accelerated growth when they towered at eight feet. The trees put out fresh green leaves and began blossoming.

Alistair turned his head and saw that even the fountain was affected. Somehow his magic had got into the inner workings of it, and water was pouring out of the frog's mouths to fill the pool.

Birds sang in the trees, and all around Alistair could hear the world coming alive.

"Finish the spell," Ambrose whispered in his ear. "Say the words to set it in place."

Alistair cleared his throat and his voice rang out as loud as he could manage. "As I will it, so let it be."

The ward settled firmly into place in William's chest, with all the satisfaction of the final piece of a jigsaw puzzle clicking into place.

The surge of magic ebbed, and although Alistair was still highly aware of how his magic was linking Thomas, William and Samal to the Garden itself, there was a definite feeling of closure. He had done it.

He dropped his hand from William's chest and wiped the back of his sleeve over his damp forehead. "That felt like it worked," he said.

William took a deep breath and let it out in a whoosh. "I think it did, too, I feel like..." he rubbed his hand absently over his chest where Alistair had just been touching him. "I feel like I can breathe properly. I hadn't exactly been choking before, but I wasn't able to take a full breath. Now I can, and the air tastes sweet and good, and like it's giving me strength."

"You're amazing," Samal said, suddenly, and hugged Alistair tight against him. Alistair chuckled and nuzzled his nose against Samal's chest.

The power of the magic ebbed still further as Samal let Alistair go. William caught him in a hug next, his grip more forceful and urgent than Samal's, which made Alistair laugh a little more. He felt giddy, the waning of the power filling him with a sensation not unlike the one he'd got from drinking wine.

"Tell me, did you expect it to work?" Alistair asked, feeling bold and not normally as shy as he might, being held in this way.

William let go of him and laughed, rubbing his hand on the back of his neck. "I had faith in you, Alistair, but I still wasn't sure if it would work the first time."

"It seems as if..." Samal said slowly. He ran a faintly glowing hand down William's chest. A sight which stirred something deep inside Alistair to see. He wanted to see more, to see them touching each other. "It seems as if the spell should counteract most of the pain. Perhaps it is too soon to tell, but I believe you'll feel a lot better, and not go into one of the long sleeps, while this ward is in place."

Thomas wrapped his arms around Alistair from behind, a

stable, warm presence, and Alistair gratefully leaned back against him.

"Thank you all," he said. "I couldn't have done this without all three of you. I absolutely love all three of you."

"I love you too," Thomas murmured.

"I do too," Samal said.

William caught Samal's hand and pulled him closer to him. "I love you too, Allie," William said.

Thomas's hand stroked up and down his stomach, and Alistair became aware of the source of his boldness. The same energy which had coursed through the garden and brought it to life was still inside him. Spring had come to the Garden, and with it the ebullience of life and energy. That was what was pumping through Alistair's veins now.

"I think," Alistair said. He spoke slowly, feeling more wicked by the moment, empowered by the force of spring itself, he pressed his rear against Thomas's hips. "I think I know just what to do next."

CHAPTER 43

*A*listair turned his head to kiss Thomas, gratified when the handsome young man with copper coloured hair and fox ears kissed him back with the same kind of passion that Alistair himself was feeling. He could feel the energy of spring in Thomas too, and he wondered, briefly, if this was how Thomas had been feeling since the first stirrings of spring, or if he was reflecting Alistair's energy back to him. Thomas was the closest to nature out of all of them, after all.

Alistair felt Thomas's grip on him change, his hands moving to Alistair's hips to move him. For a moment he thought Thomas meant for him to turn, to kiss him more easily but that wasn't Thomas's intention. Thomas guided Alistair forward and into Samal's arms. Samal still held William by the hand, but his other wrapped around Alistair's waist as he kissed him, deeply, flooding Alistair with a sense of belonging, of rightness and warmth. He hummed into his mouth, feeling the spring energy, the need to touch, to kiss, and to do more. The magical energy flowed from Samal and into Alistair, and through him to William.

Breathless, Alistair turned his head to kiss William, who returned it with a ferocity which seemed to indicate that whatever the spell had done, it hadn't removed William's vampiric tendencies at all.

Alistair moaned as William's tongue darted between his lips and he licked the inside of Alistair's mouth. Samal's hand was still on Alistair's waist, and now William's arm was around him, bending him slightly back.

Alistair wanted more, wanted so much from all of them, he hardly knew what to do next.

William broke the kiss to gaze hungrily into his eyes. "Is this all right?"

Alistair nodded, almost laughing at how very all right it all was. "Yes, but I need... I need more," he said. He shook his head and tried to put words to the urges racing through him. "All of you. On the ground, clothes off. I need to experience it all, I can feel..." he paused, catching his breath. "Spring. The new life, the promise of more, of coming alive, I can feel it all and I need to do something about it."

His hand, utterly unbidden, reached to stroke at William through his trousers, and the hardness he found there simply made Alistair's mouth salivate. He had to convince them. "Please, with all of you, please..." William moaned his assent, reaching to grip Samal by the back of the neck and pulling him in for a kiss. Alistair moaned, watching them. It felt like he might burst from how much he loved them, and loved to see them together. He wanted them so badly.

"I feel it too," Thomas said. He moved to unbutton Alistair's waistcoat. "I want it all."

William and Samal were undressing each other, so Alistair turned to do the same for Thomas, his heart beating so loud he was sure they could all hear it. Any sense of embarrassment, or indeed, of propriety was gone, consumed by the urge to show each other their affection.

Thomas peppered Alistair's jaw with kisses, and then, as he tugged him closer by the open collar, kissed his throat. Alistair's body flushed with heat and tingles shot out from the places Thomas was kissing.

Thomas pulled Alistair's shirt off him, and the sun on Alistair's chest felt divine, filling him with even more desire than he had thought possible.

Thomas sank to his knees as he pulled Alistair's trousers open and down, kissing a trail down his stomach before licking his long tongue up Alistair's cock.

Alistair's head tipped back and he moaned, a sound which seemed to summon Samal and William, because suddenly there were hands all over him, a body pressing against him on either side, both naked from the soft, silky feel of their skin on Alistair's.

He wondered, briefly, if it was possible to survive the bliss of all three of his lovers touching him without their clothes on, but decided it didn't matter what happened next. He had to experience it.

He kissed William first this time, and Samal's mouth placed soft kisses over his shoulder and back up to his throat.

Thomas's hand had wrapped around the base of Alistair's cock and was gently holding it while he licked over the head of him.

William's hand slid down Alistair's back and over his rear, before his fingers delved gently in between. The feel of it sent another wave of utter bliss through Alistair, and he leaned back against Samal, his breath heavy.

"It's your first time, isn't it?" William murmured. Alistair nodded.

"We must be very gentle, then." William withdrew his fingers, pulled out his wand and cast a spell with two runes Alistair had not heard combine in such a way. Then he pressed his fingers in between his cheeks again, but now they were warm and slick with fluid. "Tell me if you want me to stop," he said.

"I don't want any of you to stop," Alistair said. "I want

more, so much more." His hips bucked, pushing his cock deeper into Thomas's mouth as William gently probed at his hole.

"It's my first time too," Samal said. "I'm not entirely sure what to do."

Thomas pulled wetly off of Alistair's cock and reached for Samal, tugging him down to kneeling and kissing him.

Thomas was kissing Samal right after licking and sucking on Alistair's cock. The idea made Alistair dizzy. Samal could taste him on Thomas's tongue. He was distracted from this thought by William whispering in his ear.

"I'm going to push a finger in now, all right?"

Alistair nodded. "Hurry up."

William chuckled and bit Alistair's earlobe, as he pushed his finger inside Alistair. It was tight, Alistair could feel an initial sting when the finger went in, but he could also feel how incredibly good it was. The magic on William's finger seemed to help, easing the sting almost instantly to something more pleasurable.

"That's it, just breathe," he said, softly.

Alistair gasped and felt his knees buckle. "I think I need to lie down," he said, raggedly laughing. "Or I may fall."

William withdrew his finger, which made Alistair whine, and lowered them both to the ground. "Go on your hands and knees," William said, half manhandling him into position.

"Ohhh..." Alistair was aware, distantly, that perhaps he ought to feel humiliated, going to his hands and knees like an animal, bare naked and exposed to his lovers, but he didn't feel anything but needy. He planted his hands on the grass and grinned as Samal caught his mouth in a kiss.

"You look incredible like this," Thomas said. His hand stroked up the line of Alistair's back as William pressed his finger back inside.

Alistair flushed under the attention and rocked his hips

back, urging William to do more, to go faster. William pushed a second finger inside and Alistair bit Samal's lip.

Alistair's eyes kept shutting with the pleasure of it, but he forced them open, not wanting to miss a moment. Thomas's hand was in Samal's lap, stroking his large, long cock, nestled in a thatch of golden hair.

"Might I... lick it?" Alistair panted, looking down at Samal's cock.

Thomas put his hand on the back of Alistair's head and guided him down. "Gently, no teeth," he advised. Alistair opened his mouth and sunk down on Samal, tasting the hot salt of him and moaning again. Behind him the moan was echoed, William positioned himself closer, his knees in between Alistair's spreading him more open still.

Alistair reached a hand to pull Thomas by the hip, pulling off Samal to do the same to Thomas. His cock was a little shorter, thicker but just as enticing as he sank down to take him between his lips.

The taste was different, sweeter perhaps, and Alistair moaned, wondering if it was somehow possible to suck on both of them at once.

"I'm gonna fuck you now," William said. That distracted Alistair enough that he pulled up, saliva and fluid from the other two dripping off his lower lip.

"You should all have a turn," he said. William laughed, gripping him by the hip with one hand and guiding his cock against him with the other.

"You heard the man."

William pressed his cock inside of Alistair. There was another stretch, a sting instantly replaced with deep heat and intense gratification. William filled Alistair and the spring energy pulsing through the both of them exalted with it. Alistair could feel how much he wanted it.

Alistair wanted to be more upright, so he put his hands on

Thomas's knees, looking up a bit more. Silently begging for help with his goal since he was apparently unable to speak. Thomas gripped him by the arms and lifted, enough to claim his lips.

"You're doing so well," Samal said. He leaned in to kiss Alistair's shoulder again, his hands warm as they rubbed his chest.

"So well," William echoed. "It won't take me long at all to finish. But brace yourself, I'm about to start thrusting."

"Yes, please, please," Alistair said, managing those words at least. William's hand gripped his hip tighter, digging his fingernails into Alistair's flesh and making him moan with more urgency. He had no idea that the flash of pain could turn so quickly into something which made him want more. He closed his eyes, panting hard, his heart in his throat as William's hips pounded against him. The slap of skin on skin seeming to be the loudest thing in the Garden.

Alistair's lips were claimed, hot and urgent. Samal, he thought, judging from the quality of the energy flowing into him.

Thomas's hands were still gripping his upper arms, and he felt his mouth on one of his nipples. The sensation of his sharp teeth digging in there sent another electric charge through Alistair and had him moaning loud enough to startle a nearby pheasant into the air.

In a moment, William's arm wrapped tight around Alistair's waist and held him in an iron grip as he plunged deep inside. William's cry was a broken sound, his voice cracking as he groaned out Alistair's name.

Between the three of them, Alistair was lowered back into the softness of the grass, and William slid out of him with the movement, causing both of them to whimper at the sudden lack of connection.

"You now," Samal said, his voice hushed. Alistair opened his eyes to see Thomas moving in closer. Alistair was on his back, and he reached his wobbly arms up to wrap around Thomas as he lowered himself over Alistair's body.

His smile was wicked and welcoming at the same time, little sharp fox fangs which belied the cuteness of his fuzzy fox ears where they stuck out of his hair.

"You're so beautiful," Alistair murmured, half out of his head with the bliss of it all. He reached a hand to touch the softness of Thomas's ears, smiling when he leaned his head into it, encouraging more petting.

"You are," Thomas said.

He felt Thomas's cock probing between his legs and let his knees fall open, welcoming him in. His own cock was throbbing, untouched for far too long, but Alistair was drunk with it. The spring energy all around him singing the same song - more, more, *more!*

He might have said that too, but he couldn't be sure. Thomas smiled so his eyes crinkled and almost closed entirely, kissed Alistair and with a quick movement of his hand pushed his cock inside of Alistair's waiting hole.

He felt stretched even more, Thomas's cock having a bit more girth than William's. It was a delicious stretch though, a sting which promised so much more.

Thomas was slower than William, taking his time to push all the way in and then pull most of the way out again, making Alistair whine with the heat of it. The pull and push and intoxicating drag of Thomas inside him was enough to have him almost swooning with happiness. He increased his grip on Thomas, pulling him down for a kiss although once he got it he found he couldn't concentrate on it. Thomas continued his slow thrusting, and Alistair's breath was too short to maintain a kiss. Thomas kissed his jaw, nipped his earlobe, then down the line of his neck where it connected to his shoulder, sending sparks of arousal through Alistair so his world narrowed to Thomas's cock and mouth.

He opened his eyes, feeling bleary, drunk, and saw Samal's hand on William's cock, stroking it. William's teeth deep in Samal's shoulder, his fingers carding through the feathers of Samal's wings. It was too much, Alistair thought.

Thomas pulled back from his affectionate attack on Alistair's throat and looked him in the eye. "I love you so much," he gasped. "Going to come."

Alistair nodded. "Touch me, please, I need to as well."

Thomas slid his hand between them, pulling back from Alistair's hold to kneel, Alistair sprawled in his lap with his shoulders in the grass, utterly debauched and loving every second of it.

Thomas's hand went around Alistair's aching cock and stroked, and the noise which came out of Alistair was more of a keening than anything else.

In an instant William and Samal were there on either side of him, William pressing his thumb into Alistair's mouth and Samal pinching his nipples between his fingers and rubbing them slowly.

The stimulation was too much and Alistair felt himself orgasming, his body tensing and releasing in tiny pulses, his back arching, biting down on the thumb in his mouth in lieu of screaming his contentment to the world.

Thomas thrust deeper inside and there was the sensation of being filled again. Thomas and William's seeds mixing within Alistair. He almost came again just thinking that. His stomach was wet with his own spending and he relaxed back into the grass, sighing happily.

"You all right?" Thomas asked, brushing Alistair's hair off his forehead with his clean hand.

Alistair nodded although he felt boneless, the essence of Spring still pulsing through his veins. He licked his lips, tilted his head back to look at Samal. "Sam now, please."

Samal leaned over to kiss him, upside down with his nose on Alistair's chin, making him laugh.

"Perhaps you ought to rest, love," Samal murmured.

Alistair shook his head. "Rest after. I need you now."

Samal's wings fluttered slightly and Thomas moved away. "Sit up a little," Samal said. He helped Alistair to do it, and then pulled him into his lap, facing him. Their cocks slid against each other, Alistair's hard again even after the orgasm he'd just had. The magic of spring and the awakening of nature seeming to override his physicality in that respect.

Alistair slipped his arms around Samal's neck, smiling as he felt William and Thomas both press close around them. William on one side, with his arm around Alistair's waist and the other teasing at the downy feathers closest to Samal's shoulder blade.

Thomas on the other side, half leaning against Samal, his hand on Alistair's chest, stroking him gently.

Alistair wondered, hoped really, if there was a magic spell that would somehow allow them all to have sex at the same time. Perhaps it was simply a matter of logistics, and practice. The prospect of both of those things sparked even more arousal within him.

He pushed up on his knees and positioned himself over Samal's cock, and slowly lowered himself down. It wasn't as thick as Thomas's, but it was longer, and Alistair gasped as he lowered himself all the way down.

"Incredible," he moaned.

Samal's wings wrapped closer around the four of them, and Alistair reached a hand to stroke the feathers, delighting in the way Samal's cock jolted inside him. "Does that feel good?"

Samal nodded. "It feels divine," he said. "Almost as good as fucking you, and even more intimate."

Smiling, Alistair tugged gently on one of the feathers and Samal's hips jolted in response, pushing deep inside him.

Alistair tipped his head back and groaned, rolling his hips in small circles to fuck himself on Samal's cock.

"Oh Alistair..." someone moaned. Alistair wasn't sure who it was, too wrapped up in the feelings of love that were welling in him. He was aware of every place on his body where he was being touched, and there were so many of them. He ran his fingers through hair, through feathers, played with Thomas's soft ears, and tugged on William's hips. All of them seemed to do the same, caught up in the desperate need fuelling Alistair.

The four of them were all moving together now, hands on cocks and all four of them panting and moaning. The energy connecting them all flowing fast through one body and into the next. Alistair could see it, a golden, green and red sparkle, a river through bodies. The air around them clouded with it as if the river had put out a mist.

Samal came without warning, his wings first tightening around the group and then flapping wide out, spreading to their full length. The sudden rush of fresh air startled Alistair, who came immediately after. At some point he had wrapped his hand around Thomas and he was coming as well, Thomas was stroking William, Samal's fist tight around his wrist.

The orgasms ignited the magic and it warmed their skin like the hot summer sun, sparkling and then dissipating in a sparkling rain over the grass.

They fell into a tired, happy pile of limbs. Alistair pillowed his face on Thomas's soft tail. All of them touching and softly kissing each other. Alistair's energy was finally tapped out and he sighed and let sleep take him.

CHAPTER 44

They slept for a time in the Garden, and then dressed, and made their way back up to Misselthwaite Manor in time for dinner.

Alistair was famished, in fact they all seemed to be. The energy needed for the spell and then the lovemaking session after it had drained them.

It was a hearty meal, roast pork with a variety of roasted vegetables, lots of crispy crackling and apple sauce. Alistair loaded his plate and grabbed as many dinner rolls as he could balance on top of it and the four of them sat together at their customary table.

Martha joined them when she came in, smiling softly as she looked between them.

"You all look far too happy and satisfied, did something happen?"

"You could say that," Thomas said, grinning, fangs out.

"I'll explain it later," Samal said. He was too busy shovelling food into his mouth to say anything else.

"Fine," Martha said, laughing softly. "Well, you'll be pleased to know that the Birch cousins have all been banned from ever returning to the Misselthwaite grounds."

"They have?" Alistair asked, after hastily swallowing his mouthful of roll.

"Indeed," Martha said. She picked up a long piece of crackling to gesture with. "Lord Carlisle has been in talks with the heads of families, and with the Mages council, and that was the final decision. What they attempted to do was illegal and cruel, and they haven't just been expelled, they're banned for life from this school. I imagine they'll have a bally rough time getting into any other British school as well. Probably they will have to go study on the continent or even over in the Americas if they want any more education."

Alistair's heart thumped happily at that. Hopefully they would leave the country and he could put all three of them out of his mind.

Martha started eating the pork crackling and the table was comfortably quiet as they all ate their meals.

Just as they were all finishing up and Alistair's hunger was finally feeling satisfied, Medlock walked into the dining hall and made a beeline for their table. Alistair was filled with a sudden inexplicable guilt. Had she heard what they'd gotten up to in the Secret Garden? Did she know that he was sneaking in there and had been for weeks?

Her expression wasn't angry though, it was mild and perhaps almost bright. "Mister Lennox, Lord Carlisle is available to speak to you now."

"Can the others come too?" Alistair asked. He had a sudden recollection of the time faux- Medlock had lured him away.

"I don't see why not," Medlock said. She surveyed the table. "As long as you all tidy up after yourselves as you are supposed to."

William, Samal and Thomas all got to their feet and bustled the used plates and cutlery to the kitchen. Martha waved them off. "I'll see you later Sam, I'll leave my door open."

Five minutes later and the four of them were being ushered into the impressive study of Lord Carlisle.

His eyebrows lifted, seeing all of them together, but he gestured and two more visitor chairs slid into place before his desk, from where they had been waiting at the wall.

Alistair and William sat in the middle two, with Thomas and Samal on either side.

"I expect you've heard about the fates of Eleanor Birch and her cousins," Lord Carlisle said. Alistair nodded.

"Yes, sir."

"I'm terribly sorry that it happened," Lord Carlisle continued. "The stars above know the three of them were well enough behaved until you joined us, Lennox."

"Oh?" Alistair said, unsure what else to say.

William shook his head and he tsked his tongue against his teeth. "Father, I have far more important news. I believe Alistair has for the moment, halted the curse."

Lord Carlisle's eyes widened and he looked between William and Alistair.

"I'm not entirely sure," Alistair said. "But we worked a ward into him which has formed a barrier between the curse and him."

"My stars." Lord Carlisle looked quite stricken, his hand pressed to his chest. "Can it really be? The Lennoxes came through at last?"

He stood up and moved quickly around the desk, and placed a hand on William's forehead, speaking some words under his breath. William stayed quite still, perhaps used to this treatment, Alistair thought. The silence in the room was absolute. Alistair was holding his breath and apparently the others were too.

Lord Carlisle dropped his hand and turned to Alistair, his eyes lighting with a joy which seemed foreign to his features. "Incredible lad. How did you manage this?"

Alistair looked at his friends, his lovers, and then back to Lord Carlisle. "I stole a garden," he said, his voice small. "I didn't exactly mean to, but it's your wife's old garden, I found the key and inside it was a Wellspring, it all started there."

Lord Carlisle caught Alistair's hands in his own and squeezed them. "I see. I should have considered... but as soon as I locked that place, I banished it from my thoughts. It was simply too painful for me to think of it, let alone visit it. But you must tell me everything."

Alistair recounted the past weeks as best he could manage, with William, Samal and Thomas filling in details where he forgot or where they'd noticed things from their perspective. Lord Carlisle ordered in hot chocolates for them all, and when Alistair had told the entire story he had also finished his mug of chocolate.

Lord Carlisle, back in his throne-like chair, took it all in. "I expect you'd like to know the things that happened that led to all of this."

"Please sir," Alistair said. "There's much that isn't covered in the books and things we found."

"William inherited the curse from me," Lord Carlisle said. "I was bitten by a vampire in the backstreets of Paris, a man sent by enemies of my father. Perhaps, considering the number of enemies my father had, the curse began further up the line. At any rate, I was able to keep the side effects of it at bay for a time. Long enough to meet Melusine and fall in love. We did what we could when she became pregnant, preventative healing spells and the like. However it was not to be. William was born cursed, and Melusine died soon after that, a victim of it."

He paused, took a swig of something out of a silver hip flask and continued. His eyes were large, lost in the sorrows of the past.

"The Lennoxes were apparently blessed, the exact opposite of my line. They were the talk of the town, an attractive, vivacious and interesting young couple with twin boys, curse breakers, damn good ones who had proved themselves several times over. However when they came to try and heal William it all went terribly wrong. William became sicker still, fell into a coma worse than we'd seen him - he was turning into a vampire, and the little Lennox boy was killed." He paused, looking mournfully at Alistair. "I'm so sorry."

"I expect they liked the attention, of being famous like that," Alistair said, feeling not nearly as sad as Lord Carlisle looked.

"Perhaps. But the attention they received after the incident was of a different kind indeed," Lord Carlisle said. "People said they had been reckless, endangering their children for the acclaim of society. Used magic as a circus show... There was a lot said. They removed themselves from magical society by necessity. They were receiving no invitations and the gossip was cruel indeed. Perhaps I could have done something to mitigate that, but I was too ashamed of my own involvement in the matter." He sighed and rubbed his forehead. "My guess is that the curse on you, Alistair, was placed by them. To hide you from those who would see you perform, or maybe to remove their own temptation to use your gifts."

Alistair nodded, thought of how his parents had often gone to parties... they must have been trying to forget, perhaps. To drown their fears and sorrows in wine and gambling. They ignored him, because there was supposed to be another little boy beside him. How could they look at him and not see their lost son?

He closed his eyes, grieving for them now that he could better understand them. He leaned forward as tears welled in his eyes. How foolish they must have felt, when Ambrose had died. How horribly guilty.

To lose a child because of something that you had done, and then to have the daily reminder of it walking around the house. He wiped his streaming eyes.

"It's all right…" Ambrose whispered in his ear. "We're reunited now." Alistair's breath hitched and he coughed, wondering if he ought to relay that to Lord Carlisle.

"I'm sorry," Lord Carlisle said. "There's simply no good reason for any of this to have happened. Except for the love I have for William, and the hope I had that he might be saved. We were all acting foolishly."

A rustle alerted Alistair to the movement of Samal moving his chair closer, putting his arm around him. Thomas, in dog form, put a paw on Alistair's knee, and he straightened up enough that Thomas could flop over his lap. William stood, wavered for a moment, and then went around the desk to his father. They regarded each other for a moment, gazing into each other's eyes as if they were strangers.

"It's all right Father. We can't change the past, but we can move forward together into the future. We can do better and we can find a new kind of happiness."

Lord Carlisle huffed out a breath and took William's hand. William tugged him to his feet and embraced him. Lord Carlisle looked shocked, but hugged him back after a moment.

Warmth flooded Alistair's chest as he saw the good that he had in part created. Perhaps William was correct and it really would be all right.

Some long moments passed as the men embraced, and finally Lord Carlisle pulled back to smile at them all. "I would very much like to see the garden, to sense Melusine again."

"Of course," Alistair said. "Perhaps, perhaps we should leave the door unlocked?"

It felt like a big step, Alistair wanted to keep the garden to himself, for it to remain the special place that he took his boyfriends. But he knew that wasn't fair. He couldn't be selfish with it. It was a place of power, and it should belong to everyone, especially to Lord Carlisle, who had lost so much.

Perhaps it could go some way to healing him as well.

"I think that's a grand idea," Lord Carlisle said. He went to take Alistair's hands again. Thomas flattened himself on his lap and watched him warily. "I cannot thank you enough Alistair. You have brought my family back to life."

Alistair felt tears welling in his eyes and his throat closing over a lump. He shook his head. "It was the Garden."

"No, it was you," William said. Samal nodded, his arm tightening to squeeze him closer, and Thomas leaned up to lick Alistair's face once. All of them thanked him in their own way.

And Alistair realised that there was something of worth inside him after all. He wasn't the dull, uninteresting and sour boy he had been when he arrived. He had been a seed then, something cold and hard, frozen in the ground. Misselthwaite and the magic within him had allowed him to grow, to become the strong tree he was now, and he could feel that he was about to blossom.

- *To be continued*

AFTERWORD

Thanks for reading Garden of Secrets, this book was a labour of love, and it got me through some dark times.

Preorder Garden of Mysteries now.

Find me on social media
Facebook: Drake LaMarque Author
Facebook reader group: Drake's Crew
Tiktok: @jamiesandswriter

Thank you to my wonderful alpha readers/editors : K and Z you two rock! Thanks also to the wonderful denizens of Drake's Crew and my stellar ARC reading team. You are all very much appreciated.

Coming soon: Night's Melody

The opera house holds many secrets, but none are as frightening as the Opera Ghost.

Matthieu has harboured a crush on his best friend, Christophe, since they started dancing together in the Paris opera ballet troupe, but he's never acted on it.

When disaster strikes only hours before a gala performance, Christophe reveals a hidden talent for singing.

But where did he learn to hit such beautiful high notes? Why won't he tell his best friend who his singing tutor is? And what are those bruises he's covering up?

The rehearsals for their new opera are plagued with "accidents" and a dashing stranger who has a past connection with the beautiful Christophe disrupts their lives. To make matters worse, Matthieu seems to have attracted the attention of the

Phantom of the Opera himself... but who is the man behind the mask? And why is he so very alluring?

The melody heard in the darkest part of the night is terrible, but beautiful as well.

Night's Melody is an MM horror retelling of the Phantom of the Opera, as part of the collaboration Monsters & Mayhem: An MM Horror Collection, adapting some of your favourite classic horror stories with an MM romance twist.

It is a standalone story, featuring accidents of a violent nature, overdramatic characters, BDSM, why choose/ MMMM scenes and some very intriguing chambers under the opera's stage floor.

Buy now

I've never been what I was supposed to be. Wealthy sons of Port Governors aren't supposed to be ejected from the British Navy after less than a year, they're not supposed to like pulp romances or daydream about the handsome heroes of the stories instead of the heroines.

When my Father issued me an order to marry a woman, I knew I had no choice but to make my own way in the world, and I found a berth on the first ship out of Jamaica.

I didn't mean to join a pirate ship, and I certainly didn't intend to find myself the cabin boy to an incredibly charming Pirate Captain. Or that I'd also be attracted to the mysterious First Mate, or that both of them would show me all sorts of unspeakable and salacious pleasures while on board. How can I choose just one of them when I want both?

In addition to confusion on board the ship, there's also enchanting genderfluid merfolk, a cat which seems to understand a lot more than it should, an unseasonable storm and a sea witch with a serious grudge... and with all these complications, I am definitely in over my head.

Come and meet the crew:

Gideon: an innocent with a lot of forbidden desires and a lot of love to give

Tate: a huge, muscular ship's captain with a sweet side

Ezra: a dominant and closed off first mate

Ora: a genderqueer, curious and affectionate merman

KIDNAPPED BY THE GENTLEMAN -
GENTLEMAN'S BOUNTY BOOK 1

Buy Now

Cedric has been kidnapped by pirates.

...they have no idea how much trouble they're in for.

Cedric was living his best life, partying in the colonies, bedding whomever he pleased and trusting that his parents' money and affluence would get him out of any unfortunate scrapes.

Until he was kidnapped by the fearsome pirate Lucifer, who planned to trade him for a hefty ransom. Unfortunately, he's not the only one after Cedric, and the strange secret society who have Cedric in their sights might just be more dangerous than Captain Lucifer.

Now Cedric is trapped on a pirate ship with a dashingly handsome captain, a quartermaster who won't stop staring at him and an overwhelming desire to find some fun, all while saving his hide from an unknown organisation who will stop at nothing to track him down.

Buy now

A witch in the broom closet probably shouldn't be so interested in a ghost hunter, right?

That Basil is a librarian comes as no surprise to his Mt Eden community. That he's a witch? Yeah. That might raise more than a few eyebrows.

When Sebastian, a paranormal investigator filming a web series starts snooping around Basil's library, he stirs up more than just Basil's heart.

Between Basil's own self-doubt, a ghost who steals books and Sebastian, an enthusiastic extrovert bent on uncovering secrets, Basil's life is about to get a lot more complicated.

Overdues and Occultism is a sweet, no heat contemporary novella about a witch living in Auckland, New Zealand. MM romance, HEA.